Hero Rising

Anna Alexander

Also by Anna Alexander

Heroes of Saturn Series

Hero Revealed

Hero Unleashed

Hero Unmasked

Hero Rising

Men of the Sprawling A Ranch Series

The Cowboy Way

The Marlboro Man

To Have Faith

Elite Metal

Bound by Steele

Adamantium's Roar

Elite Ghosts

Thallium's Submission

www.ingramcontent.com/pod-product-compliance
Lightning Source LLC
Chambersburg PA
CBHW050911250626
47155CB00001B/192

Hero Rising

Anna Alexander

Book four in the Heroes of Saturn series

Ari Rayner's fresh start in the city is put on hold when her car breaks down on a mountain pass. Her savior is a hooded angel with haunted eyes who gives new meaning to the words "smoldering intensity". Drawn to his strength, she revels in helping him succumb to his illicit fantasies. Just because she's a woman doesn't mean she's afraid to get down and dirty.

Bale made a deathbed promise to protect those who cannot protect themselves, a vow he's done a damn fine job of upholding, but the fire burning within Ari beckons him to play in the flames, and the heat they generate brings the house down. But such brilliance sheds light on past mistakes that Bale must now answer for. With his true nature revealed, Ari uses everything at her disposal—whips, straps and a firm hand—to convince Bale he is not a monster and is worthy of her love.

Dedication

Till min familj, för alltid.

And for my sister Sarah. You know I love you more than my luggage.

Find Anna Online

Website

annaalexander.net

Facebook

facebook.com/pages/Anna-Alexander/282170065189471

Twitter

twitter.com/AnnaWriter

Newsletter

http://eepurl.com/Q0tsz

Chapter One

I F YOU'RE SUPPOSED to make lemonade when life handed you lemons, what were you supposed to do when handed a sack of shit?

Ari Rayner slammed the door shut on her '88 Toyota Corolla. "Well fuck you too," she shouted at the car, then reopened the door and slammed it again. The *thwack* of metal on metal was slightly more satisfying than screaming at the hunk of junk.

A peek to her right and left confirmed she was all alone on a long stretch of a two-lane ribbon of road bordered by fir trees so tall and thick she figured they had to have been there for centuries. Trees didn't grow so massive where she was from, and the terrain wasn't as mountainous either. She was used to brown, rolly hills of farmland, not the steep slopes of the Cascade Mountains. The congested forest surrounding her was so dense she was barely able to see through the foliage to discern if she was close to any sort of civilization.

A fine mist of rain fell from above, not enough to form definitive drops, but coating the earth in a layer of wet and soggy. At least there was a sliver of daylight left. If one could call the endless expanse of slate-gray sky daylight. Once the sun set, it was going to get cold damn quick.

From her jacket pocket she withdrew her outdated cell phone and pressed the Power button. "Please, please, please," she prayed, focusing all her energy on the cold black square in her chilly hands.

A light flickered across the screen. *Find Power Source.* Then zilch as the image zapped away.

"Nooo," she groaned and rested her head against the door of the Corolla. If only the cigarette lighter hadn't gone out a year ago, she could have made sure the battery was fully charged.

"If ifs and buts were candies and nuts, we'd all have a wonderful Christmas," her grandmother used to say. In other words, suck it up, sweetie.

Torn between laughter and tears, she settled on both. Her shoulders shook as puffs of breath fogged the window and temporarily heated her damp cheeks.

She just had to take that detour off the main highway to visit that hole-in-the-wall drive-thru she'd seen featured on the food channel. Was it the cheeseburger's fault the transmission she had hoped would last until she reached the city had finally blown? No. But it figured that would be the icing on the proverbial crap cake after enduring the month of hell. All she had wanted was a little treat. Just a small, tiny bit of goodness to kick off the start of a new beginning. What could be more harmless than sampling the best cheeseburger west of the

Mississippi?

"Was it really too much to ask to have a little fun?" she wailed to the heavens. The answering clap of thunder as the rain gained density was a resounding yes. Apparently the powers that be felt she hadn't been punished enough.

Fine. So be it. If she was meant to walk, it was time to march. Crying on the side of the road wasn't going to do her a lick of good and wasted valuable daylight, or light-grayness, as was the case. On the bright side, she now had the opportunity to burn off the calories in that chocolate shake.

She reached into the backseat and retrieved a navy hooded sweatshirt, layering it under her denim jacket for another level of warmth. Wherever she ended up next, an umbrella was going to be at the top of her shopping list. She threw her purse in her overnight bag and slung it over her shoulder. The rest of her luggage would have to sit tight until she was able to have a tow truck sent out to retrieve her car. Ugh, a tow truck. Another expense she couldn't afford and didn't want to think about.

Shake it off. Shake it off. One emergency at a time. First priority, find a power outlet.

Twenty minutes later Ari slogged down the road with no hint of a building in sight. Rivulets of rain trickled down her neck and soaked the collar and shoulders of her jacket. The fabric of her black- and red-floral-print cotton dress stuck like papier-mâché around her thighs and strands of hair kept slapping her cheeks. It figured the only item she kept from her jerk-off ex-boyfriend were the kickass Jimmy Choo Dash biker boots and now they were being devoured by the mud and roadside sludge.

With each soggy step she cursed the day she met Anthony Martinelli. Excuse her, City Councilman Anthony Martinelli. The, unbeknownst to her at the time, very married public servant who she hoped at that very moment was getting a good nut-roasting by his wife. Lord knows the woman spewed enough hate in Ari's direction in every newspaper in all of Jefferson County and most of St. Louis. Let her blow some brimstone in the direction of her adulterous hubby too.

How had she not known Anthony was a player? Was she really so bowled over by a nice suit and impeccable table manners that she completely missed the signs that he led a double life? She used to believe she was a good judge of character. As a bartender the ability to read people was an essential skill to possess. A gesture or tone of voice told her immediately who were the cool customers and who she needed to keep an eye on.

For example, she didn't need to be a psychic to guess that the two guys climbing out of the truck that pulled off the road ahead of her were bad news. Slowing down while doing a drive-by to say a fine how-do-you-do was understandable, but both of them did not need to exit the vehicle.

Both men wore what she had noticed was the Northwest uniform of scruffy beards, flannel shirts and work boots. Seriously, hadn't male fashion changed at all since the grunge-rock era? When the man on the right spat a stream of tobacco she cringed. Oh yeah. That was attractive. Excellent first impression.

Ari hooked her thumb under the strap of her bag, ready to ditch the extra weight at a moment's notice, and calmly crossed the road to the other side and prayed. Please let them only be stopping for engine troubles and not notice she existed.

"Hey, girlie."

Fuck. Well there went that wish.

One steady step after another, she walked on by without sparing them a single glance. The roller-coaster pitch in her stomach was enough to convince her she didn't need or want anything to do with them.

Through the pitter-patter of rain, the tread of booted foot-steps came up behind her. As they approached, she whirled around and braced her stance for either fight or flight. Better to see the devil coming at you instead of letting him take you by surprise.

"What?" she shouted, as if she didn't have a suspicion.

"Whoa." The spitter held up his hands. "I'm not going to hurt you, little lady."

Right. Her bullshit alarm clanged. She knew how to read between the lines. They weren't going to hurt her, if she went along with their plans.

The spitter and Billy Bob Joe Willy weren't large men, but they carried enough bulk around their middles to make her think if they tackled her to the ground she'd be down for the count.

As her gaze flicked from one to the other, she noted that their eyes appeared clear of drink, but drunk with lust as they inched closer.

A good girl, a desperate girl, might have been tempted to give them the benefit of the doubt. Just because she was a woman didn't mean they wanted to nail her like a two-by-four. But she was not an angel and not nearly that desperate.

She'd been called pretty in the past, but she knew the only thing that inspired such a look of desire in a man was the fact she had a vagina and was handy. And at the moment, she was all alone. A neon sign flashing "victim" might as well be hanging over her head. The female population of their logging camp or fishing boat, or wherever the hell they were from, must be low for them to think she was a tasty treat. Hey, she was from the Midwest, what did she know about mountain men and their proclivities?

Billy Bob Joe Willy took a step closer. She countered with one back. From the corner of her eye, she gauged the distance to the tree line.

"Easy, girl," he drawled. "Was that your sedan back there on the road?"

She lowered her head and gave him the fuck-off stare she used on grabby customers.

"A pretty little thing like you shouldn't be walking in the rain. Where'ya heading?"

With one eye on the spitter and the other on BBJW, she countered their every step.

"Kitty cat got your tongue?" The spitter chortled and wiped at his mouth. A fine trail of chaw remained on his hand.

"I don't talk to strangers."

"Well then let us give you a lift. We can become friends on the way."

"No thanks. I'm good."

His smile turned icy. "Get in the truck."

"I'm sorry. I guess I wasn't clear. Fuck off."

The smile disappeared altogether. "Fuck is right. Get her."

Well hell.

Her bag hit the ground with a wet *thunk* as she turned and raced down the road. She ditched the idea of trying to hide in the woods. If they attacked her, she wanted to be out on the open road where it was more likely someone would see them. God, let someone else see her. Like a family. With teenagers. And a big burly husband.

The rain-cloaked air burned her fast-moving lungs and in her mind she chanted, *Big dogs. Big dogs. Big dogs* just like when she was a kid playing softball and trying to reach base. Of course, she was eight then and her running skills hadn't improved much since.

A tug at her hair almost brought her to her knees, but she kept going, pumping her legs like the Little Engine That Could. The unseen fingers grabbed for her shoulders and yanked on her jacket. She fought out of the sleeves, slapping at whoever was behind her in a last-ditch effort to trip up the impending attackers.

Her brain sent the signals to her limbs to stop fighting. What was the use? She was toast. But her heart shouted "fuck that", so she dug deeper. If she was going down, she'd do so with blood under her nails and a throat raw from screaming.

One of the losers whooped with triumph as burly arms wrapped around her middle. Down they fell, both fast and in slow motion as the world ground to a halt around her. Fire raced up her legs as her knees hit the ground first and asphalt rushed toward her face. Imaginary pain exploded in her head in preparation for impact.

The hit, when it came, was nothing like she expected. Yeah, it hurt like hell, but where was the harsh scrape of concrete against her skin? Where was the crushing weight of her assailant on her back? All she felt was a lumpy hardness underneath her cheek.

She'd died. Holy shit. The blow to the head was so severe it killed her!

No. No, no, no. This could not be the end. Her eyes flew open and she tensed, ready to battle whatever god had decided this was to be her fate.

What the hell?

Her vision blurred like the lens of a camera trying to focus until the image settled and revealed a long length of arm stretching out before her. Up the black-denim-covered appendage her gaze traveled to a set of mile-wide shoulders that blocked out the sky. A black hood covered the stranger's head, leaving only the chiseled, whiskered chin and a firm set of lips exposed to the elements.

Her gaze flickered about, struggling to comprehend that it was his hand she felt under her cheek. How did this man manage to slip his hand under her head before she crashed to the pavement? Even more mind-boggling was that in his other hand he had Billy Bob suspended above her by the back of his jacket.

The stranger gently lowered her head to the ground then stood, lifting Billy Bob higher until his feet dangled in the air.

"Hey, man," the spitter shouted. "Put him down."

Despite the haze clouding her mind, she had to laugh at the ridiculousness of the command. This man was a grade-A badass. No one was gonna make him do anything he didn't want to.

Apparently the spitter had missed body language lessons as a child for he rushed the giant, who rounded about with a kick, connecting solidly to the stupid man's ribs. The crack of bone made the bile rise in her throat, even as she silently cheered. The spitter sailed through the air then landed in a heap in the gutter.

Holy shit! Was he dead?

Billy Bob was hauled within millimeters of the newcomer's hood.

"Shall I grant you the same courtesy you were showing the lady? Shall I?" he shouted in voice so deep, her throat ached in sympathy. "Who will mourn you when I kill you?"

Ari's jaw dropped at the cold, sinisterly rasped question. Not for a second did she believe the threat was said in jest.

Billy Bob sputtered as he hung limp in the man's hands. All color left his cheeks as he stared death in the face. "M-my daughter."

His lips curled as he snarled, "She deserves better. I'd be doing her a favor gutting you now. Or maybe I should find her. Tackle her to the ground and violate her like you planned to do to this girl? Have you allowed that cretin to harm your young?" He indicated the limp body of the spitter with a nod.

"N-no. No." Water droplets sprayed all over as he shook his head.

"When I put you down, you are going to run back to your vehicle and leave immediately. From this moment forth you will treat all women as if they are royalty, or I will hunt you down and end you. Understand?"

More frantic nodding and over the damp rain, Ari scented the antiseptic stench of urine as Billy Bob pissed his pants.

The man lowered Billy Bob to his feet but kept one hand on his shirt. "To remind you of your promise."

The snick of a switchblade reached her ears a millisecond before Billy Bob screamed and clutched his face. Blood gushed from between his fingers, mixing with the rain to drip onto the road.

What had she missed? One second his face was fine, then bam! His skin was flayed open like the back of a fish from ear to lip. Had the hooded man moved that fast?

Fear constricted her throat like a cheap scarf as she watched the stranger calmly wipe the blade clean on his jean-covered thigh. Who was this guy?

Billy Bob took off, leaving his *compadre* facedown in the muck. Great friend. The stranger picked up the spitter by the back of the shirt, and to her slight relief, the creep moaned at the movement. As Billy Bob sailed past them his friend was tossed into the flatbed like a bag of trash.

Once the roar of the big block engine faded into the distance, cold set into her bones. Her teeth chattered, the sound louder than the patter of rain hitting the asphalt.

Stand up! Run! This man is a total badass. Why are you just sitting here?

Yes, brain. Running was probably an excellent idea. If only her limbs would fucking move.

Her shaking grew worse as the man turned and stalked in her direction.

"Stay back," she managed to mutter, because obviously, he was going to do what she said.

Despite the ridiculousness of her command, he froze mid-step then lowered his foot one slow inch at a time.

"I mean you no harm," he rasped, holding out his hands to show her they were empty before reaching for his hood and drawing it off his face.

Hello, handsome.

Oh. My. God. Ari bit her tongue to keep it from falling out of her mouth as she stared up at a face Hollywood casting agents would bet millions on. He wasn't pretty, not by any stretch, but definitely a man's man. Square jaw, high cheekbones, a slightly cricked nose as if it had been broken once, or many times before. Big surprise there. Not. The rain hid the true length of his black hair, which she'd describe to the police if the need arose as overgrown, but his bangs were long, hanging down to frame the intensity of his dark eyes.

Okay, just because the man was freakishly gorgeous did not mean she was out of danger. She had no doubt he possessed the power and will to fuck her up, if he wanted to.

"Can you stand?" he asked in an accent that heated her from the inside even as chills made her tremble. "Your knees appear badly injured. Are you hurt elsewhere?"

She shook her head. Where was he from? Somewhere in Europe maybe. Not Latino. German, maybe Scandinavian? Yeah, when Ari was a kid, her mother loved a rock band from Norway and this guy looked a lot like the lead singer. Only darker and a helluva lot more dangerous.

"Are you certain? You're bleeding quite profusely from the head. Your hair is all bloody."

"What?" she shrieked and felt around her scalp. Nothing on her head hurt or was sore as if she'd been cut.

She pulled her hands free, but only rain covered her skin. "I'm not bleeding."

His brow furrowed. "But your hair is bloodied."

"Oh." She held up a sodden lock. "That's just the color. I

guess it does look a little like blood. But I'm okay. Relatively speaking."

His brows rose and mouth fell open as if he were stunned. "It's a most unusual color. I've never seen anything like it before."

For some reason the wonder in his tone made her want to smile.

Okay, so far he had maintained a respectful distance. She'd see if that lasted if she was upright. She climbed to her feet and bit back a moan with a wince as the skin of her scraped knees stretched. The seat of her dress was soaked through and muddy and bits of gravel and pine needles stuck to her bare legs like a strange tattoo.

"Um…thank you?" she offered, still not convinced she was any safer now than she was before he arrived.

"Was that your vehicle I passed back aways?"

She nodded and continued to stretch, testing her limbs.

"Why did you leave your vehicle? Don't you have a communications device to call for assistance?"

"You mean a phone?"

"Ya."

Damn he was cute with that accent. There was also a grit in his voice, deep and growly, kinda like a blues singer at the end of his career. The sound was sexy and harsh, which completely sucked. She didn't want to find anything else about him attractive.

"I do," she began to answer, "but…" *That's it. Confirm you have no one to call or a way to scream for help.* "I preferred to walk."

His eyebrow took another journey north. "Where are you going?"

"That way." She pointed down the road. "Look, like I said, thanks for taking care of the creepazoids. Have a great day."

With her body positioned to keep him in her sights, she walked back to where she dropped her bag.

"You are alone, aren't you?"

Yep, not gonna answer that either. She picked up the bag and brushed off as much debris as possible before slinging the strap over her shoulder. She didn't even bother with her sodden jacket and stuffed it into her bag.

"Can I take you anywhere?" He gestured to the motorcycle several yards away that lay on its side as if he had been more concerned with saving her life than parking properly. "It will be a tight fit, but I can carry you."

Though his shoulders were wide, his waist and hips were lean, not the she was paying that much attention to his physique. Sure, they'd be able to fit on the seat. Barely. She would have to be plastered to him as tight as wallpaper. Wrapped around all his muscles…and manliness…and muscles…

Shaking her head to clear the image, she marched on. "No thank you."

"I promise you, no harm will come to you while you are in my care."

"Right." Was he for real? Who talks like that nowadays?

"Female, stop!"

The barked order made her stop short. *Here it comes.* Steel formed in her bones as she braced for his attack.

He held out his hands again, this time as if trying to calm a frightened animal. "I know you have no reason to trust me, but I will see you to safety. Here." From his pocket he withdrew the knife he used earlier. With a slow bend of his knees he set the blade on the ground then took three steps back. "Take it."

"What?"

"Take it. I'll stay right here."

Between them on the ground lay the knife. The inlaid silver scrollwork pattern and deep-blue gemstones set deep into the black onyx grip caught the last bit of daylight and flashed at her with an enticing wink.

What game was he playing? This gesture of goodwill could totally be a trick, but the allure of having a weapon was greater than the voice of reason. She took half a step, then another while he remained standing as still as stone. Her gaze never left his face, watching for the slightest movement that may announce when he'd strike. By the time the hilt was in her grasp, a tiny smile softened his lips and satisfaction glowed in his eyes.

"Good," he said. "Place your thumb on top of the third oval stone on the side and press."

"Holy shit!" she shouted with a jump as the four-inch-long blade slid out with a little hiss.

"Press it again to retract the blade."

Snick. The deadly weapon was contained before she blinked. How many times in her life had she held a knife in her hand and not thought anything of the potential damage she could inflict with the blade? But kitchen knives were for utilitarian purposes, not homicidal ones. The little switchblade in her grip felt a million times more deadly than a butcher knife ever did.

"Ride with me," he said, pulling her attention away from the weapon. "Hold on to my hips with your thighs and keep the knife in your hand. Place the end right here." He pointed to a spot on his side between his ribs. "If at any time you feel threatened by me, press the trigger. You'll puncture my lungs and they will fill with blood, drowning me. You will then have a chance to continue on with my bike."

"Are you serious?" she exclaimed, completely in shock. Not that he knew how to take a life, of that she had no doubt, but that he'd calmly explain how to end his.

"Of course," he replied with nary a wink that he was anything but sincere.

Right. Okay. What were her options? Continue walking down the road and risk being hit by a car, or facing an encounter with another scumbag or accept a ride with talk, dark and scary who gave her a weapon?

Damn. None of those choices were optimal.

"My name is Bale. What is yours?"

"Ari." She shifted her weight from foot to foot, still hesitant to commit to one way or another.

"Ari." His tongue flicked each syllable in a way that made her breath catch. "There is a petrol station up ahead with a restaurant, not too far by cycle. At least let me take you that far. I promise, you will arrive safely."

Her gaze bounced from the knife in her hand to the motorcycle then to his dark eyes. Over and over she weighed the consequences of each option. The roar of a sixteen wheeler barreling down the street broke the circuit and she stepped back, but Bale didn't move. He stared at her even as the truck clamored past, missing him by mere inches and not once did he flinch. As if she needed further proof he was a major badass.

Maybe she was crazy, but she'd rather take her chances riding behind him on his bike with a knife in her hand than with a car or another big rig on the road.

"Fine," she said. "But just to the restaurant."

The stiffness in his posture eased and though his mouth never moved, she swore his eyes smiled at her with pleasure over her answer.

"Have you ever ridden before?"

She shook her head.

"Hang on to me and lean when I do. Flow with me, not against, and we will remain upright."

"Great." That sounded safe.

He gestured for her to follow, which she did while repeatedly calling herself an idiot. Try as she might not to, her gaze zeroed in on his denim-covered backside while she mentally kicked her own ass. In her deepest of hearts she knew the biggest reason for agreeing was for the chance to be pressed along his big body. She was worse than those women in those horrible slasher flicks who were killed for being stupid.

"May I secure your bag? You'll find it easier to hold on."

The formal cadence in his speech in comparison to his restless biker appearance charmed her, and before she thought better of it she handed him the bag with a smile.

His eyes widened, as if surprised to see her comply so readily, and he took her satchel, securing it in one of the saddlebags before handing her the full-face helmet.

"Will you need help with the latch?"

"I'll manage." She tucked the knife under her arm as she strapped the headgear into place. She felt as if she had placed a jack o' lantern over her head, but at least her brain would be protected. Fat lot of good it was doing her now.

"Here, take my coat." He removed the denim and held it out for her to slip her arms into the sleeves. "I'm not certain it will keep you dry, but it will at least add a layer of warmth."

"I don't want to leave you with nothing."

"I'll have my sweatshirt. Wear it, please."

She slid an arm into one sleeve and sighed, quickly sliding into the other and pulling the edges over her torso. The coat was two sizes too big, but the residual heat from his body on the fabric felt as if she had slipped under an electric blanket. Oh, the sensation was heavenly.

Bale threw a leg over the seat. "Climb on."

Suddenly her lungs refused to work as she eyed the scant space left on the seat behind his butt. Her grip on the knife tightened and she forced a lump down her throat. Gingerly, she swung her leg over the bike and sat. She had intended to rest her free hand on his waist, but the moment his heat touched her chilled bones she wrapped her arm around his middle and snuggled closer. If not for the helmet, she would have rubbed her face into his back.

"You are so warm," she moaned without thinking.

His stomach clenched under her forearm. "Here we go."

Ooo, Nelly. She snapped her teeth together as he kicked the engine into gear. With the mouth of her sex pressed over the vibrating seat and his hips wedged between her open thighs, arousal hit her unexpectedly hard. When he sent the bike into motion, she grabbed on to his belt for purchase. Against the backs of her fingers his cock pressed hard and hot through his jeans. Man, he *was* built big all over.

Hot guy. Motorcycle that doubled as a giant sex toy. She was in hell. This had to be more punishment for her sins. Who the hell had she pissed off so greatly to be tormented in such a manner?

Breathe, Ari girl, just breathe. It was only a short bike ride. She could manage to keep it together for a few miles.

The rain tapered off to nothing and Bale kept their speed at a steady clip but slow enough to minimize the wind tearing through her wet clothes. His consideration for her comfort drew him one more mark away from scary to pretty decent.

As the road passed under her knees, and with nothing else to do but hang on, Ari allowed her mind to wander. And why not? Her life had taken a turn toward Crazyville and it was healthy to cope with a little indulgent fantasy.

In her imagination they were just a boy and a girl out on a Sunday drive with a picnic lunch stashed in the saddlebags. Instead of searching for a roof and hot water, Bale was whisking her away to a secret location in the woods where he would lay her out on the grass and kiss her senseless with his firm lips. Of course with her luck, his favorite make-out spot was probably a quarry he used to stash the bodies.

God, when had she become so cynical? Except for the way he had dealt with the creeps he'd been a nice guy so far. It wasn't his fault she was terrified of him one moment, then felt the burn to ride him like a bronco the next.

She was so fucked in the head.

Around the next bend the glow of a gas station broke through the ever-increasing darkness of night. Attached to the station was a fast-food restaurant and the promise of hot water to wash her hands and face with. The front of her body was nice and toasty from being molded to Bale's back, but her rear was freezing and felt as if ice had formed along the edges of her dress.

Bale brought the bike to a stop and held out his hand for her to use as a brace. She was shocked she didn't hear her joints creak as she climbed off the seat with stiff knees and a wince. Between the cold and her bruises, she was so sore even her blood ached.

After a mumbled "thanks" she went into the restaurant. Ignoring the delicious scent of French fries, she headed straight for the restroom and turned the tap to hot at full blast, praying the water would actually be warm.

"Whoop, whoop," she hollered as the warmth seeped into her skin when she tested the temperature.

The rush of water went a long way to soothing her frazzled nerves. Blessed was the peace and quiet of being out of the elements for just a moment. Soon enough she was going to have to leave this little sanctuary, but for now there was only her and the hot water. Perfect serenity.

Tranquility lasted for all of a second as she got a really good look at her reflection in the mirror. Damn, she looked as if she just hopped off the boat from hell that encountered a tsunami. If the press back home saw her now, they'd probably add drug user to the list of false adjectives they wrote about her.

She stripped off Bale's jacket and laid it on the tiny bit of available counter space. Her hoodie she wrapped around her waist before she crouched to riffle through her bag. What the hell? Makeup, power cords, soap, undies and pajamas. No real clothes? Not even a pair of leggings? Gah, she really needed to plan better for emergencies. The soaked cotton dress, which had once been a favorite, was quickly becoming a hated entity, and at the first opportunity was going to face a grisly end.

Perhaps even burned in a fiery pyre in honor of her new start.

As best as she could with cheap paper towels and an empty soap dispenser, she attempted to clean the blood and dirt off her legs, but sadly the effort did not do much to improve her appearance.

Priorities, girl. Where are your priorities? At the moment looking cute was at the bottom of the list. First order of business was to get something warm in her belly.

Heat raced across her cheeks as a picture of a naked Bale flashed through her mind.

Food! She meant food. Geez, had she left her mind in the gutter? Maybe a slap in the head was needed as well.

She splashed another palm full of water on her pink cheeks and focused on the next few minutes. First up, food and nothing but food. Second, find an outlet to charge up the phone, then figure out how to get to the city and locate a place to stay. If she was lucky, she'd be in a warm bed by midnight.

No. She *was* going to be in a warm bed. Positive thinking.

"Let's do this," she said with the utmost conviction of succeeding and opened the door. She jumped back with a curse when she saw Bale leaning against the opposite wall, his fierce stare nailing her in the eyes.

"I did not mean to startle you," he said, unfolding his arms and straightening to his incredibly tall height. "I was afraid you had fallen. You were in there a while."

"The water felt nice." She licked her lips and shifted her weight from one leg to the other. Remembering the weight in her hand, she handed him his jacket. "Um...thanks for the ride. You didn't have to wait for me."

"I promised to see you to safety. Keep the coat. You're cold."

"I'll dry out faster without the extra layer. Thanks anyway."

He reached out with a slow hand and accepted the jacket. "Are you hungry? Can I get you anything?"

"No. I mean, I can get my own food. Can I get you anything? You know, as a thank-you."

What are you doing?

Just being hospitable. The man made an effort and a small token of thanks was not unreasonable.

Uh-huh. Riiiight.

All right. Fine. So she wanted to spend a little more time in his company. He was just so, sigh, drool-worthy. All too soon she was going to be neck-deep in adult stuff like finding a new job and getting her car towed. It was crazy, she knew, but all she wanted was to stare at him awhile and gather images to take with her to keep warm during the lonely nights to come. It would only be for a moment.

"Your words of thanks are all I require," he said with a formal nod.

All I require. There he went with the cheesy talk again. The trait was really quite adorable. "Seriously. You're a big guy. You must be hungry, or at least could use a snack. Coffee? I heard you people drink a lot of coffee out here."

The tops of his cheeks bunched and his eyes narrowed for

a brief second. Was that a precursor to a sneeze or had she amused him somehow?

"If you insist." He bowed his head. "I would like a salad."

"Lettuce? That's all you want? Are you a vegetarian or something?"

"I do not know this word."

"It means you don't eat anything animal related."

"Ah. No, I am not a vegetarian."

She waited for him to continue, but when all he did was stare back expectantly, she shrugged and headed for the counter. Handsome, but definitely an oddball.

Between the inclement weather and the time of day, the restaurant was near to empty. As she went to place their order, she noticed Bale took a table in the far corner and sat with his back to the wall. Those dark eyes of his surveyed the entire interior and she'd bet money he knew at least a dozen ways to evacuate the building if need be. His actions reminded her of the Fort Leonard Wood guys who came to the bar she used to work at. Was he military perhaps, or law enforcement?

Well, crud. Now she was intrigued and she didn't want to be intrigued by the man, but how could she not be?

He was like one of those giant, complicated jigsaw puzzles you have no intention of putting together. But then someone opens the box and leaves some of the pieces out, and each time you walk past it, you start to put a piece or two together then, wham! Before you know it, eight hours whizz by and you are still at the table trying to put the damn thing together.

The sight of the two salads she had purchased—because really was one going to be enough?—sitting on the tray next to her juicy cheeseburger and fries made her shake her head. What curiosities would she discover about him next?

She set the tray on the table and took the seat across from him. "Your salads, sir. And you have to help me eat the fries. If you don't, I'll end up eating them all."

"Then why did you purchase so many?"

"Because a small was too small, plus they looked good." She unwrapped her burger then dumped the carton of potatoes over the paper. After blowing on a hot fry, she popped it into her mouth. "Yum. They taste good too."

His cheeks did that weird bunch thing again before he began to eat his salad. His shoulders curled over and his face was tilted down, but his eyes continually scanned the room.

Wow. Suspicious much?

While she went about the task of plugging the charger to her phone into the nearest outlet, Bale continued to eat in silence. She pushed a few fries in his direction, which he ignored, until she gave him the evil eye and he took one with a grudging harrumph.

"So." She observed him over the top of her sesame-seed bun. "Your accent is—" *Sexy as hell.* "Different. Are you from Scandinavia?"

He straightened as if she had pulled a gun on him. "Did you say Skandavia?"

"Scandinavia."

"What?"

"What?"

"Yes."

"Yes?"

"Yes." He nodded then resumed eating.

Okaaay. "So, what part are you from?"

"The north end."

"Oh. Of Norway or Sweden?"

"Norway?"

"Are you asking me?"

"Why are you asking at all?"

"Just making conversation. Sorry." She picked up a fry then let it drop back to the table. "Are you going to kill me now?"

This time his nostrils flared with the cheek flinch. "No."

Fork to mouth. Fork to mouth. He finished one salad then moved on to the next.

That was it? Was she to assume all was now well? "Um, thank you?"

A sound burst from his lips that was a cross between a laugh and a cough. She was about to offer him some of her water, but the sparkle in his black eyes stayed her hand and made her heart do a little flip. Had she...had she made him laugh? Damn, there was one more thing about him to find intriguing.

"If you believe I will harm you, even though I have vowed otherwise, why are you still here?" he asked.

Good question. "I don't know. But you're right. I should be across the room, pretending you don't exist."

"Don't." His loud command drew her up short. He amended with a gentler, "Do not go. Please."

Oh, the way he said please probably made many a woman agree to anything he wished. This man was dangerous on so many levels, she was losing track of them all.

"Fine." She fiddled with the corner of the wrapper. "Is there any topic that is safe to discuss?"

"How about you tell me how you plan to get to the city?"

"I'll call a cab or something once my phone is charged a bit more."

"Won't that be expensive?"

Fuck yeah. Ugh, she didn't want to think about it. "Maybe."

"Where are you staying?"

As if she was going to tell him she was on her own with no plans. "With friends."

"Why not ask them to come retrieve you?"

"I don't want to inconvenience them."

"I would hope you have friends who are more concerned with your safety than being inconvenienced."

"Well, we're not that close."

"Ari." The way he trilled her name made little shivers run across her neck. "Are you on your own?"

"Not completely."

"I ask you again to trust me. On the souls of...my family.

You will be safe."

Something in the way he somberly said his family, and the haunted shadow that entered his eyes, robbing them of all the earlier merriment, conveyed an intent to carry through with his vow no matter the cost.

Goose bumps erupted over her skin as she drew in a deep breath, then another. Unable to form any words, she simply nodded. Whether she was agreeing or answering, she wasn't certain, but instinct compelled her to comply.

"Where are you staying?" he asked in the same low, softly spoken tone.

"Don't know yet," she whispered.

"Do you have any money?"

"Some."

"A position for work?"

"Not yet." She gulped, forcing saliva past the raw ache in her throat.

Bale nodded twice. He stabbed a cherry tomato with his fork and brought the bright-red fruit to his lips. As he chewed, he regarded her with a tilt to his head and a gaze that felt as if he were looking right into her soul. The muscles of his throat moved as he swallowed and she licked her lips, already tasting the flavor of his skin. His quickly drawn-in breath brought her gaze back to his, and she too gasped at the heat turning the black depths into a rich chocolate brown.

He closed his eyes and shook his head with a soft murmur she could barely hear. When they opened he said, "If you will permit me, I know of a place you can stay however long you will need."

"A motel?"

"No."

"A shelter?"

"No."

Ah, she knew this game. "Let me guess. Your place?"

"In a fashion."

"No." Her brain decided for her while all of her girly parts shouted, "Yahoo, when can we go?"

"May I finish the thought, please?"

She raised a brow but said nothing as she gestured with her hand for him to continue.

"Thank you." That sparkle reappeared in his eyes. "My...employer has several vacant rooms in their home that they use for frequent visitors. I am certain they will be able to accommodate you for the evening, perhaps two. My own residence is inside the same building, which is why I will be close by. Allow me take you there, please."

"Is that where you were on your way to earlier?"

"Yes," he said with the slightest hesitation.

"What kind of work do you do?"

Another hesitation as he unscrewed the cap from a bottle of water and took a swig. "I am in law enforcement," he finally answered.

"You're a cop?" Man, the criminals must piss their pants when he closed in on them.

"No. I am sorry, that was the wrong word. I look out for threats and eliminate them."

"For the government or a company?"

"Not for government."

"Oh, so you're like a bodyguard?"

"Yes?" he replied with that little up-note as if he were not sure that was the correct answer.

She folded her arms. "So if you're a bodyguard, why are you not with your employer right now?"

"I am on vacation. Or was. Please, come with me."

A free place to crash? Tempting. Tempting. "I don't want to be a burden."

"You won't be. Believe me, Prin—Amaryllis will enjoy hosting you."

Now it was Ari's turn to ruminate while sipping her water and pushing the last of the French fries to and fro. Bale was still a stranger and he wanted to take her to stay with other strangers. If this were a movie, she'd be screaming at the screen for the heroine to run away, so why was she seriously contemplating accepting his proposition?

Duh, maybe because she was out of options and her cash was running low. Unless she wanted to live on the streets for a while, she was going to have to find a low-cost, meaning free, way into town. If only she could be one hundred percent positive he was being truthful.

Her gaze landed on her smartphone. Oh-ho. Maybe there was a way.

"I will go with you, if you answer a few questions."

Tension snapped his spine straight and his eyes narrowed. "What questions?"

"Hey, you're the one asking me to trust you. Before I climb back onto that motorcycle, I want a few answers."

His lips tightened, but he gave a begrudging nod.

"Good. What's your last name?"

His eyes widened. "What?"

Oh, God. This was not a good start. "What is your last name?"

"I do not go by one."

"But you must have one. I know people from Norway usually have a last name, unless you're Bjork, and I think she's Swedish."

"I—uh." His Adam's apple bobbed as he looked to the walls, tables, everywhere else but at her.

Was he seriously not going to tell her?

As she opened her mouth to tell him no way, he answered with a softly spoken, "Llanos."

"Excuse me?"

"My name is Bale…Llanos."

"Is that with one *L* or two?" she asked, pulling up the web browser on the phone.

"Two."

Bale Llanos. Hmmm. Interesting. Especially the way the syllables rolled around her tongue. Damn, why couldn't he have a non-sexy last name, like Smith or Steenburgen?

Good news, not a single thing came up in a web search with his name. Not even anything close to his name. Bad news, not a single thing came up in a web search with his name. So, the man knew how to keep a low profile.

"Who is your employer?"

"Are you asking for their names?"

"No, their tax ID numbers. Of course their names, silly."

He drew a deep breath and answered just as softly as he had given his name. "Amaryllis Kilsgaard."

"Is she someone famous?"

The corner of his mouth quirked up. "Back home, yes."

Ping. A hit.

"She owns a restaurant? Tutala? I've heard of that place. That's cool." She scrolled past the listings of five-star reviews and went to the photo gallery to check out his mysterious employer.

Figures. Of course he'd be hired to guard a beautiful woman with long black hair, lavender eyes and more curves than the St. Louis Arch. Hey, what was this?

"Who's this guy?" She pointed to a photo of the woman with a man standing next to her with a possessive arm around her shoulder. "He's hot."

Bale frowned. "That is her husband, Lucian."

"Seriously?" Way to go, girlfriend. A successful restaurant and surrounded by two incredibly gorgeous guys? The woman was doing something right. "So, what kind of trouble does she get into in order to have you two guys watching out for her?"

"None, because we watch out for her."

Ari smiled and went back to look for more information. "What's The Cavern—"

"Will you come with me?" he interrupted in a rush. "I'm offering a nice bed. Hot shower…"

Ooo, he had to play on her weaknesses.

"Only for the night. And if I think I'm being an inconvenience for even one nanosecond, I'm outta there."

"If you wish," he said with a nod. "Are you ready to depart?"

"Yeah, I just want to make one last trip to the restroom."

"I will await you at the cycle."

Damn, she was really falling for the way he spoke. It was too cute. "Okay."

She admired the fluid way he moved as he collected their trash and walked out the door with a stride that said, "Yeah, I'm a man. Back the fuck off." A walk like that made a girl's brain misfire and wonder if he was as confident in all aspects of his life. At least, it made *her* wonder.

She let out her breath in a slow whistle and placed her hand over her fluttering belly. It was hard to tell what made her more nervous—staying the night with strangers or being plastered again to Bale's delicious backside.

Didn't matter really. She was going to face both realities soon enough.

Chapter Two

B ALE ADJUSTED THE fit of his leather gloves over his scarred hands and asked himself for the thousandth time that hour just what the fuck he was thinking. The moment they had stopped at the drive-thru, he should have ushered the little human inside and been back on the road before the door closed behind her.

So why hadn't he?

The too-too pleasant ache in his cock was an obvious answer but not the only one. The rest, well, he didn't even want to contemplate. And those reasons didn't matter. Ari was just another of the many humans who had needed his services, and she wasn't going to be the last. Taking her the last leg of the journey and seeing her to safety had nothing to do with wanting to remain in her presence and everything to do with fulfilling his mission. That was all.

Right. His dick twitched as Ari stepped out of the restaurant and glided toward him on her impossibly long legs. Although he towered over her by a good foot and a half, the female was all legs with gently swelling hips, and breasts that weren't too big but large enough to shimmy a touch with each step.

Of course the heating of his blood would be easier to ignore if he hadn't sensed the answering flare of desire within Ari. For some reason he couldn't fathom, she liked what she saw when she looked upon him. She also had a healthy dose of skepticism too, which he appreciated. When she had gazed at him with that sultry stare and a soft pout on those full lips, he had almost forgotten who he was and reached out to feel the texture of her cheek before he woke from her spell.

And that hair. In all his days he had never seen anything so glorious. On his home planet of Skandavia, everyone was light skinned and dark of hair. Well, almost everyone. Princess Amaryllis with her straight silver locks had been a much-discussed anomaly among the citizenry. Now that she'd been mated and marked by her husband, she resembled the people she once had been destined to rule.

Ari's deep-red mane was something special and another wonder he had beheld since arriving on this mysterious planet called Earth. The thick strands had dried into a soft tumble of rich maroon, the shade reminding him of the *darhan* flowers that grew in the forest of his origins. The splash of red against the gray-green foliage had always fascinated him with its elegant beauty and delicate petals. Much as Ari had when he had ridden upon her attack, only she was no fragile flower.

His empathic powers had picked up on her terror from a mile away, but it was her courage at facing her attackers that had flashed like a bolt of lightning, directing him to her location.

His two hearts kicked as he recalled the sight of Ari running with the wet strands of hair blowing around her shoulders like a flag during battle. The fear in her eyes made him wonder if his Natalia had had the same wild look when she had fallen to her killers.

"Bale, are you all right?"

Ari's softly spoken question and her compassion pierced through the haze of horror and regret that clouded his vision every time he thought of his wife. "What?"

The human stood poised on the edge of the sidewalk with her hands wrapped tightly around the strap of her bag and her big blue eyes wide with concern. She might not have his power of empathy, but obviously she was picking up on some of his volatile emotions. "Is everything all right?"

"Yes." He smiled. Or at least, he tried to force a semblance of a friendly expression. "For a moment I had a horrible vision of what could have been if I had not arrived to assist you when I did."

She shivered with a frown. "Well let's not think about that. You were there and it's all in the past now. What good does it do to dwell upon what might have been?"

"What good indeed. Maybe it's to remind me of why I do what I do."

"Oh." She clasped her hands in front of her and fell silent.

"Ready to depart?"

"If you are."

He handed her the helmet and watched as her slim fingers and delicate wrist manipulated the strap. So feminine was this little human. So completely opposite from his own brutish ways. To have killed those two bastards who dared to harm her would have taken zero effort on his part. Only her presence had stayed his hand. She didn't need to be a witness to the ugliness he was capable of imparting with a speed faster than one could blink.

Or his hungers.

He clenched his teeth against the wave of desire that lapped up his spine as she settled into place along his back. The respectful clutch she had around his waist was its own sensual torture. One inch lower and her hand would brush the pulsating head of his cock, which seemed to want to crawl out from under the constricting waistband of his jeans. The sensation intensified as the insides of her thighs pressed against his hips as he steered onto the highway. *Jesu*, if he kept thinking of the heat of her skin, he was going to drive them right into a ditch.

Laying on the throttle, he concentrated on the next bend in the road, then the one after that and the one after that. As mile after mile passed, he was able to focus less on Ari, barely, and began to formulate what he was going to say when he arrived on Lucian and Amaryllis' doorstep.

He had no doubt they would welcome Ari into their home. His princess was always willing to help those who had a need, whether they wanted her assistance or not. The difficulty was going to be explaining why he brought Ari at all. His status was lone ranger. Lone. Always. Never in anyone's company longer than it took to lend his sword or when stopping to pay his respect to the princess and his former commander. Ari's presence was going to raise a lot of questions that he had no clue how or desire to answer.

When the effervescent lights of the city bloomed over the horizon, Bale pushed aside the senseless concern and focused on seeing his charge to the end of their journey. Ari had not made a sound the entire last leg, but he felt the drugging pull of her exhaustion. The stiffness with which she had held on to him earlier had long ago melted until she draped his back like a cloak. He'd wager she'd deny her sleepiness, if he asked, which was one more thing about her to admire, and again he wondered what she was doing traveling all this way on her own.

A riddle he would never solve. Once she was entrenched in Amaryllis' good graces, he'd be off. Humankind could not be saved if he spent all his days on social visits.

"We're almost there," he shouted over the sound of the engine. "Are you still with me?"

The helmet rubbed against his spine as she nodded and her arms tightened around his waist. For half a second, he enjoyed the pressure of her touch. But only for half a second.

Their destination was located a few blocks north of the waterfront and the beautiful bay and on the outskirts of the busy downtown corridor with its row after row of skyscraping office buildings. In the middle of all that steel and glass lay an acre of park with flowering cherry blossoms, picnic tables and a velvet lawn that was perfect for a lunchtime getaway.

Bale turned into the driveway of a five-story building that opened directly across the street from the bubbling fountain that marked the entrance to the park and stopped at the gate. Careful to avoid brushing the soft skin of Ari's thighs, he withdrew a card from his back pocket and held it over the sensor. The gate rose inch by screechy inch, and with each second Ari tensed behind him, her nerves reaching across the air to tighten around his neck.

Despite the warning from his brain, he reached down and patted her fingers clenched around his belt. He kept his hand over hers as he drove into the garage and parked the cycle in the shadows near the elevator.

"Where are we?" Ari asked after stripping off the helmet.

"Our destination."

"Ha ha. You're telling me your boss lives in an office building?"

"My employer lives in a former office building. The upper floors are living quarters."

She adjusted the strap of her bag to lie flat across her torso and glanced around the garage. He noticed she took particular interest in the more expensive automobiles parked close by with a little touch of her envy tickling his gut. "What about the lower floors?"

"There are some businesses that rent out the lower floors.

Keycard access is needed to enter most of the building. Stay by me or in the main part of the house for now, otherwise you may become trapped until morning."

"I have no need to snoop around." She arched her brow. "Or do I?"

"No. No need. Trust me."

She shrugged then turned to lead the way to the elevator.

Why was having her trust so important to him? Why did the need to see the tension ease from her shoulders and a genuine smile curve her lips drive him to distraction? She was by his side, following his direction. That should have been enough. But as long as there was that invisible wall between them, he found it impossible to leave well enough alone.

The ride up to the fourth floor was silent except for the soft tap of her fingernail on the bottom button of her jacket. Again he felt the urge to reach out to grasp her hand in a gesture of reassurance, but he kept his fists at his sides. To feel the warmth of her palm against his would only make him wonder if she was as warm all over. A curiosity best left unfilled. Fortunately for him, the trip was short and the doors slid open with a hush to reveal a welcoming cream-on-cream decorated sitting area. The monotony of the pale walls and upholstery was broken up with splashes of orange and red in the paintings and pillows.

"Nice," Ari murmured and glanced around with an eye that seemed to capture every detail of her surroundings.

He stopped at the double doors and raised his hand to

press the Call button only to pause a millimeter from the lighted, pearl-colored circle. His hand trembled and throat closed up as an unnamed terror raised the hairs on the back of his neck. Deep in his psyche was a certainty as strong as the sun's pull on the Earth that once he pressed that button, his world was going to change forever. How, he hadn't a clue, but the feeling electrified all his senses to the point he swore he could hear the flutter of Ari's eyelashes.

"Bale?" Ari questioned softly. "What's wrong?"

"Nothing." He swallowed hard and pressed the button.

On the other side of the door, the chime resonated in his chest as if he were standing under the curve of one of the bells of Notre Dame as they chimed in warning.

Heavy footfalls that sounded with the gait of a man who was used to being in charge crossed to the door, snapping Bale's spine straight. After all these years away from the guard, including the many years he had spent cursing Lucian's name, the reflexive need to snap to attention at the arrival of his general still took command of his body.

The left half of the door opened and Bale sensed Ari tensing beside him.

"*Brovaro*, it's been too long," Lucian greeted and gripped Bale by the forearm in a warrior's bow.

Bale nodded, swallowing past the lump in his throat at Lucian's greeting of brother. The title wasn't deserved, at least as far as Bale was concerned. One should not forgive so easily when their lives had been threatened, especially for the one who had done the threatening. But then Lucian and his mate were not ordinary people, rather they were extraordinary.

Lucian's gentle smile and kind eyes spoke of his knowledge of Bale's internal struggle, but he was benevolent enough not to mention it. His lavender gaze switched to Ari and his brow rose with surprise. His mouth opened then shut as he looked back and forth between them before he said with a lift of his finger, "I shall wait until Amaryllis comes down, that way you will only have to tell the tale once. Please, come in."

"Thank you, sire." Bale motioned for Ari to precede him into the foyer.

"Sire?" she mouthed when she caught his attention behind Lucian's wide back.

He nodded once with absolute seriousness. Although they were no longer on Skandavia and he had once shunned his title as a *Llanos* warrior, he continued to honor his former vows and respected the old ways with the utmost conviction. It was the least he could offer in the wake of the graciousness and forgiveness bestowed on him by his betters. No matter how many times they told him his formality was not necessary, he refused to forgo the promise he made to himself to atone for his indiscretions.

If he ever needed a reminder as to the differences in their stations, he only had to step into the confines of the Kilsgaards' home. Gone were the white-and-silver color schemes of their home planet and in their place Amaryllis had created a showpiece of warm, creamy tile and bright-orange and red furnishings. Their home was pristine, but welcoming at the same time. Well, welcoming unless you were him. The genuine happiness that bombarded his senses when he walked through the doors made him achingly aware of his solitary existence and the dirt stains on his clothes and hands. The light and comfort were a stark reminder that he didn't belong, and no amount of Amaryllis' insistence would ever change that.

"Come warm yourselves by the fire." Lucian gestured to the two armchairs closest to the hearth. "You two look as if you were caught in the rain. Still riding the motorcycle, Bale?"

"Best way to travel," he replied.

"Balellanos," came the squeal from the entry to the living room.

A combination of guilt, gratitude and awe snaked through his gut every time he saw his princess. As Amaryllis bounded across the plush cream carpet with her dark hair flying about her smiling face, Bale wanted to take a step back and forbid her from sharing any of her kindness. He wasn't worthy of her care, but he knew to refuse her would cut her just as sure as a blade.

He gritted his teeth and caught her about the waist as she jumped and flung her arms around his neck. Since he was a good two heads taller than she, her feet swung above the floor as she hugged him tight.

"It's been too long, *lebshone.*" When he set her down she grabbed both his ears and shook his head with a stern frown.

"No calls. Not even a text for weeks. You know how I worry and still you do not take care to contact me. I should whip you for the insolence. But I see you have brought me a gift, so I shall forgive you. This time."

"My apologies," he murmured.

She turned toward Ari and clapped her hands with glee. "Introductions. Please."

Amaryllis' excitement at meeting this new person brushed over his skin with ticklish fingers while Ari stared at the slight woman with large, uncertain eyes.

Bale bent in a formal bow. "May I introduce Amaryllis Kilsgaard and her mated husband, Lucian. My *roylea*, I present Ari…uh, Ari…"

"Rayner," she supplied and offered her hand. "I'm Ari Rayner. Pleased to meet you."

"The pleasure is truly all mine." Amaryllis grasped Ari's hand and pulled her into an enthusiastic hug. "Welcome to our home. Sit, sit, sit. Are you hungry? Parched? Lucian, fetch us some refreshments, please."

"Thank you, your high—Amaryllis, but we have already eaten, unless you have a need, Ari?" Bale asked. Damn, he was really going to have to watch his language around the human.

"I'm fine." She perched on the edge of the suede sofa, hugging the bag on her lap while her gaze swept over the room. "Your home is lovely."

"Thank you." Amaryllis sat next to her and clasped Ari's hand between her own. "So, Bale, what have you been up to?

How did you two meet? Have you known each other long?"

"We have recently become acquainted. Ari is to be a new resident in the city, but unfortunately her vehicle could not complete the journey. I found her stranded and offered a ride. She was intelligent enough to agree. My hope is for her to stay here until we can retrieve her car and she finds a place of employment."

"No," Ari shouted then covered her mouth with her free hand. Red swept up her face from her neck to her hairline. "Sorry. I meant just for the night. I don't want to impose or intrude or be disruptive in any way. One night is all, really, unless you are busy now. I can leave and go elsewhere."

"Ari." Amaryllis stopped the litany with a finger pressed across Ari's lip, who gasped in surprise at the contact. "Not another word. We would be honored to host Bale's lady."

"I'm not his lady," she mumbled around the finger, before Bale had a chance to make the correction.

To hear Ari say the words he himself intended to speak was like a sucker punch to the kidneys. No, she was not his lady, and he had no intention of changing the label, but the thought of laying claim to such a lovely creature heated his blood. Unbidden, the image of Ari laid out on his bed clouded his mind. Her red hair, a tangled cloud on his pillow as she looked up at him with sex-drowsy eyes and lips swollen to a deep pink from his kisses. Bruises marked the pale curve of her breasts and chest, where he had bitten her, like tribal tattoos. She'd have her thighs spread wide in welcome, revealing her slick sex that glistened with his seed as he came over and over—

A sharp cough and a jab in the ribs from Lucian's elbow jarred him from his lusty thoughts.

Ari stared up at him with a confused frown while Amaryllis beamed with a smile as bright as a million-watt light bulb.

Double damn. Ari might be clueless to his dirty thoughts, but with their empathic powers, Lucian and Amaryllis possessed the ability to feel his hungers as if they were their own. By the tension humming off Lucian and the rosy flush on Amaryllis' cheeks, they both knew exactly what he had been thinking.

"I apologize," he rasped in a voice steeped with residual desire. "It has been a long journey and I am succumbing to the effects. Was there a question?"

"No." Amaryllis chuckled. "I have absolutely no questions for you."

He choked down a groan and forced himself to keep his facial expression pleasantly blank. He'd already given his princess enough cause to plot a scheme to bring him and Ari romantically together. The more he protested, the harder she'd dig in her sharp heels and force the matter.

"*Akita*," Lucian interjected. "I have a few business matters to discuss with Bale. Why don't you take Ari to the guest quarters? I'm certain she would enjoy a nice soak in the tub."

Amaryllis' eyes narrowed and her lips pinched into an expression that said she knew exactly why she was being sent away. The determined light in her irises did not give Bale confidence that any plans she had hatched had been deterred in any way.

"Very well. Is this the last I will see of you tonight, Bale?"

"Yes. I will be returning to my own quarters when Lucian and I are finished."

"Then I expect you at breakfast." She stood and crossed to his side to buss his cheek. "Good night. Lucian, let's leave him alone to say good night to his lady."

Lucian said not a word, but his amusement tickled the back of Bale's neck. Hopefully the general would remain silent about the subject when they met later.

"I am sorry for any assumptions Amaryllis may have made," he said once they were alone. "They are not used to seeing me consort with women."

"And here I thought you brought back strangers all the time." She winked and her smile made his breath catch. "She seems very nice, they both do. And they're beautiful. Freakishly so. Is everyone back where you're from gorgeous? What are they feeding you people?"

Beautiful? Was she including him in that remark? Impossible. He was scarred and somber, which left marks on his face that usually made people cower in fear. He knew females desired him. He was tall and muscular, which was a combination that seemed to elicit passion in human women. But he didn't believe himself to be an example of beauty. Masculine, yes. Beautiful, no.

Ari, now she was…exquisite. Soft in the right places, lean in others. Her femininity soothed his warrior spirit like a gentle breeze on a hot day, but there was a fire inside her that jolted his base urges like a live wire. He'd never experienced such a dichotomy before.

Not even with Natalia.

At the thought of his wife, his desire cooled and his mission became getting Ari ensconced in a guest room and then locking himself away in the solace of his own apartment. She had been enough of a distraction for one night.

He straightened his posture. "Amaryllis will see you have anything you need, and I will warn you, she will not listen to any protest you have of her doing otherwise."

"I've kinda noticed that."

"The entrance to the main house is on this floor. The floor above are apartments they lease to their employees. These floors and the garage you can access. You'll be able to roam wherever you wish, but stay away from the second floor."

"What's on the second floor?"

Debauchery in mass quantities. "Businesses you have no need to have access to."

"Like what?"

"Stay away." He bit his tongue for he realized how harsh the command sounded. "Look, I do not want you to find yourself in trouble for wandering where you should not be. I only wish for you to take care."

"Okaaay." She rose and adjusted the strap of her bag across

her chest. "So. Is this goodbye then?"

"More than likely, yes."

"Oh. Well, thank you for...you know, everything." With her left hand she held out his jacket, and her right hand for a handshake as she stared up at him with those blue eyes he felt he could lose himself in for the rest of his life and be perfectly happy.

The journey of his hand traveled in slow motion as he raised it to clasp around her dainty palm. The anticipation of the moment when their palms would meet raised his temperature. This touch was going to be different than when he had helped her off his motorcycle. This time there wasn't the distraction of the elements and the situation to detract from the texture of her skin.

An electric current raced up his arm as their hands grasped and he felt the answering jump in her pulse as she drew in a sharp breath. How easy would it be to pull her an inch closer? To lower his head enough to brush his lips against her parted ones?

Too easy.

He dropped her hand as if she burned him and took the jacket, bending into a slight bow. "Good night, Ari. Sleep well."

Without another word he turned on his heel and all but ran for the sanctuary of Lucian's office. He didn't bother to knock as he flung open the door and shut it as if the great dogs of the seven hells were after him.

"I never thought I'd see the mighty Balellanos so terrified, especially by a tiny female." Lucian chuckled from behind his desk.

"She's not that tiny." He straightened from where he had leaned against the door.

"I like the essence of her spirit. I can tell why you are attracted to her."

Bale gritted his teeth. As much as he wanted to deny it, Lucian spoke the truth and they both knew it. "She does have spirit."

"How did you meet? Truly?"

"I had passed an abandoned vehicle on the mountain pass. About a mile farther I came upon a truck that was parked off to the side of the road and the two male occupants were chasing her down. Just as I came to a stop one of the men tackled her to the ground. I was able to stop her fall."

"And prevented much worse, I am certain." Lucian rose and crossed to the bar. He gestured to a bottle of amber liquid. "What of her attackers?"

Bale shook his head at the offer. "They live. For now."

"Bale—"

"If they die, it will not be by my hand. Unless I discover them harming another."

Lucian sighed and folded his arms across his massive chest. "Bale, I understand your mission, I do. If…" He shut his eyes. His throat worked as if he swallowed down an ugly thought he did not want to express.

But Bale heard it anyway. If Amaryllis should be taken from him the people of Earth would share his anguish. And Bale knew firsthand what the general was capable of for he had been on the opposite end of Lucian's sword when he had come to take her life.

Lucian had been lucky. Bale had not succeeded and his commander was free to bask in the warmth of their love every day.

Yes, lucky bastard indeed.

"As I was saying," Lucian continued. "While I applaud your efforts to stop the persecution of innocent people, you have got to rein in the desire to end all confrontations with death."

"I only kill when it's in self-defense, and even then only for those who deserve it."

"According to you. You cannot be judge, jury and executioner."

Bale matched his imposing stance. "According to you."

"According to the laws of civility and common sense. While the humans' processes may be slow and contradictory, they must be of our utmost consideration. Do what you must to protect. And that is all. If you are discovered carrying out ultimate justice, you risk exposing all of us and our powers."

"I am always careful."

"But you are not perfect. Someday you will fail."

"And if I do, then I will fail on my own."

"No." Lucian crossed to stand in front of him and placed a

hand on his shoulder. "You are family. Maybe not by blood but because we've spilled blood together. Whatever fate befalls you, we will always be at your side."

Bale's eyes stung at the fervor in Lucian's declaration. "I do not deserve such consideration."

"But you have it. Always."

Damn him. Bale pinched his lips together. Damn both him and his mate. When he had been hell-bent on revenge no matter the cost, life was simpler. Once the two had shown him how misspent all that anger had been, he redirected his focus. They reminded him what it meant to care. What it meant to matter to someone else. To have another care for you carried the possibility to disappoint.

While Lucian's words were of caution, they were of little use. If Bale was ever to be discovered carrying out his brand of vigilante justice he'd fall on the sword before Lucian and Amaryllis felt the fingers of discovery upon them. On this he vowed with his life.

"And what of the girl?" Lucian asked.

Damn her too. Until Ari had come into his life he didn't have…wants. He didn't hunger for something soft. Until Ari he had no need for the touch of a woman, yet ever since he held her hand he had thought of nothing else.

"What of the girl?" So what if his tone was on the defensive side?

"You care for her, otherwise you would have not brought her to us."

"She was in danger and I saw to her safety. That's what I do."

Lucian's smile suggested he saw through the flimsy excuse. "What of her family?"

"She has not spoken of any. Whatever she left behind I sense was painful for her. She wants to make a new start here, but circumstances have not been kind to her. I was hoping Amaryllis could assist in Ari's new beginning."

"Do not fear. I believe my wife has found a new project in your Ari."

Bale bit back the need to correct Ari's title and chose to change the subject. "I shall only be in town for a day. I plan on leaving for the East tomorrow. Kristos and Brett may have need of my service while she is on maternity leave."

Lucian laughed. "Who would have thought one tiny baby could cause so much chaos?"

"But that little girl is loved."

"Beyond measure," Lucian agreed. "This family has much to be thankful for, and much to celebrate. Perhaps there will be more in the near future."

"Perhaps." Bale bowed. "If there is nothing else, I will retire to my quarters."

"Go. Rest, my friend." Lucian stopped him before he left the room. "Do not forget, Amaryllis expects to see you at breakfast."

"Of course. I live to serve my princess."

"Careful, Bale. She'll hold you to that if she hears you say that out loud."

Bale nodded. Yes, the princess would not hesitate to make him do as she commanded, and he had a scar on the inside of his thigh that attested to how well she wielded the whip.

✦   ✦   ✦

ARI WATCHED BALE race from the room and forced herself not to acknowledge the stab of hurt that made her eyes water. Why would she expect he would engage in something as touchy-feely as a goodbye hug? If there was one thing the man did not strike her as, that was being the sentimental type.

The appearance of Amaryllis entering the room straightened her spine and made her blink the telltale moisture away.

"Let me guess," her hostess sighed. "Bale needs a lesson on how to properly say goodbye to a woman he cares about? I swear, if I didn't love that man like a brother, I'd kick his ass into next week."

Ari had to laugh at the image. "I'd pay to see that."

"Come." Amaryllis threaded their arms together and led her up the grand staircase. "Let's get you settled. I have to admit, I am incredibly curious about you, and I do love to meet new people. Tell me, Ari. Where do you hail from?"

"Ah, well, I'm from a little town out in Missouri."

"I thought I heard a delightful lilt to your accent. I wish I had an accent, especially one as exotic as yours."

"You're kidding, right?" she asked with complete incredulity. Amaryllis spoke in the same musical cadence as Bale but with the enthusiasm of someone who grabbed life by the balls and squeezed until it screamed.

"Oh, I know, people say I have an accent, but I just do not hear it. Ah, here we are. Second room on the right is yours."

Amaryllis threw open the double doors with a flourish and revealed a plush suite that rivaled any five-star hotel Ari had seen on the Travel Channel. A California king-sized four-poster bed looked tiny in the space that held a complementary sofa and loveseat pairing, as well as a coffee table and armoire with a big-screen plasma television. The bedspread was cobalt-blue velvet and there were so many pillows on top of the tall mattress she'd need all her fingers and toes to count them.

"The closet is in here." Amaryllis opened another set of double doors on the huge walk-in that was lined floor to ceiling with cedar shelves. "And the bath is through this door."

Ari's bag dropped to the floor with a sad plop and her jaw hung slack as she stared at the marble-tiled shower that was so large there wasn't even a wall of glass or curtains to keep out the water. The tub alone looked as if it could fit four grown adults with ease.

"This…this is your guest room?" she gasped.

"Yes." Amaryllis blinked with surprise. "Is it not adequate?"

"Are you insane? This place is amazing. I've never seen anything so luxurious in my life." Her gaze dropped to her boots covered in mud and the tattered hem of her dress that had been ripped when the goober twins had tried to hurt her. God, could she look any sorrier? "Holy crap, why didn't you tell me to take off my boots? I've probably tracked mud all over." She bent down and unzipped the ruined Jimmy Choos and set them by the door.

"Do not fret. You're fine and now you are here with me. After a nice bath you'll feel as fresh as a flower after a gentle rain. Then you will sleep well and in the morning we will go retrieve your car and you can plan your next course of action."

This unexpected bout of good fortune was a double-edged sword. Of course she was grateful, but how would she ever repay such kindness? "Thank you, but I wouldn't want you to go to any extra trouble. I'm a perfect stranger and yet you've opened your home to me. I can't ask you to do any more."

"You aren't. I'm insisting. No." She held up her hand when Ari's mouth opened to protest. "It is settled."

Now Ari saw why Lucian had a private security detail for his wife. The woman was quiet the ball-breaker. "Thank you."

Amaryllis jumped up onto the mattress and giggled as she bounced. "Tell me about yourself, Ari. What has brought you to the city?"

"Oh, well." She fiddled with the edge of her sweatshirt then pulled the cotton from her shoulders and stalled for time by hanging the soggy garment up in the closet. "I'm looking for adventure. Something different. I figured this city may be a good place to start."

"Won't you miss your home?"

"Not really. There was only my mom and I, and we aren't

that close. There's nothing left for me there."

"What made you leave?"

Her fingers curled around the hanger. This was not a story she wanted to share, especially when she was surrounded by opulence and with a woman who appeared to have the world on a Tiffany platter. In comparison she was as dirty as her floral dress, maybe even filthier. The last thing she wanted was to be kicked out on her ass, or have Amaryllis think less of her.

The need to lie curled her tongue, but when she glanced over her shoulder and saw Amaryllis stare at her with those kind eyes and an expectant smile, her sense of self-preservation wilted. This woman allowed her into the sanctity of her home. The least Ari could do was grant her an honest answer.

"Bad breakup."

"So bad you had to move across the country to recover?"

"Yeah." She scratched at her arm. "The town I live in is pretty small. The biggest industries are farms and the state penitentiary. Anthony was a lawyer from St. Louis who often came to town for work. We met when he had dinner at the place where I tended bar. He was cute and high class and he made me feel special."

"How long were you together?"

"About a year. We'd meet once or twice a month, and Skyped when we could." She drew a big breath. "Then a few months ago the shit hit the fan. I didn't know that he was on the city council. And very married."

"Ouch." Amaryllis winced with sympathy. "How horrible for you. Were you in love with him?"

She opened her mouth to answer then paused to consider her response with an objectivity that came with distance. The time she had spent with Anthony before the blowup had been magical. She had had the best of both worlds with a boyfriend who showered her with gifts and attention when they were together and then left her alone to have the freedom that came with being a single woman, although she had never cheated on him during their relationship.

But had she loved him?

"I think I was more in love with how he made me feel. At least how he made me feel before the badness occurred. He made me feel sexy and wanted and worthy of being with a man with a fancy car and nice clothes, instead of the wrong side of the trailer park." She looked at her soggy sock-covered toes. "Guess that makes me sound shallow."

"Not at all. Flattery is very seductive."

"It sure is."

"How did you discover his deception?"

"A news crew showed up at my door asking me what it was like being a mistress and a home wrecker. His wife found the files of our video chats." Heat raced across her cheeks. "Apparently he had kept copies of the racier exchanges."

"The cad."

Cad? Amaryllis' vernacular made Ari smile. It reminded her of Bale. "I was quoted on the six o'clock news as calling him a motherfucking bastard."

Amaryllis laughed. "Why did the press track you down?"

"The whole thing was quite the political scandal."

"But politicians have affairs all the time, and you were an innocent party. Hadn't a bigger, better scandal come along to make you old news? What made things so bad that you had to leave your home?"

"His wife was six months pregnant."

"Oh."

"Yeah, oh. She has half the state's sympathy, and I'm the wicked, gold-digging jezebel. As I said, my hometown is small and the people thought I was more like my mom than I had appeared to be. I was shunned and it made things difficult at work. When I lost my job I decided to drive as far away as possible and start fresh. So here I am."

"Where were you planning on staying once you arrived?"

"A hostel or cheap motel."

"What about work?"

"I'm a bartender. Hopefully it won't be too hard to find work," she said then dread settled in her belly. "Will it?"

Amaryllis stood then crossed to her side to envelope her in a hug. "You are a brave girl for wanting to strive for better. You will not regret this decision. I know in my heart it was for the best."

The comforting touch was too much for Ari to resist and she sagged into the smaller woman's embrace. Finally there was a human being who didn't think she was a horrible person for falling for the wrong guy. "Thank you, Amaryllis."

"Now, I want you to march in there and take that bath. Tomorrow we will have a hearty breakfast and map out a plan for your new future." She clapped her hands with delight. "Oh, there is so much I want to show you."

"Really—"

"No." Amaryllis slapped her hand over Ari's mouth. Okay, that move was still weird. "Have you not learned yet? I always get my way."

Ari thought of her giant husband. "Always? Lucian looks like he may have some sway over you."

"Only when I let him." She winked. "Good night, *lebshone*. My home is yours. Make yourself comfortable wherever you wish."

"Thank you again."

Amaryllis skipped out of the room and the quietness that settled in the wake of her departure hit Ari hard at how much space the woman's presence sucked up.

With nothing but her exhaustion for company, Ari went into the palace-like bathroom and spent five minutes figuring out how to turn on the tub's faucet before stripping her tattered clothes from her achy body.

"Ahhh. Holy fuck," she moaned as she sank into the coconut- and hibiscus-scented water. A switch near her head turned on the Jacuzzi feature and she groaned again as the jets hit all her sore spots.

Over her head a crystal chandelier sparkled in the soft light and little swirls of steam played with the ends of her hair. Now this was the life.

Or death.

"I died. That's what happened. When I fell, I hit my head and died and went to heaven."

She closed her eyes and floated on a sensuous cloud of aquatic divinity and wished never to wake from such a lovely fantasy, because seriously, who had ever been rescued by a sexy-as-sin fallen angel and delivered into the comfort of luxury reserved for royalty and the über-famous? Not Ari Rayner, that's for certain.

An hour later when the water had grown too chilly for comfort, she switched off the jets and opened the drain. A fluffy cotton towel awaited her on a warming rack and she thanked the Lord again for her good fortune. How she wished she had fancy nightwear to match her decadent surroundings. A cotton tank and a pair of shorts just screamed white trash, especially as she slid onto the silk sheets and rested her head on the overstuffed pillows.

Within seconds the day's events sucked her into the dark abyss of mindlessness, aiding her in rejuvenating her spirit and ridding her of the stress of the last few months. The contentment that seeped into her bones heated and thickened, pooling into her womb to simmer like a pot of *dulce de leche* on the stove. Fire licked up her belly to tease her nipples and a sheen of sweat broke out across her skin.

Her eyes flew open on a gasp and she realized her hand

was nestled between the slick folds of her sex. The feel of her own pussy was not an unusual one, but usually she was conscious when working her body to an explosive orgasm. Her gaze flew wildly around the room and found nothing but furniture and shadows while her breath whooshed in and out as if she had been running for her life.

What the hell had she been dreaming of to have her on the cusp of oblivion so readily? For Pete's sake, her head had just hit the pillows.

Bale. It had to be. That bathtub was made for sensual indulgence and there would be nothing more indulgent than seeing that muscled body of his lounging back in the tub with bubbles hiding and revealing all his gloriously male bits.

She moaned and thumbed the swollen bud of her clit as the images bombarded her mind. What harm could there be in giving in to a little bit of fantasy? It's not as if Bale would ever find out just how nasty her imagination ran.

Would he let her soap up his muscles and allow her full access to whatever she wanted to touch? Would he encourage her to straddle his thighs and guide her hips up and down as he impaled her on his cock? Or would he take her in the shower with nothing but him and her in the steamy enclosure and all five showerheads roaring at full blast? His arms were so strong he'd have no problem lifting her up to pin her back against the chilly tile.

Ripples rolled up her belly as she imagined the sight of her legs wrapped around his lean waist as his hips bucked and the cheeks of his ass flexed. The skin of his back would be tan, but she was certain he was pale below the waist. He would most definitely take off his shirt in the sun, but he didn't seem the type to bare all to the world.

He'd take her hard until she howled her orgasm into the spray, and when reduced to nothing but a quivering heap, he'd set her on the edge of the shower seat and push his throbbing cock into her mouth, forcing her to suck her cream off every pulsating vein. And she'd do it too, with gusto, all the while watching him through her lashes as his face tightened with the need to come. She bet his cock was so huge it would fill her mouth to overflowing, because of course he was hung like a champion stallion. This was her dream, after all.

Did she have the ability to make him cry out or would he remain as silent and vigilant as always and grit his teeth as the yearning burned in his dark eyes? The harder she sucked, the firmer he'd grow against her tongue until his cum began to spill from the tip.

With a growl he'd pull away and make her open her mouth so he could spray her lips and breasts with his cum. As the image of the hot jet of his seed splashing across her flesh flashed behind her clenched eyelids, her sheath tightened around her probing fingers. Her hips lifted from the mattress as her core turned molten and her blood boiled through her veins. She bit her lip to hold in her cries and tried to still her writhing as shame burned through her as quickly as her orgasm.

It was one thing to milk your body for pleasure in your own home but completely different when under the roof of strangers. This wasn't her bed. These weren't her sheets. Didn't Miss Manners have a rule that said one did not desecrate the hospitality of those who host you by masturbating in their guest room? Party foul.

A scream penetrated the walls of her room and brought her upright. Another high-pitched wail reverberated down the hall, followed by a guttural moan that was distinctly male.

Ari climbed down from the bed and inched toward the door, cracking it open an inch. A wave of lust enveloped her like fog rolling off the sea and the walls of her pussy constricted in response. Helpless to resist, she crept down the hall toward the sound and paused when the cries and the rhythmic smack of something heavy hitting the wall grew louder.

"Come again," a man shouted in a voice deep with need. "Now. Now!"

"Yes. Yes! Lucian, take me with that big cock," Amaryllis screamed in one long breath that sent chills down Ari's back. The cry then broke apart in staccato bursts as if she were being ridden hard.

"Holy shit!" Ari clasped her hand over her mouth and backpedaled down the hall.

Of course Amaryllis and Lucian had an active sex life. If Lucian were her husband, she'd probably think of nothing else but getting him alone and riding him every minute of the day. However, expecting them to have an active physical relationship and actually being within earshot of their lovemaking and seeing the walls shake with the fervor of their coupling was fascinating and horrifying all at the same time.

Man, no wonder she woke up so horny. Her subconscious probably picked up on their sexy vibe and let her imagination run rampant.

As the two lovers' shouting became louder and the paintings on the wall began to bounce on their hangers, Ari raced back to her room and shut the door. Even then her brain flashed images of what the pair must look like dripping with sweat and cum and wrapped around each other's gorgeous bodies.

The shouts grew louder and more frantic, and with them her heart raced and sweat trickled down her back.

Sleeping through this noise would be impossible, and with each moan and thump she couldn't help but imagine it was her and Bale screaming down the roof.

"Crap. I have got to get out of here."

She riffled through her bag then threw it across the room when she remembered she didn't have a change of clothes. Maybe a previous guest had left something behind in the dresser. The top two drawers came up empty, but she struck pay dirt on the next where she found a man's button-down shirt. A pair of jeans in a size too large were in another drawer and she whooped in jubilation before changing into the clothes as quickly as a seventh-grade girl after gym class who had yet to hit puberty. The pants were two inches too short but were covered by her boots as she zipped them up then stumbled out into the hall and down the stairs while the sound of furious fucking trailed after her.

The noise traveled into the living room and forced her to seek shelter in the kitchen, but that too was no safe harbor. Above her head a light fixture swung back and forth like a metronome, keeping time with the couple's shouting until they spiked in a crescendo like a diva hitting the high note on a hit record.

Ari wilted against the counter as the groans faded. Whoa. That was intense. No wonder they looked so bright and happy. Who wouldn't be when engaged in a relationship as intense as that?

Creak. Creak. Creak.

She looked up and saw the light begin a slow sway back and forth that grew as another round of moans filtered through the floor.

"Oh my God." She covered her face with her hands. "What are these people on?"

The longer she remained privy to their marathon sex session, the more difficult it was going to be to look either of them anywhere near their face come morning. Ack—No, not come-come. She shook her head. Gah, just at dawn.

Hell, she didn't think she'd even be able to stand in the same room with them without her cheeks flaming. Ah, the curse of being a redhead.

She ran out of the apartment and the elevator doors stood

open as if anticipating her need for escape. She ran inside and pushed the Door-close button and released her first easy breath as silence descended. Seconds later the door slid open, revealing the parking garage.

Hmm. Right. She crossed her arms with a frown. Where to now?

She eyed the elevator's display panel. Bale had told her the upper floors were apartments. The lower floors businesses. Next to the Number-two button was a placard. *The Cavern* was printed in a bold font.

The Cavern? Where had she heard that name before? Oh yeah, earlier when she had been researching Bale's employers she had seen the Kilsgaards owned a restaurant and another business called The Cavern. When she asked Bale about the name, he had quickly changed the subject. Much in the same manner that he had all but forbidden her from going to the second floor.

What was it about The Cavern he didn't want her to know about?

A smile curled her lips. Now was as good a time as any to find out.

Chapter Three

THE ELEVATOR CAR traveled in a smooth glide as Ari's heart picked up speed with the anticipation of adventure. When the doors opened a small alcove and a dark doorway covered by a red-velvet drape awaited. The residual beat of a solid bass line echoed through the corridor and pounded louder as she walked closer. With each step she worried her lip as she crossed the threshold and prepared to walk into the unknown.

"Can I help you?"

She turned toward the voice that had greeted her the second she stepped through the entry and into another dimly lit hall.

Security. Definitely security. The man was tall and broad-shouldered and wore a dark suit complete with an earpiece and a curly wire that disappeared into his collar. While his demeanor wasn't unfriendly, there was a definite "don't fuck with me" vibe in the straightness of his posture and the furrow in his brow.

Suddenly the notion to explore didn't seem like such a good idea.

"Hi." She forced a smile and hunched her shoulders forward in a move she hoped conveyed a sultry innocence. "I'm sorry if I wandered into a forbidden area. I'm new around here and staying with the Kilsgaards." Yes, and a little name-dropping never hurt.

His smile transformed his stern features into dangerously handsome. "You must be Ari. I heard you were a new arrival. Welcome to The Cavern. I'm Jax."

"Thanks." Wow, news spread fast around here. His welcome loosened her apprehension. "This might sound like a stupid question, but where exactly am I?"

"You mean about The Cavern itself or your specific location here in The Cavern?"

"Both." She laughed. "As I said, I'm new to town and I forgot to ask Amaryllis."

"The Cavern is a place where everyone is welcome and all who enter get exactly what they need. As long as it's legal, of course." He winked.

"Like a nightclub, with dancing and stuff?"

"Sure."

"Seriously? Then why was Bale so squirrely about telling me?"

His smiling mouth fell into a frown while his eyes narrowed. "Bale's here?"

"Um, yeah." She swallowed against the sudden tightness in her throat. "He brought me here. He said I wasn't allowed on the second floor, but never said why."

"Did he now?" The tension left his mouth and he smiled with a devilish light in his eyes. "Well, I think we need to give you the grand tour, then."

"Are you sure? I'm not really dressed for a nightclub."

"May I?"

She leaned back. "May you what?"

"Relax." He chuckled with a husky edge. He reached for the hem of her shirt and released the bottom buttons. With quick fingers he tied the tails into a knot above her midriff. "Plump up the girls a bit there. A little flash of skin goes a long way around here."

She adjusted her breasts to reveal an enticing amount of cleavage. "Ah, so you cater to those kinds of patrons."

"They're the best." He winked again and lifted his arm so the cuff of his jacket was near his mouth. "Donovan, this is Jax. Our special guest has made an appearance and I'm showing her around." There was a pause while Donovan responded. Jax's eyes swept up and down Ari with an appreciative light. "Ten. Most definitely a ten."

Oh good gravy. She forced down a smile as the redheaded curse kicked in and heat flamed across her face. What was with the men of this town? Were all of them handsome and seductive?

Now more than ever she was convinced that the powers that be had a vendetta against her. Why else would they see fit to surround her with sexy men who wanted to touch and tease when her focus was supposed to be on getting her life onto the path of normalcy? Some women might think she was insane to lament the situation, but she knew better when it came to men. The sincerest of smiles could hide the most devious of hearts. She refused to fall so easily again.

Jax held out his arm. "Shall we?"

"Lead the way." She waved away the offered arm and motioned for him to go first.

"Right." He smirked and led her down the hall, still managing to touch her with a light press of his hand on the small of her back. "This is the top floor of the club. At this level is where all the playrooms are located and Amaryllis' private suite, which is through that door over there."

"Playrooms?"

"Playrooms," he assured with a suggestive wiggle of his brows.

No way. He was teasing her, he had to be.

At least that was her conviction until they passed an open doorway and got a gander at the tableau taking place within the shadowed interior.

A woman was laid stretched out on what looked like a massage table. Above her head her fingers curled over the edge in a white-knuckled grip. Her dark hair spilled over the end and swayed as she thrashed about while a man stood between her naked thighs and thrust with wild abandon. Since his pants hung loose about his hips and her skirt was rucked up to her waist, Ari had no doubt as to what she was witnessing.

Two other men stood by the woman's sides. They had her

blouse open and her bare breasts bounced with each lunge of the man drilling away. With one hand they pinched and stroked bits of her flesh as they fisted their cocks with the other.

In the far corner of the room Ari saw a man hanging suspended from chains that fell from the ceiling. A woman was on her knees before him, her head bobbing back and forth as another women dressed in full-out dominatrix gear took a whip to his back.

"Holy. Shit." Ari jumped back and looked to Jax, who watched her with a knowing grin. "This a sex club?"

"I guess that's what you can call this part of the club. As I said, here you get exactly what you need. And for these people, what they need is a good fuck. See anything in there you want to give a try?"

"Not with you." She smiled sweetly.

Bale, hmm, now that was another story.

At the thought of Bale her mouth twisted. That sneaky bastard knew exactly what went on in this club, yet he didn't say one word. Why was that?

She had an idea and it soured her stomach.

This must be his go-to place for a booty call and he didn't want her cramping his style. As if his sex life had anything to do with her. If he had his little kinks and trollops holed up here, so what? It didn't matter to her if he had a sexual past, or present. They were complete strangers.

Well, it kinda mattered. Just a little. Even though it

shouldn't. But she'd get over it. Even if it killed her.

"So, Jax, what else goes on around here?" She wound her arm around his elbow and stroked his biceps. If Bale was allowed to have a good time, then she was too.

"Down this way is what we call the alcove. You can still hear the music from the dance club, but the space allows for more intimate conversation."

They rounded a corner and entered an area with curved couches sprawled in random patterns, sectioned off by maroon curtains that hung from tracks in the ceiling that allowed them to be splintered off in myriad directions. People clustered in groups from two up to ten in their own little semiprivate areas as they laughed and flirted while sipping from glasses filled with colorful liquid.

Ooo, and it looked like fun times were allowed here as well as Ari spotted a couple off to the side. A man had a woman draped over the arm of the couch as he took her from behind. The fact that the group of men seated next to them watched as if enjoying a dinner show spoke of how commonplace such an event was.

"Whoa. I guess people feel really free with their bodies around here."

"Some more than others. It's like with anything new. The unknown is frightening, but once you dip your toe into the water and realize nothing but pleasure awaits you, you become more than willing to dive right in."

She tore her eyes away from the fornicating duo. "And

what happens in the morning when faced with the light of day?"

"Since we have a lot of repeat customers, I think the morning after only whets their appetite for more. Follow me. This might be more your speed as a newcomer."

He led her down a grand staircase onto the main floor of the club that looked more like what she expected of a nightclub in the city. Before her lay the dance floor, crowded with partygoers who surged and rolled to the beat of the tracks spun by the DJ. To the right of her was a stage where two men dressed in red metallic Speedos performed an intricate fire-dance routine. On the left stretched the main bar lined with so many bottles, Ari couldn't fathom the amount of time it would take to do inventory. In the pub where she worked there had been three shelves behind the bar, and the bottles that had lined the top shelf of the hole-in-the-wall were considered house brands in The Cavern.

"Are you thirsty?" Jax asked.

"No. Not really. Besides, I didn't bring any money down with me."

"No worries." He rapped his knuckles on the bar twice. "Hey, Noah. This is Ari, Amaryllis' friend. Whatever she wants, all right?"

The cute young thing behind the bar nodded and flashed her a killer white smile. "Sure thing."

"For real? Whatever I want?" There had to be a catch.

"You're a friend of the boss lady. Whatever you want."

"*Whatever* I want?"

Both men nodded.

This was a theory she had to test. Her gaze went right to the top row and she smiled when she saw a full bottle of Johnny Walker Blue. She pointed. "Has that been opened yet?" It wouldn't do if the bottle had sat too long and gone stale.

"Not yet. A single or double?" Noah asked.

"Why the hell not? Let's have a double."

"Yes ma'am."

Noah turned and expediently climbed up the stepladder and retrieved the blue-labeled bottle. Within seconds he set a tumbler of amber liquid and a glass of ice water before her.

She reached for the glass of water and took a sip, then slowly went for the tumbler of amber liquid, fully expecting one of them to reveal that this had all been a joke and they weren't going to allow her to imbibe a whisky she knew retailed for fifty bucks a shot. When the glass touched her lips, she paused and breathed in the fumes, tasting the smoky fire on the back of her tongue. Both men watched her with bated breath and she noticed Noah's mouth part along with hers, his tongue peeking out to touch his lips as the first drop of whisky hit her palate.

She held the fiery liquid on her tongue for several heartbeats before swallowing with a loud sigh. "Smooth."

Jax laughed and shook his head. "You're going to be quite the troublemaker, I can tell. No wonder Bale is trying to keep you on a short leash."

"Bale's back?" Noah asked, going visibly pale beneath the dim lighting.

"Yep. If you're cool here, Ms. Ari, I'm going back to my post. Noah will see to any of your needs."

"Thanks, Jax." She settled onto a barstool and leaned over the bar to be heard better by the bartender. "Okay, Noah, spill it. Why does the mention of Bale's name make y'all nervous?"

His Adam's apple bobbed as he shrugged and began to load the glass washer. "Have you met the guy?"

"Yeah, he brought me here."

"Really?" He looked as if she had slid ice down his back. "Are you two like a thing?"

"No. We're friends. Kind of. Sort of." She shook her head. "Whatever."

"I thought he was a loner."

"I'm pretty sure he still is." When no more information came forth, she pressed on. "So what's the deal?"

Another shrug. "I don't know him that well, but he has a reputation of being something of a badass."

"Lucian seems to be somewhat of a badass too. So does Jax." She took another sip.

"Yeah, but at least they can crack a smile, or at least, Jax can. Lucian is a pretty somber guy, but he's like Barney the fucking Dinosaur compared to Bale."

"Why do you say that?" Damn, this was fine whisky.

Focus, brain. Intel on Bale.

"I've never seen him with any expression other than a

scowl. And I've only heard him talk once, and my vocal cords hurt just listening to him."

Oh, but she liked his raspy voice. Especially her nipples. They seemed to peak to attention whenever he spoke.

"And I've heard," Noah continued, "that if anyone asks him a question he just stares at them until they walk away, and if he does answer, it's only with a grunt."

"Yeah, he does seem to enjoy the single-syllable responses. But he's not *that* scary." Unless, of course, you were a potential rapist, and then he was downright pants-shitting frightening. "Did anyone stop to think that maybe he was lonely, or perhaps homesick?"

"Homesick? Maybe. Lonely? Only by his choice. There are a lot of ladies who've come through here and tried to break through his ice. I haven't heard of one who's been successful."

Interesting. She twirled the last of the whisky in her glass and fought back the bite of jealousy that was also stirred with the confirmation that other women found the brooding hunk of maleness as desirable as she did. At least he was discreet about his relationships, or at least that was how it sounded. She didn't believe Noah's story that Bale never took anyone up on their offer. Just because Noah didn't know about it didn't mean it never happened.

She tipped the last of the whisky down her throat and hopped off the stool. "Thank you, sir."

"Do you want another?"

"Not if I want to make it back to my room later. Another

time, maybe."

"Let me know if you need anything."

"Right now, I need to burn some energy."

Even with the hour being well past her bedtime she wasn't ready to return to the main house. Now that she knew Amaryllis and Lucian owned a sex club, who knew how long those two would be at it? If she was going to survive a night under their roof, she needed to run herself to the point of exhaustion before attempting to venture back.

The dance floor beckoned and the JWB helped her float on a cloud of mellowness and heightened her excitement for this unexpected pleasure. She loved to dance, but the only establishments back in her hometown were for Texas two-step or line dancing. The techno clubs were in the city and she never had the opportunity to spend the night sweating to the latest beat.

"Well, girl, you wanted new and exciting. Here's your chance," she murmured and rubbed her hands together as if she were taking a running start off a diving board and prepared to step onto the dance floor.

She bobbed back and forth, matching the sway of the crowd then slipped between the backs of two dancers and then shimmed around another pair. A few steps later she reached the middle of the floor and felt the press of bodies all against her and the thump of the bass beating inside her chest.

Yes. This was exactly what she needed. Complete mindlessness as she rode the wave of humanity, gyrating in syncopated beats as flesh rubbed against flesh and her heart beat in an accelerated rhythm. Her head tipped back and she lifted her arms in the air and closed her eyes. Hands came from nowhere and everywhere to brush across her shoulder, the small of her back or the curve of her ass in touches that ranged from gentle caresses to full-on groping. If a hand strayed too close to her breast or her crotch she gently moved it away and was delighted when her silent request was obeyed. This moment was only about her and dancing.

After a few songs went by someone became bold enough to snake a hand around her waist and pull her close against a leanly muscled body.

"Need a partner?" a husky voice asked in her ear to be heard over the music.

She opened her eyes and saw a cute cowboy-type guiding her hips into a bump and grind. "A partner for what?"

"Whatever you want, sweetness."

"I just want to dance."

He pulled her in tighter. "I can oblige. I like how you move."

"Thanks." She wrapped her arms around his neck and fell into the rhythm of his hips. "Keep your hands above the waist."

"How about this?" His fingers curved around her ass.

"I will walk away."

"Okay, okay. How about one hand? To keep us synchronized."

Oh, the man was smooth. But his dimples were so cute she couldn't resist. Plus, if he became too fresh her scream in this crowd would end his advances immediately. "One hand only. If you squeeze, I will take you out at the balls."

"Understood." He laughed with a wink.

Another song went by and her partner stayed true to his word and kept his hands in the authorized areas. But it wasn't much longer until she felt the ridge of his arousal pressing into her belly and his lips began to travel in gentle brushes along her cheek.

She really should stop him and end the tease immediately, but it felt so good to be held, to feel the heartbeat of another against her sternum. To be wanted.

The entire altercation with Anthony had battered her psyche. He made her afraid to enjoy something as simple as flirting. To always be on her guard was exhausting. Would she forevermore be anxious and wary to trust another, to love again? For how long would she meet a potential partner and count the minutes until he broke her heart? She didn't want to approach every relationship with a filter over her emotions. She wanted to be free to live for the day and say to hell with the rest.

Maybe the need to dance was about more than burning off steam. Maybe it was a tiny step toward reconnecting to another human being. Was it wrong to allude that she might be willing for more? Absolutely. Did she have the strength to walk away? Nope. In this she was a complete wuss. A weakling who was a slave to the desire to matter to someone, anyone, even if for the three and a half minutes it took to play the latest dance track.

Geez, she was such a—such a girl. And a needy teenage girl at that. She needed to run away from this stranger's arms, especially when she kept wishing the one holding her was a certain giant with stunted emotions and not the cute cowboy with the killer dimples.

As she tightened her fingers in preparation for pulling away, her partner stepped back as if she had kicked him in the nuts.

"What…" she began to ask and the words died on her lips as she noticed the terror in his wide eyes.

His chin rose up and up as he stared over her shoulder. Actually, all the dancers in the nearby vicinity had taken several steps backward and were looking behind her as if being stared down by the Terminator.

Despite the heat caused by the collective mass of bodies, a cold chill brushed over the exposed skin of her back and the tiny hairs on her neck raised in alarm. Something big and scary was behind her, she just knew it. She didn't want to look. Really, she didn't.

"Fuck," she sighed and turned around.

Uh-huh. Why wasn't she surprised?

Bale stood like an avenging angel with his feet spaced apart and his hands fisted at his sides. The fringe of his hair hung in his eyes, but the blaze of fury burned from between the strands and matched the intensity in the firm set of his jaw. His nostrils flared and for half a second she thought he was going to barrel toward her like a bull seeing red.

"You will leave with me now," he commanded in a low growl.

Ah, hell no. She struck her own Wonder Woman pose with her hands on her hips and straightened her shoulders. He dared to get bossy with her?

Taking a cue from his book, she kept her reply simple. "No."

His nostrils flared again. "You do not belong here. Leave now."

"No."

He took a step forward and the crowd gasped. "I will not coddle you like a child."

"Then stop treating me like one."

"We go." He dropped low, pitching his shoulder into her middle and carried her like a sack of potatoes off the dance floor.

"Are you fucking kidding me?" she screeched. "Put me down. Bale, put me down, you domineering asshole."

His brisk strides never faltered, so she reached between his legs and pinched at the soft underside of his testicles.

He barked in surprise and his knees buckled, pitching her to the side and dropping her to the ground.

"Why did you do that?" he shouted as he rounded on her.

"You have to ask? What the fuck are you doing?"

"You do not need to use such language with me."

"Oh, I'll use whatever language I want. I'm an adult and I am having adult fun. Who do you think you are, demanding I jump at your command?"

His nostrils flared again as his chest heaved. "It is for your protection that you do not remain here."

"Is that so?"

"Yes."

"Or maybe it's because you didn't want me to stumble upon your supply of booty calls."

His head snapped back. "I do not know what that means."

"Right. Whatever. Look, your business is your business, and mine is mine. I'll stay out of your way, you'll stay out of mine, and right now my way is back on that dance floor where I was having a good time."

"By letting men touch you in inappropriate places?" He grabbed her elbow as she turned. "Never. No man here shall touch you."

"Why do you care what I do? If I wanted to fuck every guy in this joint, that is my right and my choice. You have no say."

"I have every say."

"Why?"

The fingers of his left hand bit into her hips as he hauled her up against his chest. "Because you are—"

Mine.

The unsaid word hung between them as thick and elusive as smoke. The anger in his eyes had deepened, turning the irises dark and decadent with a fire she felt lick her cheeks. His jaw was clenched so tight she swore she could hear his teeth grinding over the music. His body vibrated, his entire being shuddered as his hands clenched and unclenched and all the thoughts he refused to give voice to played out in his amazingly haunting eyes.

Hungered. He hungered for her. Here in the middle of this vibrant crowd the intensity of his need blinded her to their surroundings, stroking her from neck to clit and everywhere in between. They might as well have been naked, pressed breast-to-chest for he was already on her, in her, driving deep with a desperation that bordered insanity.

Her lungs burned as she gasped for air and clutched his biceps, struggling to remain upright. Had she lost her mind? What was this happening between them? "Bale?"

"Ari." He groaned and lowered his forehead to hers. "Please." His voice cracked and his breath shuttled in and out over her lips in a light kiss. "Please come with me. You do not need to go back to your room, but please leave. There are people here who will use you, hurt you. I cannot allow that. Please."

As he begged he curled around her, protecting her from all the dangers he imagined were out to harm her, and at that moment she would do anything to soothe the anxiety creasing his handsome face. There was a time for every battle, and this moment was not it.

"Okay."

He deflated in her arms and hugged her tight for a brief second before releasing her and turning them toward the main staircase. He kept his arm around her waist as they walked. The touch of his palm on the bare expanse of skin tightened her nipples and made her thighs clench. As they passed the playrooms on the second floor his arm tensed and his entire posture went ramrod stiff. He hurried them in the direction of the elevator and drew up short when Jax stepped from the shadows and blocked the doorway.

"Ari. Done so soon? I thought you were just getting started."

"I guess I was more tired than I thought. But thank you for showing me around."

"Believe me, doll face, it was my pleasure."

Bale's giant hand slid around to her front in an attempt to cover as much exposed flesh as possible. The motion drew Jax's gaze, which narrowed with calculation.

The security man's smile broadened. "Let me know if you ever want another tour. I'll show you *anything* your little heart desires."

She scowled and stuck her tongue out at him as Bale issued a warning growl deep in his throat. Was the man insane baiting the beast?

"I'll keep that in mind. Good night, Jax."

"Good night. Sweet dreams, pretty lady. Bale," he acknowledged the other man with an icy nod.

Bale grunted in response and whisked her into the waiting

elevator.

When they were ensconced within the little car, the silence was just as oppressive as the pounding dance tracks in the club. Of course, that might have been due to Bale's harsh breathing and the overwhelming presence of his restrained emotions.

Damn, he was a volcano ready to blow. On the outside his expression was blank and he stood rock-still, but she could feel him, sense the tight leash he had coiled around his mental well-being. Was this why he was the way he was? Silent. Observant. Always watching with a quiet intensity because when he allowed himself to feel it overwhelmed his ability to remain in control?

She had the insane urge to push him as one would a bear with a sharp stick, just to see what would happen when the lid popped. Lucky for them all she wasn't drunk enough to perform that little science experiment.

"So." She licked her lips. "Where are we going?"

"Are you certain you do not wish to return to your room?"

"Ah, no. I don't think Amaryllis and Lucian are aware that the walls of their home are rather thin, and it didn't sound like they were finishing any time soon. Let's leave it at that."

His eyes widened, then he nodded. A red flush stole across his cheeks. "Then we shall go up."

He pressed the button for the top floor. When the doors opened, he led her to the emergency exit and a short flight of stairs up to the roof. Amongst the ventilation shafts were several garden boxes growing a profusion of flowers and vegetables in an abundance of variety. An outdoor kitchen took up the center, complete with a pizza oven and a grill. Normally she would have found such luxury fascinating, but her entire focus was on Bale, who had come to a stop at the balcony's edge. He gripped the iron railing with his eyes closed and took long, drawn-out breaths as he visibly struggled with whatever held him in its choking grasp.

"Bale, are you okay?" she asked from a respectful distance.

He shuddered and glanced at her from over his shoulder. "I apologize. I am sensitive to the emotions of others. I don't— I have difficulty amongst large groups of people. Especially those whose sole purpose is to act contrary to how they would behave otherwise."

"Then why were you inside the club?"

His eyes darted around. "Why was I inside?"

"Yes." She planted her hands on her hips. "And don't stall by repeating the question."

"I...had to retrieve something from my motorcycle. I was exiting the elevator as you entered the club and I was surprised to see you out and awake. I followed to make certain you didn't fall into any trouble."

Really? It sure took him a long time to reveal his presence if he had been following on her heels. The tingle in her gut told her he was hiding something, but for now she'd let his secrets lie. She had more pressing questions she wanted answers to. "Why is everyone afraid of you?"

That snapped his spine straight. "They do not know me. Because they do not know me, they fear me."

So he wasn't oblivious to the others' impressions of him. Interesting. "Why do I get the feeling you haven't done much to make friends?"

"My mission is not to make friends."

"Your mission? What is your mission? Protect Amaryllis and nothing else?"

"I...I also watch out for those who cannot protect themselves."

"What does that mean?"

He sighed and looked around as if the line of questioning were uncomfortable. "I keep my eyes and ears open. For anyone. Who may have need. Of. My strength," he answered in halting sentences.

"Like how?"

"There is no how, I just do. Much as you would help someone pick up a dropped item or open a door for another."

The swirl of disquietude continued in her stomach as she folded her arms across her chest. "Are you telling me you're like a Boy Scout on steroids?"

His eyes danced again as he sorted out his thoughts before he responded with a solid, "Yes."

"Why?"

"Why with all the questions? I am certain you help others as well, and without anyone asking about your motivation."

"Sorry, I'm just trying to understand why you've shut

yourself away from people. It sounds so lonely."

He shrugged. "It is who I am."

The conviction and acceptance of his solitary existence evaporated the last of her anger. Not five minutes earlier she had craved the touch of another, and here stood a man who purposefully cut himself off from contact even though it hurt him. Bale might have fooled himself into thinking he wanted to be left alone, but his actions of the night screamed otherwise. The man was adrift and in need. Why else would he have dragged her out of the club and up to the roof if he wasn't seeking some form of connection?

What was it about Bale that made her want to crawl inside his skin and smooth the frown from his brow? They were strangers, yet she felt a connection as if they were on a similar journey, two pieces of the same puzzle she wasn't allowed to put together.

All night long she had seen the signs and recognized him as one who had lost the ability to trust in others. In this regard they were the same, yet they couldn't have been more different. She ached for him, felt his isolation to her core and wanted to weep for the man who thought he couldn't belong.

The muscles in her arms and legs bunched, ready to run and wrap him in a hug, which instinct told her was not his style. To do so would probably make him shut down and place mental and physical distance between them, a possibility that made her heart hurt.

Bale closed his eyes and his hand went to the center of his

chest. His lips pinched together and he shook his head as if to refuse the unspoken compassion she knew shined in her eyes.

He cleared his throat. "We should go below. You need some rest."

"Why are you constantly trying to get me into bed?" She winked with a teasing smile to break the tension as a breeze stirred the nearby tree branches.

The corner of his mouth kicked up into the closest thing she'd seen him do to a smile and she wanted to give a victorious fist-pump in honor of progress.

"Perhaps it's because of the lines of strain I see on your face. I think you need your beauty rest."

Her brows lowered with mock anger. "Do you want to get your ass kicked? You may have everyone shaking in their shoes, but I can take you on."

This time he smiled for real and the breath whooshed from her lungs at the transformation of his features. Had she thought him merely handsome before? With that smile he was panty-dropping gorgeous.

Her chills turned into shivers as she imagined planting kisses along his chiseled jaw. She better change the subject before she did something stupid like drool. "So, how long have you known Lucian and Amaryllis?"

"Since I was a youth."

"He called you brother. I think. At least, that's what it sounded like."

Was that a wince? "Lucian was once my commander in

our military unit. You are cold."

Another sore subject? The man had more landmines than the beach at Normandy during World War II. "It's nothing. I don't want to go back yet. Talk to me. Tell me a story, anything."

He arched a brow and his shoulders went back. "Why?"

Because I don't want either of us to be alone. "Because I like the sound of your voice. Please?"

He was silent for so long she thought he was going to refuse, but then he motioned for her to join him on one of the reclining lounge chairs. "Sit by me. I'll keep you warm."

Nestle herself next to his hard body? Like he'd have to ask twice.

She bit her lip to stop the victorious grin from spoiling the moment and settled into place along his side on the wide chair. This idea was either brilliant or going to be a huge mistake.

Her head rested against the perfect pillow of his chest as he wrapped his arm around her back. Dear Lord, she was going to melt right there. "Ooo, you're warm. You're always warm."

Was that a chuckle that made his chest bounce? When he spoke, his steady voice rumbled under her ear. "Look up at the sky, Ari. See that bright-blue star over that skyscraper?"

She nodded and forced her eyelids to stay open as drowsiness swept over her. Pharmaceutical companies could make a fortune in sleeping aids if they could bottle what Bale provided with his embrace.

"That is Saturn. Two-thirds the size of Earth and the center of six moons. A planet consisting of an enormous compilation of gases and rock, yet if I hold up my finger, I can cover its light and pretend it doesn't exist. But it does exist, and its place in this universe is important, whether you recognize its existence or not." He looked down at her and she fell into the fathomless pool of his eyes. "Do you want to know what my mission is, Ari?"

She nodded, hypnotized by all that was Bale.

"It is my job to ensure that all life is given a chance to shine. Whether their existence is recognized or not, because you never know if one tiny spot of life is the center of the universe for an entire race of people."

"Why does that job fall on you?"

He reached up and trailed his fingertips over her cheek. "Because I said so. Now, good night, Ari."

She felt the press of his thumb against her neck and then there was blackness.

✦   ✦   ✦

SO BEAUTIFUL.

Bale released the pressure on the vein that put Ari to sleep and swept his fingers down the milky column of her neck. Not for one second was he sorry he invoked the Skandavian sleeper hold to force her to rest. The woman was beyond exhausted and didn't know when to stop being so damn intriguing. Another moment longer, he might have forgotten his vows and crossed a line of no return.

Again he wondered what it was about her that had him running in eight different directions that all lead right back to her. She was sunlight and sin. Magic and adrenaline. She had a special light that made him want to sweep her away and horde her like a rare treasure. She was everything he wanted but couldn't have.

However, just because he refused to give in to her charms, that didn't mean he couldn't enjoy the sight of her in his arms. With featherlight touches he traced the supple line of her lips and the curve of her cheek. He didn't dare go below her collar, as it was the tempting swell of her breasts pressing against his ribs was torture enough to endure. To give in to the urge to fill his hands with her softness would make him no better than the scum he rescued her from in the club.

At the thought of the club his anger rose anew. Damn Jax for not seeing to her safety. He knew Lucian had alerted security that Ari was a special guest and Jax should have sent her right back to her rooms the moment she stepped off that elevator, not given her a VIP tour of the place. After what Bale had witnessed, the man was lucky to be alive. So too was the human who dared touch Ari so intimately.

Bale bit back a roar of displeasure as he recalled the sight of Ari's red hair bunched in the man's hands as he groped her back and buttocks. Bale's powers had sensed how the male had been patiently waiting and priming Ari for the right time to remove her from her clothes while all Ari had desired was comfort, someone to hold her. The sweet purity of her need had clashed with the man's fiery lust and manipulation and made a foul cocktail that had burned Bale's throat raw. What if he hadn't made it in time to stop her from doing something foolish? *Jesu*, what if he had found her in one of the play-rooms? Sweat broke out across his forehead at the thought. Blood would have most certainly been shed.

Ari moaned with distress and stirred in his embrace. With his thoughts on what might have been, his arms were con-stricting her breathing. He loosened his hold and brushed a kiss to her forehead while whispering hushes until she settled down. Funny how that trick worked just as well on Ari as it had his child.

Once he was certain she was asleep, he rose to a stand and cradled her to his chest.

Where was his mind at? She was only a woman, a human who had needed his protection but for a brief moment. Why was he now so determined to see to her every need? For over an hour he had tossed in his bed, wondering if Ari had taken to her new surroundings until his worry drove him to seek her out.

When he had discovered she had left the apartment, he about had two heart attacks, and the anxiety quadrupled when he found her in The Cavern. The tension eased only slightly when they had reached the open air of the rooftop. She was not his and yet the yearning and sense of propriety was there, driving his every action. Whatever spell she weaved upon him had to be broken, and only distance was going to do the trick.

He used his house key and juggling skills to enter the main house and return Ari to her room. The thick scent of woman and the sight of damp, rumpled sheets made his cock instantly hard. Apparently Ari was not immune to the sexual charge Lucian and the princess generated when they made love. It was told that the night they bonded, half the state went into orgasmic shock and ten months later a mini baby boom occurred.

To know that Ari had been twisting amongst the sheets, searching for relief made the cum boil in his balls. What had she been thinking about? Had she dreamt of him?

No. Do not think on it.

He laid her upon the bed and without a second glance he ran from the room before his libido took over. By morning's light she would be on her way to the next great adventure she had been searching for and he would be back in the shadows. Where he belonged.

The image of her in bed pleasuring herself dogged him with every step down the hall. The tropical scent of her bath soap clung to his shirt, teasing his senses with the possibility of having that fragrance rubbed into his skin. Damn it all to the seven hells! How was he to go to sleep now when his body demanded action?

Hmm. Simple enough answer. He wouldn't.

With a quick stop back at his apartment he retrieved his sweatshirt, jacket and long sword and went back to the rooftop. He climbed on top of the railing and closed his eyes, filtering past the noise of the city and the cacophonous cloud of thousands of people's emotions. Even after a year of learning how to deal with the constant bombardment of mental noise, he still found it difficult to funnel his concentration, which was another reason why he hated The Cavern. The den was a bubbling cesspool of contradictions. It was a wonder he had been able to locate Ari there at all.

He puffed out two short breaths and strengthened his focus, skipping over surges of annoyance and petty anger in search of signs of stomach-clenching terror that left a person incapable of defending themselves.

A sign such as the one he sensed came from an area to the north of his location.

He drew the hood of his sweatshirt over his head and with a flinch of muscles he was off, leaping off the ledge and landing in an elegant crouch five stories below. He became a black blur to those he ran past, a figment of their imagination if they were ever pressed to ask. The beacon of distress intensified as he entered the main shopping district. At this time of night the upscale department stores and specialty shops were empty but for the occasional janitor or security staff, yet a sharp jab punched him repeatedly in the gut, pulling him deeper down the dark street as if he were a fish on a hook.

Ah, there. At the jewelry store. Through the windows the store appeared dark and empty, but a malicious presence was most definitely inside. He slipped from shadow to shadow to the back of the room where he found the service door closed but unlocked.

The hinges creaked as he opened the door, but he moved so quickly, he was hidden in a dark corner of the hallway by the time anyone came to investigate.

A man-child, for he appeared barely old enough to shave let alone carry the gun he gripped in his trembling hand, entered the hallway and scanned the area. Bale calculated that whatever had brought the male to this location was a last-minute decision based on his attire of jeans, red t-shirt and brand-new bright-white Nikes. Not exactly the uniform of a seasoned thief. He hadn't even bothered to cover his face.

"It's nobody," the man shouted over his shoulder and turned to go back into the only lit office.

Bale followed and paused outside the doorway, hiding in plain sight. Since he wasn't an expected presence, their lack of attention was a perfect disguise.

Inside the office a second gunman held his pistol on a young girl who was sobbing in hysterics as she fumbled with the dial on a closet-sized safe. An older gentleman lay passed out on the floor. Blood seeped from a cut near his temple and a purple bruise colored the exposed side of his face.

All four occupants in the room appeared to be descendants from the same nationality with their straight black hair, olive complexions and almond-shaped eyes. Somewhere from East Asia, if Bale remembered from his lessons about Earth.

As the girl fought to control her crying she stuttered in a

language he did not understand, but the tone in her voice pleaded for mercy in a way that sounded the same in any language.

Also universal was the malice glittering in the man's eyes as he barked at the female and waved his gun to spur her to move faster. A narcotic of some type coursed through his veins, amplifying and scattering his emotions like broken shards of mirror, distorting the true reflection.

Once he obtained whatever treasure was within that safe, Bale was positive the girl was going to be destroyed. It wouldn't matter if she physically survived, the woman she had once been would be gone forever.

Bale drew in a breath and allowed his arms to swing free in preparation. With his skills and speed he could decapitate both men before they heard the sound of his blade clearing the sheath. But he had promised Lucian to spare lives if he could, and full-out murder was not his style. The quickest course of action was to render them unconscious and hold them until law enforcement arrived.

An anticipatory smile curved his lips. But what would be the fun in that?

He rapped on the doorjamb. "Excuse me, may I join the party?"

Two guns whipped around in his direction. "Who the fuck are you?" the mastermind shouted in broken English.

"Your worst nightmare." He nodded at the girl. "Do you speak English?"

She responded with a single jerk of the head, her terror grew as she stared up at him.

"Don't answer him," Foul-mouth shouted and smacked her in the back of the head. "Tinh, kill him."

The scout jumped. "What?" Then volleyed a fevered dispute in his native language.

Terse sentences and wild hand movements ensued while Bale gestured to the female with a slight wave of his hand to remain calm. Her eyes widened but she pressed her lips together and tensed her muscles as if to will her body to settle down.

He nodded his encouragement then looked back to the quarreling duo. "Gentlemen, gentlemen. Allow me to settle this argument for you."

The woman screamed in surprise as he traced across the room, knocking Tinh's gun from his hand and breaking his arm at the elbow in the space of a heartbeat. As Tinh fell to the floor in howling agony, Bale had the second gunman up against the wall by the shirt front. He wrapped his hand around the bony wrist holding the gun and applied enough pressure to make the man wince and drop his weapon.

"Have you sounded the alarm yet?" he asked the girl without taking his gaze away from the squirming worm.

"N-no."

"Do it now. Then gather any rope or cord you have and bring it back here. Even a telephone line will suffice."

The patter of her shoes as she ran out the door indicated

she followed his directions and that he had about five minutes before the police arrived.

Bale tightened his grip and soaked in the man's adrenaline-laced terror like a junkie getting his fix. Screams drowned out the sound of bones turning to dust as he pulverized the wrist. The man better pray he was ambidextrous.

"You will never pick up a weapon to cause harm again. You will never touch another in anger. One step out of line and I will be there to strike you down. Do you understand or shall I continue the lesson with the left wrist?" he taunted.

A lot of nodding and agonized whimpers was the response.

"Alarm is on," said the girl as she ran back into the office, carrying an armful of extension cords and spools of metal wire.

"Tie them up, little one." He dropped the thief on the floor next to his partner.

"Tie them up?" she repeated in shock.

"I cannot be here when the police arrive, and I will not leave you alone with them if they are still mobile. Tie them up. Secure the restraints as you see fit. May I suggest you show them the same courtesy they bestowed upon you?"

"Oh, no." She tried to push the ties into his arms. "It not proper."

"Tell them I did it."

A light entered her eyes as the possibility of partaking of the forbidden chased her fear away. "Yes?"

"Yes."

She dropped her supplies onto the floor except for a length of extension cord. She began with Tinh's feet and wrapped the cord around his ankles several times, securing the ends into a knot. The fine metal jeweler's wire she used to wrap around his wrists. When she pulled on his arm to position them in to place, he cried out in pain. She hissed in sympathy then her eyes narrowed and a shy smile emerged as she bound his hands with an extra vicious twist for good measure.

Bale left her to finish her task as she started on the second assailant and he sensed her satisfaction in having a tiny outlet to express her displeasure. By the time he reached the rooftop of the building across from the store, blue and red lights flashed as the police roared up the street and skidded to a stop.

Two more lives saved. Who was next?

Chapter Four

WHAT THE HELL happened?

Ari rolled out of bed and held on to her head as she staggered into the plush bathroom. If she hadn't seen the bartender pour her drink, she would have thought she had been slipped a mickey. She was usually better at holding her liquor, especially when she only had the one. And most especially when snuggled in the arms of a ridiculously hot guy.

Had that whole event even happened or had she hallucinated the entire moment? Maybe she had been more exhausted than she had realized. One minute she was feeling groovy and relaxed next to Bale's heat then wham, nothing. Complete blackness until she woke up, still fully dressed and tucked into her borrowed bed.

The idea of Bale carrying her in his arms and laying her down on the fluffy mattress sent a surge of heat through her veins while her brain kicked her in the ass. While the fantasy of Bale doing wicked things to her was nice, she had a future to begin, like, now. Bale was going to have to reside in the place of might-have-been. At least for now. The future was still undecided. Maybe in a month or two things would be different.

In a month or two, she reminded herself and set about facing the day.

She splashed cold water on her face and changed into another borrowed shirt before racing down the stairs where she was greeted by a smiling Lucian.

"Good morning," he said with a slight bow.

"Morning." She brushed a lock of hair behind her ear and sneaked a glance at him from beneath her lashes.

Lucian was dressed in black slacks and a white button-down shirt that made his tan skin appear golden. It stretched dangerously tight across his melon-sized biceps. He was what she'd call tongue-tying gorgeous, so handsome he robbed her of the ability to form a sentence.

But that was before she met Bale. Yeah, after spending time with tall, dark and silent the only thing that made her nervous around Lucian was that now she had a good idea of just how well he used his cock. A mental image that was not going to go away any time soon.

She felt the heat of the redhead curse steal across her cheeks. "I'm sorry to have slept so late. I'm sure y'all have lots going on, so I'll be out right quick. If it's all right though, I'd like to grab some toast before heading on my way."

He laughed. "Do not fret. You needed to rest and we are happy to have fulfilled that need. And I know you require more than toast to fill your belly. Come with me. Amaryllis has been cooking all morning. She loves to have people to fuss over."

"She shouldn't have, really. I don't want to be a bother."

"We know, and you aren't." He gestured for her to precede him into the kitchen, which she did while wishing her embarrassment to die down.

"Whoa." She stopped short and gaped at the buffet spread across the center island where bowls of fruit cut into decorative shapes bookended platters of eggs made three ways and the entire roll call of pork, from sausages to ham steaks. "Is she expecting an entire football team?"

Lucian chuckled and reached across her for a slice of bacon. "No. We men can eat a lot."

"Men?" As in plural?

"Good morning," Bale rasped by her side and she nearly jumped ten feet into the air. Damn, that man took silence to an entirely new level.

"Morning," she mumbled and took a sudden interest in the star-shaped pineapple and melon balls as the heat in her cheeks returned.

What else was there for her to say? *Sorry for passing out on you,* or, *Were you the one to tuck me into bed?* Yeah, that sounded real classy.

Lucian rescued her from having to break the silence. "Bale, is all taken care of?"

"Yes sir." He bowed. "It is with the repairman."

"Good. Well, take a seat everyone. Amaryllis? Where are you? We're starving."

"Eat then," she called out as she entered from the pantry with a green bottle in her hands and a smile stretching her lips. Bacon grease and strawberry juice dotted her purple apron and tendrils of hair fell from her ponytail, but there was no mistaking her happiness at providing for her family. She held up the bottle. "I thought mimosas would be fantastic this morning."

Ari saw Lucian lean over and whisper into Bale's ear, who then nodded with a twitch of understanding in his brow and offered Amaryllis a slight smile. "That sounds lovely."

What was that about? Had he never heard of the orange-juice-and-champagne cocktail before? Granted, she had never heard of it either until she was fifteen and saw them in a movie, but Bale was surrounded by people who owned food and beverage outlets. Maybe the drink wasn't popular in Sweden.

Her curiosity was interrupted when Amaryllis hugged her tight and said, "Good morning, Ariel."

The woman might as well have hit her upside the head with the bottle of champagne. Her heart pounded hard and for several seconds she couldn't breathe. When the need for oxygen overrode her surprise she gasped, "What did you call me?"

"Ariel. That is your full name, correct?"

"I—how?"

"And it is a beautiful name."

"Unless you're a redhead," she managed to sputter. How in

the hell did Amaryllis know her real name?

"Why would that be?" The woman blinked with innocence in her lavender eyes.

"Ha ha. Funny." A long silence ensued as three pairs of eyes stared back at her without comprehension or teasing. "Seriously. Seriously?" Nothing. "Look, I know y'all aren't from around here, but you're from Sweden, which is like, right next door to Holland, right? I know you've heard about *The Little Mermaid.*"

"Ah." Amaryllis clapped her hands. "That is a cartoon, correct? One of the girls in the club dressed like the character last year at Halloween. Is that who you are named after?"

"Unfortunately, yes. Do you know how many times I've been asked to show my tail? People can be cruel." As well as the press. *The Naughty Little Mermaid* had been a popular headline when the scandal broke out.

"Did your mother not suspect this name may cause you strife?"

"At sixteen my mother wasn't much older than a child herself when she had me. She thought it would be cute. She was wrong. Please, just call me Ari."

"As you wish." Amaryllis handed her a champagne flute. "Mimosa?"

Ari ignored the glass. "How do you know my name?"

"When we retrieved your car, we had the vinny number researched to make certain it was yours."

"You what?"

"Vin number, *alskata*," Lucian corrected. "Ari, please have a seat and all will be explained."

"Yes, Ari, fill your plate and we will chat." Amaryllis thrust a plate into her hands.

Only because the Kilsgaards were smiling at her and not emitting malicious intent, she followed the directive and kept quiet.

"I'm sitting," she said the moment her butt hit the lushly upholstered chair.

"Take a bite."

"Amaryllis," she growled but took an obligatory bite of fluffy eggs. "Oh, that is good."

"Thank you." Amaryllis dropped onto a chair next to her husband. "Now, this morning Lucian and Bale located your vehicle and had it sent to a local repair shop to be taken care of. Once it is in working order, it will be sent here. In the meantime, you and I will go out and do some shopping and celebrate new beginnings."

"While shopping sounds great, I'll need every dollar to go to the car."

"Nonsense. Everything is my treat."

She froze with a full fork near her lips. "What? That can't mean what it sounds like."

Lucian chuckled behind his napkin as Amaryllis nodded enthusiastically. "Yes. I've covered the costs."

The fork clattered to her plate as she was again struck dumb. She really needed more rest to keep up with all of these surprises. "You—why? I-I—How?"

"Say thank you, Ari." Amaryllis saluted her with her champagne flute.

"Yes, yes, thank you, of course. Both of you. It's more than I could ask for. But I can't accept such a generous gift."

"Why not?"

"Because I'm a stranger."

"And?"

"Isn't that enough?" She looked at Bale, who had inhaled an entire plate of food and was going back for seconds. "Bale, tell her it's too extravagant."

He paused like a child caught doing something naughty. "No."

"What do you mean, no?"

"I have learned not to argue when Amaryllis is being generous. It is a losing battle." He turned his back to her and scooped up a platter of fruit.

"I still can't accept."

"It is already done."

Well, crud. "I'll repay you. I promise."

Amaryllis smiled. "You will, in a way. I've been checking up on you, Ari. You weren't just a bartender at your last place of employment, you were an assistant manager, weren't you?"

"There wasn't a whole lot of competition for the position." If she hadn't watched the inventory and the daily take, the bar would have gone out of business due to theft years ago. Of course, that diligence hadn't mattered when public opinion of her turned ugly and they booted her on her ass.

"My restaurant, Tutala, is in need of a bar manager. Someone who has grace and poise, as well as the ability to handle the occasional unruly customer. What do you say, Ari? Would you like to give it a go?"

"Are you offering me a job?" she squawked at the same time she heard Bale bark with just as much incredulity, "What did you say?"

"Yes, and before you ask if I am insane, or believe you are unworthy of such an offer, this is not a done deal. What I am offering is an opportunity to prove yourself. We will start slow and I'll introduce you to the right people to get your feet wet, and then I'll throw you into the deep end." She grinned.

"Your highness—" Bale began and was stopped with a shush from Amaryllis and her palm held an inch from his face.

"No." She shook her head and closed her fingers together in a "close your mouth" motion. "No."

And he obeyed!

Well, he fumed, with those expressive nostrils flaring and his lips pinched tight, but he didn't say another word.

Whoa. Ari felt her eyebrows hit her hairline as she tried to decide what surprised her more, the fact Bale addressed Amaryllis like royalty or how she silenced Bale as if he were a child, and he didn't put up one iota of an argument.

Just what exactly was going on here? Bale had mentioned Amaryllis had been some sort of a celebrity where they were from. Perhaps she was a secret princess and he was part of her secret service detail? If that were so, then why would he be allowed to leave her side?

"Ari." Amaryllis interrupted her train of thought. "Do you agree?"

Of course! Yes! Absolutely!

But the words refused to leave her tongue. Free car repair, a place to stay, a job. Twelve hours prior she had nothing, and now she was being offered the world. She should be ecstatic, jubilant, on the ground and kissing the feet of her hosts. It was a Christmas miracle, only it was February.

Why her?

That was the question she couldn't comprehend. Why was she suddenly so deserving of such good fortune? Everything she ever had, from her crappy car to the two-bedroom apartment she had left behind, she worked hard for, scraped together every penny she earned with her sweat and tears. The only time something had been handed to her was when she had met Anthony and he had lavished her with presents and attention.

And look how great that turned out.

"I still don't understand. Why me?"

Lucian reached for Amaryllis' hand. "We have all been where you are now, Ari. Alone, in a new land, with only what you carried with you. However, I was fortunate enough to have had my brother with me, unlike Amaryllis and Bale. But we all found someone who was willing to take a chance on us. Whether we felt we deserved it or not." He shot a pointed glare at Bale, who stared down at his plate. "They provided us with an opportunity and that is what we offer you. What you do now is your choice."

Was it really so simple? Had she really stumbled upon the kind of people who did things out of the goodness of their hearts? Had fortune finally decided to smile down on her?

Okay, Ari. What are your options?

Say no thanks, give them a hearty handshake and walk out into the big city and stick with the original plan of hoping to snag a job quickly and make do in the low-rent motel she had booked for a month, living day-to-day on a hope and a prayer.

Or...

Stay with the Kilsgaards, who probably saved her a boat-load of money on car repairs, in a penthouse apartment and try her hand at managing the bar in an upscale restaurant that even she had heard about all the way in Missouri.

Yeah, this was going to be a tough choice.

"Okay. I accept. But I want to pay rent and for my own groceries. And I'll move into my own place as soon as I find one."

"Agreed." Amaryllis clapped her hands together with a little squeal. "I know just the apartment for you too. But first we'll have a girls' day out and I'll show you all around town. Tomorrow morning we'll go together to the restaurant. Sound good?"

"Yeah." She felt twenty pounds lighter with the decision made. "Sounds great."

Lucian beamed a huge smile and she felt her lips stretch to match until she looked at Bale. He remained frozen in his seat with eyes cast down and a hard line where his mouth should have been.

For half a second she felt her breakfast swirl in her tummy but then quelled the sensation with a fit of temper. What was his deal? Did he not want her around? Did he think she was encroaching on his territory by becoming friends with his bosses?

Well, screw him. She didn't ask for them to be nice to her, and did the idiot forget it was he who had insisted she come with him? And if he was worried about her being near his female hunting grounds, he could go suck an egg. If the option was to face his displeasure or be out on the street, she'd deal with his sourpuss mug anytime.

Amaryllis rose. "Ari, I'll leave you to finish your breakfast while I take a moment to freshen up. Bale, please join me in the study. I have an errand for you to make for me."

Bale nodded once and stood, bowing at both her and Lucian before exiting the kitchen without a single word.

Exclamation point on the snubbing.

"Try not to let Bale bother you," Lucian said once they were alone. "He had a difficult time before he joined us here and he's still adjusting. As you can tell, he's not exactly a— what is the phrase?—people person. I too have to remember that myself on occasion."

"He's mentioned something about that." She pushed her

breakfast around on her plate and fought the compulsion to indulge her curiosity. She didn't want to know any more about him. She didn't. Really. But... "I thought you all had traveled to America together."

"No. Circumstances sent us from our homes at different times. Fortunately we were able to find each other once again."

"You said you had a brother. Does he live in this building too?"

"No, he and his wife live in the mountains in a little town called Cedar. They just had their first child, so we don't have the opportunity to see each other as often as we'd like."

"It sounds as if you're close."

"We are. Until we annoy each other. Do you have any siblings?"

"Nope. Well, I don't know, actually. My dad ran out when I was born, so there is the possibility of half-siblings somewhere in the world."

"It sounds as if your childhood was rough."

She shrugged. "Others have had it worse. Since I didn't know any different at the time, I didn't have the idea that I was doing with less. It was what it was."

Lucian nodded and offered her half of his croissant, which she accepted with a small smile. "I believe it is the innocence of youth that allows us to survive the trauma of growing up. My sister-in-law is the town sheriff, so you do not need to fret about falling into the hands of nefarious people. She's very good at keeping everyone on the right side of the law." He winked.

"I didn't think y'all were nefarious."

"You should have. We are strangers to you."

As if she hadn't had this conversation in her mind a million times in the last twenty-four hours. "Are you trying to get me to change my mind?"

He chuckled. "Ari, there are two things I want you to understand. One, I love my wife to the point that it's probably an unhealthy obsession and I will do everything in my power to see to her happiness and safety. No one harms her in any capacity. No one," he repeated in a low, vibrating warning that set the hair on her arms up in surrender.

"I—" She swallowed down the lump of fear in her throat. "I would never try to hurt Amaryllis, or you."

"I know." He blinked the intensity out of his eyes and Ari noticed that he shared the same unusual lavender shade with his wife. "I sense it is not in your nature to hurt another, and if I suspected you had ulterior motives, you would have never made it beyond the front door. But my mate attracts a lot of admirers. Some of them may think to use you to get to her. Do you understand?"

She nodded and wondered again if Amaryllis wasn't a political refugee or fleeing celebrity.

"My wife has developed a fondness for you and will do all that she can to see to your needs. It's what she does. I am not saying you have to bow to all of her wishes, but please remember that what she does is out of love." He held up the first two fingers on his left hand for emphasis. "The second item for you to understand is that people she cares about become people I care about. If at any time you have a need, please come see me. Your well-being is of utmost importance. Transversely, if you do anything to place yourself in danger, you will find out firsthand exactly what it is like to have an overprotective big brother."

She laughed. "Thanks for the offer, but I can take care of myself."

"It is not an offer. It is a vow. To us, friends and family are one and the same. You may have been on your own before, Ari, but you have been accepted into this flock. Solitude will take on another meaning and believe me, it will be an adjustment. For a long while it was just me and my brother. To have others to rely on, who rely on you, was not an easy concept for me to accept. Bale is in the midst of that struggle right now, however, once you fall into the cloud of that belief," his smile softened and the lavender of his eyes turned liquid, "it is good."

Lucian's kind words brought tears to her eyes. A family. Not of flesh but of one forged by circumstance was never a dream she dared to have. Since she was old enough to feed herself, it had been her against the world, and life taught her that the only thing blood ties counted for were genetic diseases and a whacked-out sense of familial obligation.

These people were opening up not only their home, but their hearts as well. It might not have been their intention, but she was going to do everything in her puny power to do right by them. If they followed through on half of what they promised, she would not let them down.

"Thank you, Lucian, for everything. Did Amaryllis tell you about why I came to the city?"

"Nothing specific, only that you had a broken heart and needed a new start. While we do not keep secrets between the two of us, we will honor discretion if we are told something in confidence. When you feel it is right to tell me your story, I will be willing to listen."

"God." She dabbed her napkin against the corner of her eye. "You guys are like, frickin' make-believe. You can't be real."

He chuckled and brought his glass to his lips. "Do not think we are perfect. Far from it, in fact. Wait until you know us a week. Your opinion may change."

"Maybe. Maybe not. To me, you're like…like…superheroes."

Lucian sputtered, spraying mimosa over the tabletop. As she jumped from her seat to help dab up the mess, Lucian began laughing with a booming bass that was infectious and soon had her joining in, though she had no idea what had inspired the laughter.

"Ah, Ari," he said when he caught his breath. His mouth worked as he stopped and started several sentences before he shook his head. "Ari, welcome to our world."

✦   ✦   ✦

FOR THE SECOND time in less than twenty-four hours Bale was ordered to the study like a wayward child, only this time it was Mom who was about to come in with the smackdown.

Amaryllis rounded on him when she reached the center of the study. Her black hair settled around her shoulders in a straight, silken sheet. It still unnerved him to see her once-silver tresses in the same shade as those of her bonded mate. With her dark hair, she looked so much like his Natalia that at times it hurt to look at her. She was a reminder of what he once had and had been too afraid to accept.

His muscles tensed, waiting for her to lay into him. Of course she would have sensed his displeasure at the recent turn of events, and since she had an opinion on everything, he knew she would be determined to change his.

She rested one hand on her hip and watched him with those eerie, all-seeing eyes. Not once did she blink as she stared him down. But he wasn't going to break so easily. He held himself motionless. No need to add fuel to the fire by launching the first volley.

But Amaryllis would have none of that. She arched her brow and gestured with her free hand for him to speak first. "Spill it."

"What do you mean?" He could play obtuse with the best of them.

"I offer Ari a job and you flare up in annoyance. More precisely, joy followed by fear, panic and then annoyance. Why?"

He drew in a breath to stall for time. What would be the

most diplomatic way to speak his mind? "I do not think it is wise to… allow a human stranger to be in such close proximity to our kind."

"You brought her here."

Damn, she had him there. "She had a need."

"She still does." Amaryllis walked forward until she was a hairsbreadth away. Despite the fact she barely reached his shoulder, her presence made up for the difference in height. "Be truthful, Bale. You do not want Ari here because she makes you feel something other than guilt and self-loathing."

He sucked in a breath and pressed his lips together. No way in hell was he going to admit that, even though she was correct.

The hungers Ari stirred within him had been manageable when he had thought their time together was limited. With her living in the same building, within viewing distance, within touching distance, she'd be a constant temptation.

The night before had hammered home a terrible truth. Ari made him want. He wanted to wrap her hair in his hands and hold her still for his kisses. He wanted to pin her under his body and plow into her slick heat. He wanted to take her in every way a man can penetrate a woman until they passed out from exhaustion then resume as soon as they awoke.

Amaryllis had taught him that pleasures of the flesh were not evil. As long as all parties were consenting, they made their own rules as to what was off-limits.

And therein lay the issue. Ari might have acted blasé about

the activities that went on at The Cavern, but how would she react when asked to recreate some of what she had witnessed? Ari was so bright, so shiny, he doubted that underneath her wholesome appearance lurked a woman who could match his appetites, despite the flashes of lust his powers sensed. He had been afraid to share his darkness with his wife and had kept it secret. When she died, the loss of what he might have had with her had he been braver drove him to madness and a life of killing to make up for his failures to his family and as a husband.

If he had been worried about hurting Natalia, one of his own species, he was terrified of the damage he could do to Ari if he let go and fed his needs. Hell, he had caused her discomfort with a simple hug when he had held her too tight.

And what of his mission? Overriding all those concerns was the risk of losing his focus once he took a sip of her nectar. His sole purpose was to protect those who could not do so for themselves. Lounging betwixt Ari's thighs was a selfishness he did not dare entertain. His wife's memory deserved more.

"Bale." Amaryllis laid her palm against his cheek. "If I were still your queen, I would command you to open up your heart and believe in the power of love again."

He bit back a smile. Only a royal would believe they had the power to order another how to feel. "But you will do so anyway."

"No. I am going to pray for you, Balellanos. I am going to make a plea to every god of every faith in existence that you will find your heart again, because you are worthy."

His vision blurred as a band wrapped around his chest and up over his throat to squeeze the breath from him. He wanted to shout at her to not waste her energy, to deny her words, but he didn't have the strength.

When everyone had wanted him dead, Amaryllis was the only person who believed he had merit. She fought for him when no one, not even himself, thought him worthy to live. Her faith in him was both a gift and a curse, and why he swore fealty to her although she no longer wore the crown.

"Will that be all, your highness?" he asked in a voice as smooth as coarse sandpaper.

Her slight smile made his stomach clench as she uttered the words that struck fear into the hearts of every *Llanos* warrior.

"For now."

Chapter Five

CAPTAIN MARCO DEWINTER stomped down the aisle between the cubicles that made up the organized crime and vice divisions of the city's police department. The dramatic slamming of a door would have made his exit so much more satisfying, but since the only person with an enclosed office on this level was his POS commander, the pounding of his steel-toed boots on the paper-thin carpet had to do.

God, he wished he had a cigarette. Not that he smoked. Actually never touched the cancer sticks, but the idea of feeling his lungs catch on fire then letting it all out on a long, slow exhale sounded like an excellent distraction. Well, a good fuck would do that too, but he couldn't develop an ill-timed hard-on by fantasizing about cigarettes.

"What's the word, humming bird?" his lieutenant Cassidy Coulter asked as he held open the door to the elevator.

"Just a minute." Marco bit his tongue during the short ride down to the parking level and the hundred and thirty steps across the pavement to the police-issued Jeep Cherokee where he slid onto the passenger seat. "Drive," he ordered as soon as Cassidy stuck the key into the ignition.

The moment the vehicle left the garage and turned onto the paved road, Marco let loose with a bellow, "Motherfucker," which then led into a litany of curses that questioned the legitimacy of every one of Commander Asante's relations going back several generations before launching into a detailed description of what exactly Asante could do with his directive and ending with a hurled insult at the Lord and Savior because, hell, why not include the Big Guy too?

"Went well I see," Cassidy said and pulled into the nearest parking lot.

Marco wiped his hand over his mouth and focused on controlling the pounding of his heart and the ability to speak without shouting. "The Smithwick case has been dropped."

"Fuck," Cassidy spat and slapped the steering wheel with the flat of his hand, then again for good measure. "Why the fuck for? We're so close to nailing that bastard."

"Until evidence presents itself that can directly implicate the suspect, we are forbidden to pursue the matter further, quote Commander Asswipe."

"Right, like evidence is just going to fall into our laps. He's on the take, he's gotta be, we just haven't linked him to Smithwick yet. There is no good reason to stop now."

Marco wanted to agree, but his gut said there were other reasons why his team was pulled away from apprehending one of the biggest crime lords in the state. Asante was too lazy to be on the payroll of a crime boss. He'd have to actually work to make sure he held up his end of the bargain.

"I didn't say I'm stopping." Marco reached into his jacket pocket for the pack of gum he kept on hand and pulled out a stick. "What I do on my free time is nobody's business but my own."

"No." Cassidy shook his head. "No, no, no. You go rogue, you get busted, you get fired. Then I'm stuck with one of Asswipe's cronies as a captain and life sucks. Is it bullshit the case was dropped? Yes, but do not do something stupid, you hear me?"

Marco chomped on his gum.

"Captain. Do you hear me?"

"Yup." Didn't mean he was listening.

Cassidy sighed and leaned back in his seat. "Where to now?"

"We've been assigned to a new case. Head to Nguyen and Son's Jeweler."

"Theft? We've been assigned a case of B&E where the perps have already been captured? Double bullshit."

"Nope. We've been assigned to a case of vigilante justice. The Hood made an appearance."

"Triple bullshit."

"Just drive, Coulter."

Marco snapped his gum and focused on reining in his anger on being pulled from a case he invested three years of his life on. If he spent another second thinking about the manpower, the extra-long nights and the resources that had gone into working out the intricate thread of Smithwick's network, that was now all for naught, he'd go apeshit.

Taking down an organization as large as Smithwick's was not an easy task, and the commander should have understood that. No matter how much evidence he had presented to the commander as to why to keep the case open, the dickwad had done nothing but shake his head and repeat that department resources were too low to continue to track down a ghost.

The most galling thing of all was that he almost had him too. A fact which made Marco want to punch the wall with his head.

Almost a year had passed since the night he had had the drop on Smithwick. A year since the capture of the piece of shit had been so close, Marco had heard the snap of handcuffs clicking around the man's wrists.

The crime lord had gotten sloppy and kidnapped the girl-friend of one of his enemies. A good guy who had asked Marco for help in her rescue. For a second he had the little bald-headed criminal in his sights, then all hell had broken loose and the bastard got away.

The memory of Smithwick running to the fire exit as gun-fire erupted all around them woke Marco up many a night. In his dreams he played out over three hundred different scenari-os where he succeeded and Smithwick had been captured, only to wake up on the break room's couch and head back to his cubicle to renew the search.

All that time, and now his team had been pulled off the case and assigned to track a different ghost. A goddamn vigilante.

Cassidy pulled to a stop behind a police cruiser in front of Nguyen and Son's Jewelry. At this time of morning the only other people out were the street sweepers and delivery trucks making their daily runs.

The front door chimed as they entered and both men paused inside the entry to scan their surroundings. Not a thing looked out of place that he noticed at first glance. The glass door was in one piece and all the display cases were intact. A medic was in the corner administering first aid to a gentleman with blood splattered on his collar and one hell of a bruise coloring his face. The young woman seated beside them rocked in her chair, her arms wound around her body like a straitjacket.

Two officers from theft were gathering the last of their supplies and nodded at Marco with sly grins on their faces. They knew what he was there for and probably couldn't wait to give him a hard time.

"Where's Sanchez?" he asked.

"In the back. Surveillance room is on the left." The grin spread wider. "Do you want me to pick you up a shield? That's some sword your boy carries. You may need a full suit of armor when you go after him."

"I'll take my chances."

"What about some chainmail, or a horse? A noble steed for a noble stud?"

"Funny." He turned his back on the officer and headed for

the woman. "Hello, are you Ms. Nguyen?"

She nodded.

"I'm Captain Marco DeWinter, this is Lieutenant Coulter. I know you've had a really long night and we don't want to take up too much of your time, but we have a few more questions for you."

"No, no, no." The older man jumped from his seat and waved his arms. "You talk to me."

"And you are Mr. Nguyen, correct?"

"Yes. I her father. Anything you say, say to me."

Marco restrained his eye roll and reiterated the information he had already been given by Asante. "Correct me if I'm wrong, sir. I was told that after your nephew and his friend surprised you last night by entering the shop with a stolen key, you were knocked unconscious by one of the suspects. Is that right?"

"Yes, yes." His answer was accompanied by lots of nodding.

"And is it also correct that you did not regain consciousness until after the paramedics arrived?"

"Yes."

"Great. I'm going to talk to your daughter now since she is the only eyewitness present at the moment. Now, Ms. Nguyen, can you please tell me what happened after your father was knocked out?"

The girl looked toward her frowning father and remained silent. Apparently Daddy had her on a tight leash.

"I can go look at the surveillance footage, but I'd like to hear your version first."

Her eyes widened before she looked down at the floor. Her cheeks pinked as she stuttered out the words. "Tinh's friend, Danny, he pushed me at the safe and yelled at me to open it."

"And did you?"

She shook her head. "I've only opened it once before. I couldn't remember how."

"Then what happened?"

"Danny said he'd hurt me if I didn't open it quick. And then Tinh said he heard a noise and went into the hall. When he came back, he said it was nothing."

"And was it nothing?"

She peeked up at him and shook her head.

"What was it?"

"I do not know, but soon a man was in the doorway."

"What did he look like?"

"Big."

"And?" he prompted when she fell silent.

"Really big."

"I need a little more than that. Skin color, body size? What was he wearing?"

"Black. He had on a hooded sweatshirt, black coat, black pants. Everything was black."

"Gotcha. Did you see his face? What color was his skin?"

"Not very well. Only this part." She drew a circle around her mouth and chin. "And his skin was white. Very pale."

"Did he carry a weapon?"

"Yes, a sword."

"And what did it look like?"

"It was very big."

Coulter snorted with laughter and continued to scribble notes on a small pad of paper.

"Got it." Marco sighed. This girl was going to make a spectacular witness. "Did he say anything? Was his voice deep, high? Did he have an accent?"

"His voice sounded like his throat hurt. Deep and scratchy. Very nice. Very manly." A sparkle winked in her eye before she realized what she said and looked back at the floor. "He said for them to go and leave me alone. Danny told Tinh to kill him and they yelled at each other. Then the man moved..." Her brow furrowed.

"What happened next? How did he move?"

"Fast. So fast. He broke Tinh's arm and slammed Danny into the wall. Boom. Quick like. Then he told me to sound the alarm and get rope."

"And did you?"

"Yes. Well, I got jeweler's twine. We didn't have rope."

"And then he tied them up?"

She sneaked a glance at her father and leaned forward to whisper, "I did."

Marco raised a brow. Whatever happened after she retrieved the twine, she obviously didn't want her father to know about. This could be interesting. "What else did he do?"

"Nothing. He left right after."

"Thank you, Ms. Nguyen. I'll call your father if I have any other questions. Fine by you, Mr. Nguyen?" He raised his voice so the eavesdropping man could hear.

"Yes. Fine. Fine."

"Right. Let's go check out this video," he said to Coulter and headed down the hall.

Marco remembered the first sighting of this mysterious crusader during the prior winter when a gang had been set upon by a man wielding a sword of all things. Three members had been slaughtered before another maniac with his own sword showed up and the two had gone all *Crouching Tiger, Hidden Dragon* before a peanut gallery of shocked witnesses. Eye-witness accounts of what happened that night were pretty fantastical. Too bad the traffic cameras in that part of town had been shut down due to budget cuts. Physical evidence would have been nice to support the stories that had flown around the station.

Since that night all had been quiet but for the odd rumors popping up every few months about a guy wearing a hooded sweatshirt and carrying a sword being spotted around town and dispensing his own brand of justice. His victims had been found bound, gagged or with limbs missing. Sometimes all of the above. Whoever it was, he was good at hiding his trail, never leaving a speck of DNA and keeping his face obscured. He was a ghost no one could prove existed.

Until now.

Marco paused at the entrance to the scene of the crime and issued a low whistle when he saw the three-foot-wide hole in the drywall. "Damn. No wonder he's in the hospital. I heard one had a broken arm and the other a pulverized wrist and broken back. Now I can see why."

"Impressive, huh?" Officer Sanchez asked from the dark closet of a room across the hall. "Wait until you see the footage."

In the small floor space that was available he had set up a tiny portable table to hold the laptop he had plugged into the server that fed the security system. Not willing to swim in the stench that seemed like half a bottle of Polo, Marco watched from the doorjamb.

Sanchez motioned them to gather around the computer then typed in the commands to begin the video. "I heard you and your team were the lucky SOBs who get to apprehend this caped crusader."

Marco snorted. "Nope. Our guy doesn't wear a cape."

"Ha ha." Sanchez flipped him off. "I also heard the Smithwick case had been closed."

Good news traveled fast. "Hiatus. We are on a hiatus."

"Sure. Sure." He smirked. "Okay. Let me fast forward a little here to the good stuff. This part here is where Tinh Nguyen and his boy Danny enter the shop and find Mr. Nguyen and his daughter in the office. Judging by the expressions, it looked as if the boys thought the place was empty."

Sanchez slowed the video down at the moment Danny

Phong hit Mr. Nguyen in the head with the butt of his gun. Mr. Nguyen went down hard, crashing into the corner of the desk as he fell. The video didn't carry any sound, but Marco could imagine the screams coming from the daughter as her mouth opened and her body shook.

Phong slapped her across the face twice and pushed her toward the safe. The girl's hand slipped off the dial several times as she turned to say something to Phong over her shoulder. While this was going on, Tinh maintained an eye on the hallway, the hand holding the gun swung wildly with his agitated movements. The kid had no idea how to hold a weapon.

"That's cold letting your family be knocked around like that," Coulter muttered.

Marco grunted. Coulter had only been on his team a few years. He had yet to build up his intolerance to the cruelties of humanity. Marco wasn't sure if that was a blessing or a curse.

"Ah. Here we go," Marco said as all the players on the screen froze as one. Phong motioned to Tinh, who then moved out of camera range. "Do we have any footage of the hallway or back door?"

"We have the alley but not the hallway," Sanchez answered.

He nodded and bent lower to focus on the screen.

Both he and Coulter exhaled at once as their vigilante came into view. The guy was huge. Compared to the others in the room he looked as if he'd just stepped off the beanstalk.

While Tinh and Phong blustered about like chickens the hooded man was statue-still, almost as if he were a freeze frame to their fast forward. One second he had been in the doorway and in the next frame Tinh was on the floor and the stranger had Phong up against the broken wall as if he were hanging a piece of artwork.

Marco straightened. "What happened? Why did the video skip?"

Sanchez smiled. "It didn't."

He raised a brow. "Are you telling me this guy moved ten feet across the room in one second?"

"The video says it all. Look, I'll even rewind and slow the frames down."

As each frame ticked by, yes indeed, The Hood had two men incapacitated in less than ten clicks of the mouse. Marco would have thought the feat impossible except he had seen someone move with that kind of speed once before.

Well, I'll be damned.

Life just got a hell of a lot more interesting.

"Hey," Coulter whispered. "Doesn't that remind—"

"Shh," he hushed. "Burn me a copy, Sanchez, and include any other footage with him on it from the other cameras." He nodded and gestured for Coulter to follow. "Let's head to the hospital."

"Are you thinking what I'm thinking?" Coulter asked as he slid into the driver's seat.

"Probably. Let's concentrate on finding the man first." He

unwrapped another piece of gum and chewed in silence as he organized his thoughts.

Going to talk to Phong and Nguyen was a mere formality in his opinion. He doubted they'd have anything else to add to the investigation. Even if they had seen the man's face, he knew whoever was under the hood was not easily traceable. The only way they were gonna find this vigilante was to capture him in the act. Marco's options were either have his team launch a sting operation or track down the guy to where he lived and wait for him to make a move.

Fortunately Marco had an idea of where to start, and the hospital wasn't it. But if he didn't interview the two victims it would look odd on the police report. No need to give Commander Asswipe a reason to poke his nose into the case.

They made the visit to the hospital short and to the point and an hour and a half later returned to the station. He sent Coulter on the task of checking in with the other two members of their unit who were finishing up a case indirectly tied to Smithwick while he presumably went to grab a quick bite to eat. Instead of heading to the nearest coffee shop, he drove home and to the privacy of his one-hundred-year-old craftsman.

The scent of lemon furniture polish tickled his nose as he entered, reminding him it was Tuesday. Once a week his baby sister came over to tidy up his house for extra spending money. Since he was rarely home, her duties consisted of vacuuming and wiping down the flat surfaces. She refused to do his laundry, but did make sure his kitchen was stocked with enough food for the week. Without her premade meals at the ready, he'd probably be a hundred pounds heavier from eating fast food seven days a week.

"Abby? Are you still here?" he called out and made his way into the kitchen. A notecard with looping handwriting in purple pen was propped against the coffeemaker.

Hey Bro,

I bought you a few salads. I expect them all to be eaten by next week. Don't make me hide the chocolate. I know where you stash it.

Love ya, Abby

He opened the refrigerator and took out a plastic carton and read the label. "Kale? What the fuck is kale?"

Damn, now he was going to have to hide his candy bars.

He flung the carton back inside and snagged an apple and a bowl of beef stew. As the seconds on the microwave whirled by, he crunched on the fruit and paced across the tile floor as he contemplated just how to make his next move. It wasn't a matter of figuring out what had to be done but the thought of taking action had his palms sweating and his heart beating a mile a minute. Fuckin' stupid, he knew. It was only a phone call. Really, how hard could it be?

The timer dinged and he tossed the apple core into the compost bin and went into his office, sitting hard into the chair behind the desk. The bowl of lava that was his lunch needed time to cool anyway. Might as well man up and do the deed now.

With a deep breath he scrolled through his contacts on his phone until he found the one he sought and pressed the Call button with his thumb. He tapped a drumbeat on the top of the desk as the phone rang, and rang, and rang.

God, did he really want to leave a message?

The ringing stopped. "Sheriff Briggs." The smoky answer went into his ear and down his spine.

"Brett. It's Marco," he choked out.

Damn it. All these years later the woman still had the power to tie him in knots.

The day they had met he thought the newest rookie from the academy named Brett was a man. Shook the hell out of him when a blonde bombshell walked into the room. Her confidence and no-nonsense demeanor was a target for every man in the department to try to get under her blues, but she never softened. Brett had been the hardest-working cop on the force and refused to indulge in any interoffice love affairs.

But he had tried. Oh had he tried. Several times he had attempted to get her to see him as a man and not a fellow uniform. The closest she let him get to her was as a friend. Schmuck that he was, he accepted whatever she offered just to be near her.

Then she moved away.

Inside that hard shell the girl was as soft as a marshmallow and the years of ambivalent citizens and overly aggressive cops had taken their toll on her sense of justice. So she moved to the country where she became a sheriff. From what he had heard, she went and married some adrenaline-junkie river rafter and was now living in freakin' happyland. Good for her.

"Marco," she exclaimed with a smile in her voice. "This is a surprise. What's going on?"

"The usual. Is all that fresh air making you long to return to our smog-filled streets?"

"Oh yeah, not." A high-pitched wail came over the receiver. "Crap, just a second."

Holy shit. Acid from his apple burned his tonsils. Did he hear what he thought he heard?

"Sorry," she said a moment later, a little breathless. "I'm still getting the hang of this baby thing."

"Are you babysitting?" he asked, though he knew the truth as he stretched out the query.

"No. Didn't you hear? I'm a mom now. Yay," she finished in a strangled cheer. "Believe me, I question my sanity at times too. She's only two months old, so she doesn't do much but eat, sleep and poop, but I've been torn in a thousand different directions and have no idea what's going to happen when I return to work. Kristos has been great, but I swear I'm screwing things up big-time."

"I'm sure that's not true." The words stuck in his throat, but it hurt him to hear her distress. "As long as I've known you, you never once failed to achieve what you've set out to accomplish. You're just a perfectionist, Briggs."

"I guess we'll find out in twenty years. If she's clean, sober and rap-sheet free I guess I did a good job then, huh?"

"You couldn't ask for much more. What's the little rug rat's name?"

"Moira Rose."

"That's pretty, just like her mama. Bet she looks like you too." He took a breath and said half in jest, "So, I guess you leaving your husband and running away with me is only a pipedream."

"It always was, Marco. You know it never would have worked out between us."

"Guess we'll never know for sure." He cleared his throat. "Anyway, back to why I called. There's a guy running around the state carrying a sword and tying up bad guys and he's shown up in my jurisdiction. Have you heard anything about that?"

There was a slight pause. "Yeah, I've heard some rumors."

Uh-huh. "Well, we have footage of him in action. Funny thing is, the way he moves reminds me of that fellow we helped out with last year. Your friend, the Chameleon. Has he relocated to the city?"

"No, no, he still hangs out here in Cedar. Did your suspect wear a uniform? Could you see his face?"

A tingle buzzed across his neck in warning. Brett might have sounded all concerned and helpful, but she was hiding something. "No, we couldn't make out his features, and he wore street clothes. Let's just get down to brass tacks here,

Brett. With all my years on the force I've seen some strange shit, and your superhero friend ranks right up there on the top of that list. I've never seen anyone move as fast as he did the night we tried to take down Smithwick. Now I have some kind of copycat in my backyard with inhuman speed carrying a similar weapon. Do you know who this guy is?"

"I'm sorry, Marco. I don't."

"He's hurt people, Brett. Maybe even killed someone."

"I've heard the stories."

"Then give me something to go on. I know you must have some sort of idea who this guy is. I don't want to pull the friend card, but damn it, I hope that our friendship would mean enough for you to lend me a hand. I was there for you when your guy's girlfriend was kidnapped. Don't make me say it."

"I know, I owe you," she snapped. "Let me put the baby down. I'm about to swear and I don't want her little brain to be damaged." A moment later she was back on the line. "Don't be an asshole, Marco. And how dare you throw our past into this. If I knew anything, I'd tell you, you little fucker. Look, Cam is special, but he's also very, very private, as you can imagine. We all suspect that he's not exactly local, but he has never con-firmed or denied, well, anything really. Since he doesn't interfere in my business, I leave him alone. I understand what you're going through, I do, but I don't have any information."

"What about him? Cam? Let me talk to him. What's his number?"

"I can't give you that. As I said, he's very private. But I can send him a message and let him know you have questions. I can't guarantee he'll talk, but I'll make the effort."

"Thanks, Brett." It wasn't what he wanted, but it was a start. "And you're going to be a great mom. You've got the ass-whooping thing down pat."

"Thanks. Take care, Marco. If I hear anything, I'll let you know."

After a quick goodbye, he scarfed down his lukewarm lunch and headed back to the station. All the information pertaining to the night he met the Chameleon was still in his desk because that was also the night they came the closest to capturing Smithwick. Brett may have been telling the truth that she didn't know who his hooded assailant was, but he'd bet his house the Chameleon did.

Chapter Six

B ALE STOOD IN the shadows outside Tutala and peered in through the window like a stalker. Well, maybe he was a stalker, the way he'd been trailing Ari around town the last week. The constant monitoring was madness, he knew it, yet he could not let more than an hour go by without making sure she was safe and happy. He half expected a track to be worn out in the pavement between the apartment building and the restaurant, he vacillated between locations so often.

Ever since her first day on the job she had been working twelve-hour days, staying much later than required. From what he'd heard, she was taking the responsibilities of her new position with the utmost seriousness, which didn't surprise him. The girl was proud and strong, so much so it made his eyes water just to look at her. The determination he sensed in her made him straighten his own posture as he watched her flutter around the bar like a hummingbird.

A cloud formed on the windowpane from his breath as he released a sigh filled with longing and denial. She was so beautiful in her new pale-purple dress. The cut of the fabric was a maddening tease of professional and sexy. The belt under her bust and the way the fabric clung to her hips emphasized her femininity, but she was mistaken if she thought the modest neckline made her appear proper. The stretch of cotton over her breasts drew the eye to the soft mounds and made a man want to test their softness.

And he wasn't the only one having such lascivious thoughts. Several men tracked her movements like wolves stalking a wounded doe. She did make a tempting treat, especially when she smiled and leaned over to talk to a customer. To her credit she never encouraged unwanted advances, however, it only took one asshole to misread her intentions and cause her harm, and that he would never allow.

A pack of lechers occupying a corner booth brought a frown to his face. Lust and liquor glittered in their eyes every time Ari passed by their table. One of the fools was going to make a move on her, Bale was certain of it. While other men had attempted to ask her out over the last few days, he had seen Ari turn them all down with a smile and witty retort that effectively stopped the conversation but maintained her professionalism. This time his stomach rolled with impending doom that she wasn't going to be as fortunate if one of those fuckers made a move.

Bale straightened the lapels on his jacket and ran a hand through his hair. Tutala was one of the city's premier restaurants and attracted the suit-and-tie crowd. In his jeans and hoodie he'd most definitely draw attention, but his wardrobe could not be helped. What did it matter anyway? His clothes were clean and free of holes, they were sufficient, even for the task at hand.

He swept inside, past the grinning hostess and made a bee-line for Ari, who stood at the bar talking to the bartender. She did a double take when he stopped mere feet away, her eyes widening in surprise before the corner of her lip curled into a shy smile.

"Bale. Hi. Long time no see." The smile fell and her brow crinkled. "Wait. Why are you here? Is there something wrong?"

"No. I..." Damn, maybe he should have put some thought into what he was going to say before charging in. Simplicity was probably the best course of action. "It is late and I am here to escort you home."

"Oh." She issued a little laugh. "Thanks. That's...nice of you, but I do have my own car. I can make it back alone."

"I understand, but I want to escort you."

"Thanks for the offer, but I'm not ready to leave yet."

"Why not? You've been working hard, every day. You deserve a rest."

"Have you been talking to Amaryllis? Did she send you? You would think she would be happy to have an employee who liked to be at work."

"No. I've come on my own. Ari, please. Let me escort you home. It's late and the streets are not safe."

"So were you planning on following me home on your bike?"

Shit. "No. I walked here."

"Oh," she said again, but with a touch of disappointment coloring her tone. "Bale, did you need a ride? Why didn't you just say so? Look, I do have tasks to finish, but you can wait if you want to."

"Ari, no—damn it," he muttered as she swept past him in a cloud of hibiscus and coconuts and went to give directions to one of her servers.

"Hey, Bale," Ted the bartender greeted. The restaurant staff had yet to learn about his reputation at the club and therefore treated him with politeness. "Can I get you anything?"

"How about her undivided attention?"

"Ha, good one. That woman is constantly on the go. But I like her. I hope she sticks around."

He did too.

Bale pushed the thought aside and turned to go walk down the hallway that led to the office. She had to be keeping her purse locked away in there, and if he had the keys to her vehicle, she'd have to go with him.

Two steps was all he traveled when a tendril of disgust slithered down his back. He whipped around and found Ari standing by the corner table. Her posture was ramrod stiff and she barely restrained the sneer on her lips. She inclined her head to one of the men, who was slapping the tabletop with an open palm and suggestively wiggled his eyebrows as she issued an icy good-night.

As she walked back toward the bar, she kept her gaze fixed straight ahead and never faltered in her stride.

"Ari," he said as she neared. "What did that man say to you?"

Her eyes flickered in his direction and she shrugged. "Nothing."

"Do not lie. He did or said something to upset you. Tell me."

She sighed with a roll of her eyes and a pink flush streaked across her cheeks. "It was nothing but juvenile banter. I've been working in bars since I was eighteen. I'm used to it. Doesn't mean that I like it, but I'm used to it. Just let it go."

"Ariel. What. Did. He. Say?" He lowered his head and gave her his most intimidating glare.

With a small shake of her head she murmured, "He asked me if the carpet matches the drapes. I told you. It was juvenile. Geez, Bale, you don't have to get so growly."

He stopped her with a hand around her wrist. "What does that phrase mean?"

"Ha ha. Funny." She tried to push past him.

"What does it mean?"

"Are you serious?"

"Am I ever not?"

The flush turned crimson and covered her face from hairline down to the swell of her breasts. "Well I'm not telling you. Let it go, Bale. It was stupid."

She all but ran down the hall. Her embarrassment

slammed into his gut and wiggled up to squeeze around his chest as he felt his ears and the back of his neck burn hot.

He rounded on Ted, who he noticed had been eavesdropping on their exchange under the guise of wiping down the bar top. Leaning over the counter, he snarled, "Explain what she said."

Ted swallowed hard and uttered a shaky laugh. "I don't think I should."

"Explain or else you will be eating that bar towel."

"Ah. Yes, well, it's an old joke about hair color. You know, since women color their hair. Is the hair on her head the same color as the hair…" He gestured around his groin.

Blood rushed in Bale's ears and his vision darkened as he comprehended the innuendo. Before he realized he had moved, he was across the room and hauling the little prick from his seat. The pissant struggled as he was lifted by his shirtfront, his feet flailing as he dangled above the floor.

"How dare you," Bale spat into the terrified face, "treat a fine female with such vulgarity? Tell me why I shouldn't break you in two right now."

The man gurgled and squealed as he clawed at Bale's fist.

"Answer me!"

"*Balellanos. Drakeros le bajo. Commanedo e ta aura.*"

From the corner of his eye he saw Amaryllis standing by his side. Attired in a light-pink silk dress, she looked like a fairy princess as she calmly demanded the human be set down.

"This pig degraded Ariel with his vulgar words and should

pay for his insults," he responded in their native language.

"I see. Put him down, Bale. I will deal with the human." Her voice was calm and steady. A lion tamer calming the beast.

Bale's fingers flexed and seams popped as the fabric stretched under the pressure.

"Bale," Amaryllis warned. "Ari is watching."

Actually, the entire bar area was looking on, but his gaze homed in on Ari, who stood across the room, her hands hung loose at her sides and her eyes wide. Unbelievably he sensed no emotion rioting within her like he did with the other patrons. Despite the bombardment of sentiments aimed in his direction, she was a blank space in the storm. An unexpected response that made him falter in his course of conduct.

With a snarl he tossed the human back into his seat and focused on controlling the murderous rage coursing through his veins.

Amaryllis stood between him and his target. A pixie defending the weak from the dragon. "My apologizes, gentlemen. I ask that you forgive my dear friend. He is a firm believer that women should be treated as treasures and not whores. Your meal is on the house tonight, so please enjoy, for it is the last you shall receive in my establishment. Thank you, and I bid you good night. Bale, come with me."

He followed his princess back to Ari and felt the shame of losing his temper sting his cheeks with a thousand needles as he realized the spectacle he must have made before her employees. Would he do it again? In a heartbeat, but that still didn't make his actions right.

"Ari, why don't you go on home?" Amaryllis smiled and touched the girl on her arm. "You've done so well this week and I thank you, but I also don't expect you to devote all your time to the restaurant. Go rest and I will see you tomorrow. Take your man with you. Make sure to see to all of his needs." She winked and walked into the kitchen after ordering a busboy to attend to the ruffled party.

It took a herculean effort to lift his gaze to hers. "Ari. I apologize if I embarrassed you in any way."

She shook her head. "Let's go," she said in a quiet voice that to him was as powerful as a shout.

Neither said another word as he followed her while she retrieved her purse and coat, then led him to her vehicle. The silence stretched during the drive home. A pressure that expanded and pressed on his body, much like being submerged deep underwater. His empathetic powers should have made reading her emotions an effortless endeavor, but all he sensed was a deep sense of concentration. She was thinking hard about something, but damn if he could tell what it was as he watched her from the corner of his eye.

With each passing second he pressed his lips tighter together, refusing to ask what was on her mind. If her thoughts were positive, then he didn't want to ruin it by saying something stupid. If they were negative, he didn't want to know.

They arrived at the apartment building and Ari used her

keycard to gain entrance into the garage before coming to a stop near the elevator. The closing slams of their car doors as they exited echoed across the floor in a wave that mimicked the pounding of his hearts.

Inside the elevator she pressed the button for his floor and the one for hers, and his stomach dropped. Was she really not going to say anything? Even with his limited knowledge of human women, he realized this to be an anomaly. Gods, how badly had he fucked up?

"Look, Bale," she finally said and he practically wilted with relief she had spoken. "I'm not quite sure what to say right now. Part of me is glad that you put that little shit in his place, but you can't go around manhandling men like that. What if he called the cops or pulled a gun on you?"

"As if he could overtake me," he scoffed before thinking.

"Bale!" She rounded on him.

"I am sorry."

"My point is, I work in an industry where there are creepy people. It comes with the territory and you have to build a thick skin. If I needed backup, I would have asked for it. Don't put yourself on the line like that for me."

"I am going to anyway."

"Well stop it."

"I can't."

"Well you're gonna have to."

"I will not!" He stalked forward, inching her backward until the wall stopped her progress. "I cannot stop protecting you."

Her eyes widened, the yellow flecks in the iris sparked as a shudder shook her body, yet he sensed no fear of him as she whispered, "Why?"

"Because." He paused to swallow. "Because…"

A thousand reasons why he should follow her wishes engaged in a battle with the thousand why he refused to yield. There was no place in his world for a female, even one as fiery and passionate as Ari. But the thought of walking away made his stomach turn inside out with the familiar ache of regret. There was so much in his life he wished he had done differently. Was this moment to become another?

"Why, Bale?" Ari whispered again.

"Because I care about you. Your well-being means everything to me."

"Can't you show it in a different way?"

He shook his head. "This is the only way I know how."

No. That wasn't entirely true.

He raised his hand and placed his palm against her cheek. She stilled beneath his touch as his thumb brushed over her lips. Words were never his strength, so he'd just have to communicate without them.

With the decision made, he struck. His lips covered hers, stealing her breath as she gasped at his sudden movement. With a turn of his head he pressed deeper, sweeping his tongue into the well of her mouth. Her groan of pleasure vibrated down his torso to his tightening cock. At the touch of her little hand against his chest, her fingers digging into his pecs, he lost his mind.

Sliding his palm around to cup the nape of her neck, he swept his other hand over her backside to lift her into the cradle of his pelvis. In his arms she became a live wire, twisting and grinding her soft curves into his hard planes as if she wanted to crawl under his skin.

She tasted so good. Sweet and peppery, like a fine liquor that shot straight to both heads. Though her lips looked petal soft, the strength with which she kissed him back was so fierce, for the first time since he landed on Earth he felt weak.

With a strangled cry, she latched on to his shoulders and climbed up his body as if he were a tree. Her skirt rose over her ass as she wrapped her legs around his waist. *Jesu*, she tested his control as the hot press of her sex against his stomach tempted his inner animal to claim what was his. Somehow he found the strength to resist and wrapped his hands around the handrail of the elevator, the metal bending in his grip as if it were made out of aluminum cans.

"Woo-hoo!"

"Holy shit, man. They're fucking!"

They wrenched away from each other with startled gasps. The elevator door was held open on the parking level for The Cavern. A half-dozen club goers watched them, some with smirks, some with wide eyes and others giving them a round of applause.

One man turned to his friend. "See, I told you this place

was wild. Don't stop, dude. You're doing great."

Bale roared out a battle cry and pressed the button for her floor. As the doors slid shut, the expressions on their faces fell, and he thought he might have detected a hint of urine as one boy began to cry.

Ari giggled as she caught her breath. "Well, that was interesting."

Fuck. What in the seven hells was he doing?

Not more than thirty minutes prior he was ready to draw blood because a man dared to disrespect her, and here he was doing far worse as he rutted against her like a beast. In public of all places. He should be hanged for such crimes.

"I am deeply sorry, Ari." He set her on her feet and did his best to smooth out the wrinkles in her skirt. Damn, feeling her curves against his palm was not helping his control. He pulled away as far as the car allowed. "I did not mean to hurt you, or compromise you in any way."

"You didn't." She tilted her head and regarded him with watchful eyes. A smile flirted on her kiss-stung lips and he felt her amusement tickle his skin like tiny bubbles. "I liked it."

"I was too rough."

"That's what I liked about it." She took a step forward just as the elevator doors opened.

Ah, room to escape.

He dashed into the hall and drew up short. Lust, need and self-recrimination tore him in different directions. The result made his feet stay planted as if his body knew where it wanted to be.

What was he running from? Happiness? The past? Guilt?

Yes. Yes and yes.

He ran a shaky hand over his face. "Ah, Ari, you are driving me to madness."

Delight touched her smile as she stalked closer. "How so?"

"You make me forget."

"Is that bad?"

To forget was liberating and terrifying all at once. Ari made him forget that he was dead inside. She reminded him what it was to be a man with needs and wants.

But he wasn't a man. He was something else altogether. A creature who was a hundred times stronger than she. A creature who had a past. A history. A wife.

A wife.

Bale closed his eyes on a ragged breath and tried not to think of the delicate, dark-haired female who had agreed to be his wife. It wasn't Natalia's fault she died, just as it wasn't Ari's fault she had come into his life second. The two women were different in so many ways, yet he cared for both as one would a lover, a confidante, someone to share his innermost self with. Yet his insecurity had prevented him from letting Natalia see who he truly was, and here was another woman silently asking to be let in.

If he joined with Ari, she would steal into his soul, for Ari was not an instrument of pleasure. Even he with his stunted emotional capacity understood that. And while Natalia might have been content with only the parts of himself he allowed her to share, Ari was going to demand more. She already was. Could he give her what she needed?

"I don't want to hurt you." He fingered a lock of her hair. Somehow, some way, he'd find a way to fuck this up.

She took his hand, kissing his knuckles. "Why do I think you couldn't, even if you wanted to?"

"I'm starting to question your sanity. You should be running as far away from me as possible," he said, helpless to resist brushing his lips across her forehead.

"I know." She laughed. "I shouldn't be thinking about men at this time of my life. But I do. I think about you. All the time. I want you, Bale." She pressed her belly against his erection. "I need you."

There were the words. Combined with her desire pooling in his loins and the fire building between them, he felt his resolve crumble. Could he be what Ari needed? Dare he take the risk?

Amaryllis had once told him that he had been given the gifts of today and the possibility of tomorrow. Natalia was never coming back. Ari was here. Now. His present and potentially his tomorrow. If he dared.

"Damn you, woman." He took her upturned mouth and ravaged her lips again until the sound of the elevator bought him two seconds of sanity. "Your place. Now. Before I take you right here."

The excited flare in her eyes toyed with his control until

she gasped. "Oh, wait. I don't have any supplies. I don't suppose you do?" There was a hopeful yet jealous color in her query.

"Supplies?" What did *that* mean? Was there some unusual ritual or requirement for sex here on Earth? From what he'd seen from his employers, it looked very similar to intercourse on Skandavia.

"You know. Condoms. Until my insurance kicks in, I can't get on birth control, and condoms weren't on my shopping list this week."

Ah. Yes. She must be speaking of the rubber-looking balloons he'd seen down at the club.

Stupid man. His hearts beat an irregular tempo as the implication of just how mixed-up his thoughts were sank in. Thank the Gods one of them had been thinking. A woman in his life now was a complication of its own. To add a child to that mix? A nightmare of epic proportion.

"Go to your home and I'll go retrieve some. I won't be but a minute."

"Okay." Her flirty smile and goodbye kiss almost made him say fuck it all, but he remained strong and raced down the stairs the second she turned her back to go to her apartment.

The word condom was a constant litany in his mind as he brushed past the doorman and strode down the darkened hall toward the playrooms. Without bothering to knock, he burst into the first doorway, startling the occupants inside.

"What the fuck?" a petite woman he recognized as Mistress

Jasmina shouted with her hand raised mid-swing. At her feet a man kneeled with his bare ass raised to the sky. The globes of his cheeks were pink from where she had been striking him with the paddle in her hand.

"Condoms. Now," Bale growled.

"Seriously? A knock would have been polite. As you can see, I'm working here." She tossed her dark hair over her shoulder and rested her hand at her hip. Her nails tapped a rhythm against her stiff corset as she raised her brow in expectation.

"What?" he bit out.

She looked pointedly at the door.

Grrrr. "Fine." He knocked on the wood. "Condom."

"Please."

"Woman."

"Then leave."

"Fine!" Damn Dominatrix. "Please, Mistress Jasmina. I need condoms."

"Was that so difficult?" She sashayed to a chest of drawers, pulling one open to reveal a rainbow of thin packets. Her gaze alighted on the erection threatening the fabric of his jeans and she smirked. Handing him a couple oversized packets, she said, "Looks like you're an extra large. Lucky girl."

He didn't bother with a thank-you and left the woman to continue with her work, cursing the tiny wench for wasting precious seconds he could have been in Ari's arms.

Outside Ari's apartment he raised his fist to pound on the

wood, then pulled back at the last second. Judging by the way his muscles twitched, he was going to tear her apart. He had to get his shit together or leave her be.

As if he were out in the field, preparing for battle, he focused on slowing his breathing and stemming the effects of the adrenaline overstimulating his senses. Very gently he raised his fist and knocked, but even with the conscious effort to curb his strength, the walls rattled under the demand of his knuckles against the oak.

Ari opened the door, all smiles and softness. "That was fast. I barely had time to take my shoes off."

With one deliberate step, then another, he entered her home, closing the door behind them until they were the only people who existed on the planet.

His voice rumbled like a cement mixer. "Take off your dress. I don't want to tear it."

A siren's smile flirted with her lips and her eyes sparkled like gemstones as she slowly reached for the tab under her arm and dragged the zipper down catch by catch. Without dropping her gaze, she slipped the garment off her shoulders with a little shimmy and let it pool at her tiny feet.

Jesu. He fell back against the door. Not in his most illicit fantasies did he imagine a sight as sinful as Ari dressed in nothing but scraps of white lace cupping her curves. So sexy, so alluring...

And so Gods-damned human.

He beat the back of his head against the door and closed

his eyes. How in the hell was he going to keep from harming her?

"Bale, what's wrong?"

He opened his eyes to see her earlier confidence had vanished. Her hands fluttered across her chest as if to shield the sight of her cleavage.

"Don't, Ari." He raised his hand. It wasn't her fault he was fucked in the head. "You've done nothing wrong. You are so beautiful, and I am so not. I'm afraid I will crush you."

"And I'm afraid I'm going to faint right here unless you touch me."

Didn't he know it. Her arousal reached out with an invisible hand and grabbed him by the base of his cock and twisted in agonizing delight.

Man up, brotkja. *Take what is yours.*

He clenched his teeth and sucked a breath in through his nose. He could do this. He had to do this. He'd die if he didn't.

Resolve strengthened his spine as he stalked toward her. Control was all in his mind. He'd have to remind himself that he was fully capable of restraining his depraved hungers as he had in the past. To touch her, taste her, even with the tightest leash on his control, would be well worth the effort to be gentle.

"Take off the lace," he ordered. He'd do it himself, but he hadn't a clue as to how to work the complicated-looking contraption binding her breasts.

Her hand trembled as she reached for the left strap. "I want to see you naked too."

And reveal his scarred body? No. "That will take too long."

The bra hit the floor, followed quickly by her panties. "I can wait."

But he couldn't. The site of her rosy nipples and the pink flush of arousal painting her creamy flesh made him want to fall to his knees and bury his face against the soft pillow of her belly.

"Ariel. You're beautiful," he rasped.

The pure joy in her smile made his throat tighten. "Take off your clothes. Please."

As a concession, he pulled off his boots and jacket and sweatshirt then removed his belt before sweeping her up in his arms. He drank from her lips as he strode into the bedroom and sat upon the mattress, settling her across his lap. Without the barrier of her clothing, her wet heat burned through the denim stretched across his erection and the tips of her breasts prodded his chest in teasing glances. Under his palms the muscles of her back flexed as he smoothed his hands up and down. Curling his fingers around the fleshiest part of her ass, his fingertips discovered the moisture seeping readily from her slit.

"Bale, please." She panted into his mouth. "I need you."

She was wet for him. Ready for him. Aching.

For him.

Next time… Next time he'd spend hours learning her body, but his need was just as great. Reaching into his pocket with one hand, he retrieved the crinkly packets while wrestling with his zipper with the other. Ari trailed kisses down the column of his neck, teasing the beast within him. He ripped the pouch open with his teeth and promptly sputtered as the foul taste touched his tongue.

Ari laughed. "You're supposed to use your fingers, silly."

Gods, that was horrible. He licked along her shoulder to replace the unpleasantness, then did it again because he loved the sigh she made when he did so.

Behind her back he withdrew the rubber disk from its package and eyed the foreign object over her shoulder. How the hell did this work?

"Let me." Thank the Gods Ari interrupted his confusion by taking the condom from his hand with a sultry smile and looked at his lap. Her smile fell and her eyes boggled. "Oh my God."

"What?" He looked as well. Nothing unusual, just his turgid, pulsating cock pointing to the sky.

She began to giggle and slapped her hand over her mouth. "Sorry. Sorry." She giggled again. "I just...never... Oh my God."

"Ari," he grated out in a strangled moan as she wrapped her hand around his length and gave him a firm squeeze.

"I'm sorry." She stared transfixed as she rubbed up and down the shaft. "I've never seen anything like this in my life."

His hips bucked. "Woman," he growled.

"You're right." She jerked up and rolled the balloon down

his shaft with a deft hand. "Screw foreplay."

Fore what? The thought was obliterated as Ari pushed him back and straddled his hips. They both gasped as she notched the crown at her opening and began a slow descent.

Sweet heaven. She was tight. And hot. And glorious with her red hair flowing over her shoulders and her breasts shimmying ever so slightly as she worked to impale herself on his thick pole.

The only thing marring this perfect moment was the cursed condom preventing him from bathing in her wetness. A man had invented these torture devices? Hopefully whoever the sod was had met a grisly end.

Ach, never mind. It was a necessary evil, and if he had to choose between no contact with Ari or sex while wearing raingear, give him the fucking coat.

The kiss of her wet pussy lips brushing his pelvis made the cum roll in his balls, the hold on his control weakening with every jerk of her hips.

Too soon. Too soon. This perfect moment was going to be over before either of them was ready.

Reaching for the headboard, he ground his teeth so firmly, he'd be shocked if he had any left by the end of the night. If anything, he had to hold out until Ari reached her peak first. Gods grant him the strength.

He stared up at the ceiling and shifted his focus to the texture of the drywall and not on the press of her hands on his chest as she rode him in a steady rhythm. *Jesu*, he needed a distraction immediately. Mayhap he could count the number of stars he had passed on his journey to Earth. There had been, what, trillions of them? Ah, he knew! A listing of the names of every Skandavian monarch and their offspring. Please let the endless roll call temper his desire enough to hold on.

With every name that passed through his mind, the urge to come relented and the pressure in his cock eased until only a pleasant fullness remained and he was able to release an easy breath. Now to concentrate on Ari's pleasure.

A glance at Ari's face and stiff posture made him sit up in alarm.

"What is wrong?"

She shrugged and her gaze fell to his chest. Her folded arms tightened more across her breasts and he sensed her lust had all but disappeared. "You tell me."

His throat tightened as if he could taste the burn of her unshed tears, and that telltale flush stained her cheeks. She was embarrassed. Why? "I do not understand."

"Look, I knew you weren't a talker, but a sound of some kind would be nice. Am I boring you?"

"Are you insane?" he yelled before he could temper his incredulity. "You have me a hairsbreadth from losing all control and I'm doing all that I can to stop it. If you were any sexier, I wouldn't survive."

Her eyebrows rose, revealing her doubt of his statement and he wanted to shout at the heavens with frustration.

How could she be so unaware of her effect on him? The

fact she hadn't a clue crushed him as surely as if she had slapped him. Again he cursed her humanness, for if she had his powers of empathy, she'd never question how she twisted him into knots with a single glance.

Damn. Damn it all. He sighed and held her against his chest. The blame was entirely on him. Here he had been determined to not make old mistakes and he was doing just that, relying on old habits to convey his feelings. He had to learn some new tricks. Fast.

"How I can please you?" he whispered in her ear and felt the first flickering of hope when goose bumps erupted across her skin.

"I like it when you touch me," she said in a small voice.

"Like this?" Starting at her neck, he ran his hand along her shoulder, down to her breast and cupped the full mound.

"That's nice," she sighed and pressed forward, forcing her breast against his palm. Around his shaft her sheath softened and grew damp again, allowing his cock to sink deeper. She released a moan. "That's really nice."

Emboldened by her sighs, he cupped her other breast and plucked lightly at her nipples with each pull stronger than the one before, testing the limits of how much of his strength she could handle.

"You like this?" He twisted the tips harder and was rewarded with a throaty growl. "What else do you like?"

"I—oh—your mouth. I like your mouth on me."

"Ya?" He pressed a line of kisses across her sternum, tickling her skin with flicks of his tongue until he reached a dusky peak and sucked it deep into his mouth with a firm draw.

Her fingers dove into his hair, holding his mouth to her breast as her hips rolled, stroking his shaft with shallow thrusts. Oh ya, his woman loved his tongue on her flesh, and his teeth too. He smiled when she squealed in delight at his bite.

"What else do you like?"

"I like how you feel inside me," she panted.

"I like that too."

"You do?"

"Ah, Ari. It's taking all my strength not to hold you down and ravish you."

"But I want to be ravished." She pulled his hair. "Don't be gentle. Take me. Take me hard."

"You don't know what you ask."

"I do." She squeezed her inner muscles as she rose and fell on his shaft. "I want you. All of you."

Dare he?

"Please, Bale. I need you," she cried then bit into his shoulder, the fabric of his shirt a slight barrier against her teeth.

"Ari," he moaned. How could he not do as she wished when she pleaded so prettily?

He reclined onto the mattress and held her hips still as he lunged up, again and again, experimenting with the force.

"Yes. More." The ends of her hair tickled his hands as her head tipped back. "Harder. Yes. Harder."

Using her gasps and cries as a barometer, he soon had them racing at a punishing pace with her bouncing on his cock and the need to come tightening in his belly.

"No," he barked when she palmed her breasts. The sight of her bobbing mounds as she took each thrust fascinated him to no end. "Leave them be."

"Ah, so that's how it is." Her laughter sizzled across his skin. "That's it, Bale. Fuck me harder. Make my tits bounce."

The vulgar choice of words shocked him even as his cock jerked in agreement and surged within her soaking sheath. The ripple of muscles stroked him as firmly as a tight fist and her answering moans were a hammer on his preconceived notions. To have her revel in his possession, wanting more and not being afraid to ask for it spoke to his need to claim her and his hips responded in kind.

He was close, so close. And Ari was too. Her orgasm twined around both of them in a razor-sharp thread that hurt with a pleasure-pain that brought tears to his eyes. The mist of ecstasy bathed his face, the abyss was so close.

She balled the front of his shirt in her fists as she hung on for the ride. Her fingernails clawed at his chest, scoring his nipples in another bite of pleasure. Over her cries he heard the tear of cotton as she tore the seams.

"Bale," she sobbed, caught in the throes of near completion, her frustration mounting with each lunge. "Please."

"I have you."

He slipped his hand between their bodies and found the

wet, swollen nub of her clitoris. A few hard circles pushed her over the edge.

Her eyes rolled back as she screamed and her pussy clamped down, milking the seed from his loins. Her orgasm reached out to punch him in the chest and turn him inside out. His release shot up his cock like sweet fire, flooding the inside of the condom in spurts and obliterating the barricade he had built to keep out the bombardment of emotions from the world around him.

Elation, fear, both hers and his, wrapped as sharply as barbed wire around his chest, climbing up his arms and neck to paralyze him with the intensity.

Too much. This was all too much. Feeling. Experiencing emotions with all the subtly of a sonic boom. Colors, sounds, textures so crystal clear his mind burned under the onslaught.

"Bale?"

Too much. Too much. To handle.

"Bale?"

The world pulled him in, sucking him in like a tree branch through a wood chipper and spitting him out the other side in a million tiny pieces.

"Bale!"

Air's terrified shout made his eyes fly open as he gasped as if surfacing from the ocean. She sat beside him with strands of red hair clinging to her wet cheeks. Her blue eyes glimmered with her tears.

"Ari?" he croaked.

"Bale. What's wrong? Are you all right?"

"Need. I need. A minute."

A newborn foal attempting to stand had more grace then he did as he slid from the bed and beat tracks to the bathroom, slamming the door behind him so hard, the walls rattled.

Knees buckling, he crashed to the floor, the cool press of tile on his hot cheeks woke him up enough to feel the sensation of Ari's fear and humiliation rolling across his skin.

"I'm sorry, Ari," he moaned. "It's not you. It's me."

It's all me.

Chapter Seven

WELL. THAT WAS a first.

Ari wrapped her arms across her chest and clenched her teeth to stop the chatter caused by the sudden drop of adrenaline. If she didn't know better, she'd have thought she was on drugs by the way tracers floated in her vision and her mind splintered into several directions of what the hell happened? Come to think of it, what the hell did happen?

Once Bale had relaxed, he had taken her on a journey beyond her wildest imagination. For several glorious minutes she had been deep in the grip of one of those out-of-body experiences she had only read about in books. Even now the walls of her pussy fluttered, hungry for more of his possession, and there was no mistaking, Bale had possessed her. She might have been on top riding him like a mechanical bull at her former place of employment, but he had her completely under his command with the weight of his hands on her hips and the fire in his gaze as he had watched her breasts bounce.

And now he was shut in the bathroom, sounding like a wounded animal as he moaned an apology. What exactly was he apologizing for? The amazing orgasm?

Or maybe he felt bad for scaring the ever-lovin' crap out of her when he fell into convulsions after he erupted inside her with the force of Mt. Vesuvius.

She climbed off the bed and pulled a nightgown and a sweater over her trembling body. Geez Louise. Could this night get any stranger?

The man all but disappeared for almost a week with nothing but a tight-lipped nod in passing then, wham! At the first opportunity she's spreading her legs and begging him to plow her. Classy.

But she liked him. She really, really liked him. And the way he had been about to put the smackdown on that creep? Oh, wicked awesome. He reminded her of the Punisher or Wolverine, all badass and sexy. What hot-blooded woman wouldn't want a taste of that? She was human, after all.

Apparently Bale had more in common with those superheroes than rippling muscles and attitude. The man had issues. Major ones.

She glanced back at the bathroom door. At least the moaning had stopped. Whether or not that was a good sign remained to be seen.

Sooner or later, he was going to open that door. Then what? Did she want to know what set him off? Would he even tell her? The man was a statue when it came to talking about...well, anything.

And if he did? Was she ready to deal with his personal demons? It was early in their relationship. She still had the power to walk away. All she had to do was say thanks for the orgasm and send him on home. Potential craziness averted.

With another glance at the door, she shook her head. Who was she kidding? There was no way she could leave him now.

There had been a moment when she had looked into his eyes and seen forever. Not the live-happily-ever-after kind of forever, but a kindred spirit. The yearning for more than a quick lay and the discovery of finding "the one". For a second she had thought she had seen into Bale's soul, and it was lonely and hungry for affection.

Of course, that might have been the hormones talking, but she never experienced that type of magic. It was addictive, frightening and wonderful all at once. When Bale had asked her to come with him to the city, she had taken a leap of faith and received more than she thought possible. She owed it to herself, to them, to take another leap. If she didn't try, she knew she'd think about it for the rest of her life.

She went into the kitchen and popped a pod into the coffeemaker. Who cared if it was after midnight? It was either caffeine or whisky and the caffeine was probably the better choice to face the next few minutes.

After the last drop of dark brew fell into the mug, she settled onto a barstool and faced the bathroom with the warm ceramic cradled to her chest. A few sips in and the door opened.

A weight filled her chest when she saw the stamp of shame

carved into his features. His bangs hung in wet strands over his eyes and the front of his shirt was damp, as if he had splashed water on his face. So much tension rioted inside him she swore she felt him vibrating to the point of breakage. Part of her wanted to run and throw her arms around him and hold him close, while the other half feared whatever, if any, words he'd say next.

"I fucked up, didn't I?"

Her fingers tightened around the mug. "Truthfully, I don't know what's going on right now."

He wiped his hand down his face then stared at the floor for several long moments, and again the urge to offer him comfort made the muscles in her arms twitch. Self-preservation and prudence kept her butt in the seat. At some point in time, Bale was going to have to open up and give her a glimpse at his thoughts. If he couldn't do that now, she might as well kiss her fantasies goodbye and show him the door.

Another two minutes passed and just when she thought she'd have to kick him to the curb, he lifted his tortured gaze, which struck her like an arrow through the heart.

"I—" He grimaced and rubbed at the back of his neck. "I don't know exactly what to say right now. I don't…share. Ever. But you deserve… You deserve more."

Ari pinched her lips together and didn't dare lower her gaze as he began to pace in the tiny space of the living room. It was as if she were deep in the jungle observing a panther. One tiny peep and she might scare him off.

"I told you that I am sensitive to people. What we just experienced was...intense. Overwhelming. Spectacular, but overwhelming, and I couldn't handle the rush. I'm sorry. You—you were, are, wonderful. And that's—that's why I'm fucked."

The stop-start of his sentences made her heart climb into her throat, as if she were watching a scary movie and the hero was in danger. How she wished she could just fast forward to the end and find the ease that came with knowing everything turned out all right.

"Ari, I have done...things," he continued in that stilted tone that made her ready to scream. "There is a darkness inside me. And you are so passionate, so brilliant. You make me want."

She made him want...what?

"What do I make you want?" she asked, daring to interrupt.

"That is all. You make me want."

"Is wanting so bad?"

"Yes, when I'm afraid my darkness will snuff out all of your light. You deserve so much better than me."

"Shouldn't I be the one to decide that? From what I've seen of you so far, I think you're pretty great."

The corner of his mouth twitched. "Even if I'm ready to maim any man who looks to be harboring an illicit thought about you?"

"That," she sighed, "you may need some help with."

He chuffed. "The terrible thing is, I can't really blame them when I have the same thoughts myself. Even more so. I'm just as vile as they are."

Now why did the idea of Bale having dirty thoughts about her make her skin tingle instead of feeling repulsed? "Like what?"

He shook his head. "I cannot tell you. I do not want to shock you more than I already have."

Fool. Didn't he know his refusal to tell her made her want to know all the more? "How do you know I'll be shocked?"

"I just do. Ari, allow me to apologize and let it alone."

"Stop, just stop." There was only so much teeth-pulling she was willing to do. She set her mug down and marched up to him. Clasping his cheeks between her palms, she forced him to look at her. "Stop trying to shelter me. I'm a big girl, if you haven't noticed. I like you, Bale, but I want to be with the real you. Not the version of you you think I want to be with. So what is this all about, really? Are you trying to tell me you have a kink? Most everyone does.

"My last boyfriend always wanted me to wear schoolgirl uniforms during sex, which is disturbing on so many levels now that I know what his real job is, but that's not the point. My point is I like being with you and want to do it again, without you holding yourself back from me. That's not fair to either of us. The least I can say is no. Unless it involves knives and/or small children. To that I'll say no right now."

"Is that so?" The light in his eyes and his deep drawl sent

shivers down her spine that weren't anything close to fear. "What if I told you that whenever I look at your lips, I imagine how they'd look stretched around my cock?"

Oh yeah. Now they were getting somewhere. "Are you speaking truth or hypothetically?"

"One of the most honest things I have ever said out loud."

"Then I say that whenever I look at your hands, I want them all over my body. Pinching, twisting, filling me until I scream and beg for you to take me hard with that big cock you want me to suck. I want you to hold me down and take me so hard, I can't walk the next day. What do *you* say to that?"

A shudder shook his big shoulders as his nostrils flared. "Do you mean that?"

"You're the one who's supposed to be sensitive to other's emotions. You tell me."

His eyelids fell to half-mast and he reached out a hand, cupping her cheek. "Ari."

That was all he needed to say to have her in his arms, her mouth meeting his in a kiss so hot, she swore it singed the ends of her hair. Those big hands of his gripped the fabric of her nightgown at her hips and pulled, dragging her into the curve of his body.

"Wait. I like this nightgown." She broke away and swept the garment and sweater over her head then reached for the hem of his shirt. "But I'm not going to be the only one naked this time."

He gripped her wrists. "Don't. I have scars."

The note of distress in his voice was unmistakable, and with it he stole another piece of her heart.

She placed a soft kiss on his lips. "Why do I have the feeling that the worst of your scars are on the inside? Let me in, Bale."

After another big shudder, he let go of her wrists. She kept their gazes locked as she pulled the cotton up and over his head. As the fabric fell to the floor, she scanned the massive area of his chest and stifled a chuckle. The man was insane to have such body issues. He had the type of physique that reminded her of the gladiators of old. Six-pack? The man had a case of muscle feeding into sculpted muscle. Was he scarred? Yes. A line here, a pucker there. There was a particularly nasty one dominating his right biceps that looked as if he had an enormous chunk of flesh cruelly hacked out of his arm, but even so, he was still a beautiful specimen of man.

The rasp of his zipper sent shivers over her skin. Did he really think she would be offended if he asked her to suck his cock? *Pul-eeze.* She was ready to fall to the floor, claw at his jeans and beg for the opportunity to get up close and personal with what he was packing.

Hands down, he had the biggest cock of any lover she'd had, and she was certain to ever have again. She never considered herself a cock snob before. After all, it wasn't the size of the ship, but the size of the waves rocking her ocean that mattered. But after Bale, how could any man compete?

She sank to her knees as she pulled his jeans down his legs

and sighed like a schoolgirl gazing at her crush when his erection bobbed before her. Behind the flare of his crown, the stalk was narrow then grew thicker at the base. The memory of the way he filled her pussy so perfectly made her mouth water to taste the satin skin.

She licked her lips and wrapped both hands around the shaft, feeling the pulse of his heartbeat echo down to her core.

Bale stifled a groan and fisted his hands at his sides, which made her smile. So this was how to make him talk. After a few more strokes, she touched the tip of her tongue to the bit of flesh under the crown, loving the way his eyelids grew heavy as he held his breath, waiting for her next move. She didn't keep him waiting long.

She parted her lips and swallowed halfway down the shaft in one move. With the narrow tip, she was able to fit him comfortably into her mouth without fear of suffocating. Lightly sucking in her cheeks as she drew back, she reveled in his groan as she worked to take more of his length down her throat.

"*Liera*, you undo me." His hands dove into her hair, his fingers flexed, but he did nothing to control her movements, allowing her to take the lead.

She smiled around his rod and made sure his cock shined with her saliva as she pulled back and forth. Under the shaft she rolled her tongue, flicking beneath the head with each draw. In seconds his cock went from firm to hot steel within her mouth.

Bale was afraid to reveal his more depraved side, was he? So far, this was pretty tame in her book. What would he do if she were the one who pushed the envelope?

Reaching between her thighs, she found the lips of her sex swollen and drenched. She swirled her fingers in the syrup then reached up to slide the wet tips across the dark hole of his anus. He gasped, his fingers tightening in her hair as his cock flexed against her tongue.

"Witch," he barked. "You push me too far."

Slowly she worked one finger into his ass, watching from beneath her lashes as sweat broke out across his flesh and his abdominal and pectoral muscles twitched. She moaned her encouragement around his throbbing shaft and sucked harder, rubbing his base with her other hand.

The pupils in his eyes expanded then contracted and his lips pulled back over his teeth as he snarled her name. "I'm close, *liera*. Fucking close. Where do you want it, vixen?"

The question was more like where didn't she want him to come? If she could, she'd bottle his cum and use it like lotion, she was so turned-on by watching this big man wrestle with his control.

"Ari. Choose," he gasped in a tortured groan.

The saltiness of the pre-cum slipping over her tongue was delicious, but since he was such a fan of her breasts, she wanted to reward him for sharing a small part of himself he was afraid to allow her to see.

His fingers pulled on her hair and gave her the split second of warning to pull back and aim the head of his cock at her left nipple. As he shot jet after jet, she directed the milky fluid across her chest, her smile growing as he bellowed with his release. Wow. Who knew he was able to produce that much sound?

As the last little bit of cum dribbled out of his shaft, she licked the slit clean then made a show out of rubbing the cum into her skin, making sure to pull and pluck at her nipples while never once dropping eye contact.

The muscles of his thighs quivered and his knees wavered. The only bit of strength he displayed was in the intensity of his gaze and the rough command in his voice as he ordered her to climb onto the bed.

"Spread your legs for me." He fell to his knees beside the bed. "It's my turn to feast."

He didn't have to tell her twice. She parted her thighs, showing him how wet and needy she had become while sucking his cock. "I ache, Bale."

"I'll see to your need, *liera*. Always."

Fire burned in his black eyes as he bent and swiped his tongue from clit to anus. His tongue dipped into her cunt then followed with the thick press of his fingers as he wrapped his lips around her clit and sucked hard.

"Yes," she shouted and clutched his head to her pussy. Subtlety was not going to convince Bale that she wanted whatever he dished out. "That's so good. More. More."

Her eyes crossed and her lungs burned as he rocketed her

to the brink of madness. The calluses on his fingers stroked the neck of her womb, coaxing more of her cream to ease the way for a third digit to fill her to overflowing.

Just a little more, she panted as if she'd been without water for days, just a little more. She hunched her hips, desperate for that tiny bit of pressure against her clit to push her over the edge.

And then he was gone.

"No!" she cried and opened her eyes.

Bale climbed between her spread thighs. A flush of red painted his cheeks and those dark eyes glowed with a possessive fire. With a quick thrust, he seated his condom-covered cock into her sheath to the hilt. Before she could draw a breath, he lunged again, then again.

Her legs fell open and she stretched her arms up over her head, luxuriating in the slide of his sweat-slick chest across her nipples and the grind of the base of his shaft against her needy clit.

"Yes, Bale. I want it all."

At her words, his lips curled and his pace gained speed and power.

With a shift of his hips, the crown of his cock stroked along all her nerve endings and lit her on fire. Tears gathered in her eyes, but it wasn't from pain. No, the sight of him over her, taking her, was so beautiful, so bestial, the intensity was blinding.

The punishing pace was exactly what she wanted. The reverence in his touch and gaze as he caressed her from breast to hip was unexpected. Not because he had led her to believe that once he loosened his restraint, he'd become a raving maniac, but because the touch unlocked the gate between lover and loved one.

When her confidence in the men of the world had been at its lowest, Bale's care for her in and out of bed gave her hope that there was someone out in the world to entrust with more than her body.

She ran her fingernails through the dusting of hair on his chest and placed her hands against the hard muscles. The pounding behind his ribs was so fierce, she felt as if she held his heart in her palms.

This was the new dream. She wanted to have his heart. She wanted to take this man from the shadows and bathe him in light. Dear heavens above, she wanted him to love her.

The first wave crested and her fingers dug into his chest. In response, Bale released a stream of curses in a foreign language and intensified his thrusts, tossing her into the deep end of the abyss.

"Bale," she cried as shock waves radiated out from her core.

"I feel you, Ari. I feel you. Gods," he roared and his eyes rolled back. Inside her rippling sheath his cock jerked in a way she didn't think was humanly possible. "That's it, *liera*. Give me your all."

Anything he may have said after that was lost to the roll of thunder in her head. As her pussy suckled on his shaft, his hips undulated, drawing out the last of their orgasm in a slow yet electrifying descent.

Damn it, she didn't want this feeling to end. All too soon she was going to have to open her eyes and face the fact that she was falling for a man who carried secrets.

She'd have to be an idiot not to recognize the signs. He was a lone wolf. A wounded warrior. To trust was not in his nature. In fact, she believed he'd rather cut off his dominant hand than trust another with anything.

Tonight he may have trusted her with his desire, but that was sex. Matters of the heart were much more complicated and messy. The lead weight settling in her gut warned her that to continue the journey from lust and affection to love would be difficult and paved with many hurdles. What would it take for Bale to trust her with his heart?

The price, she feared, would be more than she could pay.

✦   ✦   ✦

"SON OF A bitch. You have got to be kidding me." Marco wadded the front page of the newspaper into a ball and tossed it into a nearby waste bin.

Commander Asswipe withdrew another copy of the paper from behind his back and slapped it on top of his desk. His pudgy fingers framed the headline, *Who Is the Claymore?* Underneath the big block print was a grainy photo taken from the video footage from the botched jewelry heist.

A nickname. The press had gone and given the mother-fucker a goddamn nickname. What was next, a Bat-signal? Fuck.

"I thought you had this contained, DeWinter."

Marco clenched his fists to refrain from slapping the mustache off his boss's face. On the other side of the glass wall thirty faces peeked around cubicles or people stood out in the open to watch their interaction as if they were the latest YouTube sensation. He was not going to give them more of a show.

"It is contained," he gritted out from between clenched teeth. "At least within my team. Theft also had access to those pictures, remember? You might want to ask one of them if they've had an info leak."

"I need this guy caught yesterday." Asante stepped from behind his desk and came to a stop next to Marco's chair. "I have the chief and the mayor breathing fire over this. We need the people of this city to have faith in the police force. Not some bozo running around like a fucking superhero. I don't want copycats coming out of the woodwork."

"Believe me. I want this case closed more than you do. I've got a good lead and I'd be out there right now checking on it, if you hadn't pulled me in here to show me this comic strip. Are we done now?"

"Watch it, DeWinter." Asante's eyes narrowed and he pulled his shoulders back, as if that would make his five-foot-nothing height appear more intimidating. "You've been a thorn in my ass for the last three years. Get your shit together or I'll have you rounding up stray poodles with animal control, you hear me?"

"Yep. So will the union. May I be dismissed? Sir?"

Asante stared him down. The corner of his moustache twitched as he restrained his sneer. The feeling was entirely mutual. A minute later he jerked his head toward the door and Marco was out of there as if his ass were on fire.

What a shitty, shitty morning.

Not only was the press making this Claymore fucker out to be the city's savior, just before he was called into that fantastic meeting, one of his informants had sent word that Smithwick was making a move into human trafficking. That was where he needed to be, fighting real crime, not chasing after a hooded freak.

"Hey, DeWinter." One of the goons from homicide stepped out from his cubicle and waved around a letter opener. "Do you need a sparring partner? Looks like you may need lots of practice if you want to compete with a sword that big."

"My wife's a seamstress," another shouted from across the room. "I can ask her to make you a costume. How 'bout something with a cape?"

"He needs a name too! How about Captain Underpants?"

"That's a kid's book, you idiot."

"Oh. No wonder it sounded familiar."

Marco kept his gaze forward while he marched back to his

desk and shoved two sticks of gum into his mouth. At the rate he was going, he was probably wearing out the ligaments in his jaw.

"Hey, boss." Coulter appeared from around the partition and dropped onto an empty seat.

"Thank the fuckin' Lord. Tell me good news."

"I checked into Briggs, like you asked." He leaned forward to murmur with a knowing grin. "Have you seen the size of her husband's family?"

"No. How would I? I've never met the man."

Coulter's smile widened. "Don't you know what family she married in to?"

"No. That's why I had you dig up dirt. If I did it, she'd find out and castrate me. Obviously you have something good, otherwise you wouldn't be a shit about it now. Spill it."

"All right. Calm down. Man. Can you, like, start smoking or drinking or something? You need to lighten up."

"No." He double-clicked a ballpoint pen as if he were flicking open a switchblade.

Coulter eyed the potential weapon and sighed. "Fine. Anyway, Briggs' husband Kristos is a river guide and some of his clients have posted pictures of their excursions with him online. The man is a giant."

He laid printouts of vacation photos across the desk.

Shit. Marco frowned as he looked at the pictures of groups of women surrounding a man who stood at least a foot and a half taller with muscles stacked on muscles. No wonder Briggs fell in love with the guy. He was a freakin' Adonis. Even he felt a little turned-on staring at photo after photo.

"Wait. Whoa, whoa, whoa." He pulled out two photos and laid them side by side. In most of the photos Brett's hunk of a husband sported thick, luxurious black hair. The bastard. Then all of a sudden he turned into Fabio.

"He bleached his hair? Why?"

"This one," Coulter pointed to a dark-haired shot where Mr. America was fighting rapids and looking like an action hero, "was taken a few years ago. And this one is more recent."

His shoulders slumped. "Briggs married a guy who colors his hair? The world is coming to an end."

The younger man's stifled chuckle turned into a snort. "Moving on. His cousin, who happens to be a cop on Brett's force, was married a few months ago to a woman named Fiona Corrione. Sound familiar?"

Fuck yeah. "She's the woman Smithwick kidnapped. She was also the Chameleon's girlfriend."

"That's right." Coulter flashed a dazzling smile and pulled another sheet of paper from the file folder on his lap. "There was a lovely announcement about the wedding in the local paper."

The last time Marco had seen Fiona Corrione she lay pale, almost lifeless on a hospital bed where the worn, white bed sheets held more color than her flesh. In the photo Coulter handed him, she was breathtaking with flowers in her hair and a smile so filled with happiness, he couldn't keep his own lips from twitching, ready to share in her joy.

He had always felt horrible that the girl had gotten caught in the dangerous crosshairs in the war with Smithwick. Questioning her about the kidnapping had only strengthened his resolve to see the man behind bars. To see her so happy lightened his heart.

But the sight of her groom brought his frown back. Good Lord. Another good-looking giant. "I'm starting to hate this family."

"And there's a brother."

"Let me guess. He's another gigantic son of a bitch too."

"Yep. And he's local."

"Reeeally." Now they were getting somewhere.

"Lucian Kilsgaard married the owner of Tutala. Ever eaten there?"

"Of course, because I have that much disposable income. What'da ya think?"

"She also owns The Cavern."

His brows rose. "The sex club? No shit."

Coulter straightened in his seat. "It's a nightclub that caters to those with an open mind."

"Been there, have you?"

"Once. Maybe twice." He shrugged.

"Ah-hmm. What have I told you about playing where you work?"

"Hey, the city is where it's all happening. You can't get that kind of action out in the sticks."

Marco shook his head and tapped at the photos. "I'd bet my left nut the cousin is the Chameleon. And I'm positive Briggs is close to our guy."

"You mean the Claymore."

"God." He winced. "Not you too."

"Me? No way. I think it's a stupid name. Anyone can tell he carries a long sword."

"And you know this how?"

"I used to date a girl who studied medieval history."

"Sounds kinky." He was learning way too much about his lieutenant.

"It was, kinda."

"Right. Now, I don't think The Hood is Brett's husband. She just had a baby, and I don't think he'd risk pissing off a new mother who can shoot a target two hundred feet away by leaving her to travel all the way to the city to bust some heads. My hunch, it's the brother."

Coulter rubbed his hands together. "I'm thinking a field trip is on the horizon."

"For me." He stood and gathered a pair of night-vision goggles and other surveillance supplies from the cabinet behind his desk. "This will be a solo trip."

"Ah, come on. Between the two of us, I've had the most experience inside the club. You need me."

"You can fill me in on the details as I stake out the joint before they open."

Coulter trailed behind like a little brother as Marco headed for the elevator. "You seriously can't think of leaving me behind."

"Where did you meet that history chick?"

"At The Cavern," he mumbled.

"Case closed."

Chapter Eight

MARCO DISCREETLY FLASHED his badge at the doorman. "I'd like to have a friendly word with your boss."

The man raised a beefy eyebrow then motioned with a jerk of his head. "Right this way."

With one step, Marco left the familiar white noise of the city street and entered a world of loud music and flashing lights. At first glance The Cavern appeared to be like any other nightclub with several bars, clusters of tables and a bevy of sweaty bodies grinding together on the crowded dance floor. If he was honest, he'd have to admit that the interior was much nicer than any of the other clubs his work brought him to. Nicer than even the few he'd been to in Vegas. The club had class, no doubt about that, and as he waited by the bar where he was escorted, he saw why Coulter had been so eager to tag along.

Stories abounded throughout the police force about free-for-all sex taking place in every corner of the club, and while Marco didn't see anything more scandalous than some heavy groping and a hand job going on at a nearby table, he'd bet money they were all true. There was a heightened sense of excitement pulsating in the air. A sensation of impending action that made him shift on his feet and continually scan the room for any unusual movement. Tiny pinpricks raced across his skin, and under his lightweight jacket his blood heated. Perspiration beaded on his lip and induced the urge to shed his clothing to relieve the pressure of his zipper against his stiffening cock.

He glanced up at the ceiling, searching for a source of ventilation. What were they doing? Pumping aphrodisiacs into the air? His heart sped up and he fought the need to walk out onto the dance floor just to feel some friction against his tingling skin.

The crowd parted and a woman walked toward him with a smile curling her luscious lips. Woman? Ha! This girl was unreal. She was an ethereal bombshell straight out of a comic book, with her shining straight black hair, curves like a '55 Bel Air and lavender eyes that seemed to look straight to his soul and stir up all the desires he thought were dead and buried. A pale-pink gown hugged her body like extra-cling plastic wrap, and if he squinted his eyes, she appeared to be wearing nothing at all. The effect did not help temper his raging libido.

Damn, he had to make this fast and get the hell out before he did something embarrassing.

The enchantress held out her hand. "Good evening. I'm Amaryllis Kilsgaard. I was told you wished to speak to me?"

This was Briggs' sister-in-law? Holy hell. Now he really, really hated the Kilsgaard men.

To his surprise her handshake was as firm as any man's he'd encountered. She might have looked like a fairy princess, but she had the grip strength of an ogre. "Mrs. Kilsgaard, I'm Police Captain Marco DeWinter."

"Oh," she squealed, throwing her arms around his neck and peppering both his cheeks with kisses. "Captain DeWinter. Thank you so much for what you did for Fiona. My family will always be grateful for your assistance with her rescue."

"Ha. Funny you should say that. I'll have to remind you of that in the future." He made sure he canted his hips back so she couldn't feel the effect of her wiggling against him. He released a mental sigh once she stepped away. "Actually, I was looking to speak to your husband, Lucian."

She arched her brow. "I was told you asked to speak to the boss. That's me."

"Ah." He rocked back on his heels, certain the little minx was testing him. "Why don't I doubt that you rule everything around here?"

"Because you are a smart man."

"I apologize for the error. I guess I should have been more specific with the doorman. I have a few questions for your husband. Is there a quiet place I can speak with him?"

"I can arrange something. Please, follow me."

As if he could resist following the swish of her backside encased in that pink satin. And he noticed he wasn't the only one watching her as a few men followed her progress across the room.

Amaryllis led him up a grand staircase and down a long hallway. As they passed door after door he heard the sounds of flesh on flesh intermixed with screams of "Fuck me harder." Marco didn't dare look into the rooms with open doors, but by facing forward his eyes were drawn to his hostess's delectable ass. No matter where he looked, he was fucked.

"Is this your first visit to The Cavern, Captain?" she asked with a glance over her shoulder and her hair falling across her eye with supermodel precision. The smile in her light irises made him think she knew exactly what he had been thinking and thought it was hysterical.

"Yes ma'am."

"Oh, you must come again for a more social visit. I can arrange a private tour. Show you all the best parts of the club."

"I couldn't ask you to do that. Besides, I don't go out much."

"That's a shame. A balanced life is a happy life. The offer still stands."

"Thank you, ma'am. I'll keep it in mind. That is an interesting accent you have there, Mrs. Kilsgaard." And an awfully familiar one. "Where exactly are you from?"

"Please, call me Amaryllis. I'm from a little village in Sweden. Very remote. Not many people have heard of it. That's why I love this city. So very different and much more exciting. Are you from here?"

Nice deflection. "Yep. Born and raised."

"Local son done well. Good for you, Captain. Right this

way."

Amaryllis breezed through the only doorway guarded by a bouncer. More on the cautious side, he paused at the entrance and surveyed the interior.

The change from the loud, boisterous first floor to the mellow, almost tranquil private suite was a jolt to his senses. The plush interior was large enough to hold a party of fifty. A fully stocked bar of black granite and gold fittings was to his left and fed into another dance floor. Floor-to-ceiling windows offered a sniper's view of the crowd below and a stripper's pole anchored each corner with clusters of chairs and chaise lounges in different sizes awaiting their next show.

Instead of the orgy he expected, only two other fully dressed couples were in attendance, lounging on the floor against huge crimson and white throw pillows and sipping goblets of red wine. On the floor in front of them lay a Twister board. Okay. Maybe they were a little kinky.

"Come on in, Captain." Amaryllis winked. "We don't bite."

The man who approached him was most certainly Lucian Kilsgaard. Standing at over six and a half feet tall, he had the same massive build and freakishly good looks as the rest of his family. After Amaryllis made the introductions, Marco found his hand engulfed between two massive paws.

"Captain DeWinter, it is good to meet you," Kilsgaard said with an accent that was reminiscent of his wife's. Jesus, was it possible the entire family was capable of being supers? "We can't thank you enough for the assistance you provided last year."

"You're welcome, but I was just doing my job. I saw that the Chameleon and Fiona were married recently. Congratulations." He kept his smile pleasant as he waited for the verbal grenade to detonate.

The couple exchanged a quick glance and Lucian's hands stilled mid-handshake. "I'm sorry, I don't follow. Fiona married my cousin Dhavin. The Chameleon ended his relationship with Fiona after her rescue. He felt she was safer without him in her life. She began dating my cousin sometime thereafter."

So that was their story. "Perhaps I was mistaken. Your cousin is a similar size to the Chameleon, and I have to admit, I don't meet very many guys as big as the men in your family."

"It's genetics. The women in our family are very strong. Have to be to birth us men." Kilsgaard motioned to a seating area away from the other couples and took a place on the couch. His wife tucked her feet beneath her butt as she curled up at his side. "How can I assist you, Captain?"

Marco took a seat in a buttery leather chair across from the lovey-dovey pair. "It appears as if masked crusaders are not exclusive to your former hometown of Cedar. There's a man running around interfering in police work. I've been tasked to bring him in before someone gets hurt, or killed."

"I have heard this is an issue most metropolises are facing recently. Average citizens doing what they can to take back their streets. I agree, it is a potentially dangerous situation."

"Yes, but the man I'm looking for is not an average citizen. Just like the Chameleon is not an average citizen. In fact, there is a lot about the two men that is strikingly similar."

There was a telltale widening of his eyes for a split second, but his features remained politely interested. "Do you think they are one and the same?"

"No, I don't. But I wouldn't be surprised if they knew of each other. Were maybe even related." Pussyfooting around was not his style. Time to shoot for the bull's-eye. "Tell me, Mr. Kilsgaard. Do you know if the Chameleon may have any associates or relatives in the city?"

"None that I am aware of. Then again, the Chameleon is not exactly what you would call a sharer. He's a very private individual."

"So I've gathered. Where were you the night of the tenth between the hours of 11:15 p.m. and midnight?"

He arched a dark brow and his lips softened into a knowing smirk. "I was at home with my wife."

"And what were you doing?"

"Fucking," Amaryllis answered and stroked her hand down her husband's chest. "It's our usual routine. You can ask anyone in the building. We aren't exactly quiet."

"I see." Marco worked to clear his suddenly tight throat. Great, now he'd have to live with that image burned into his brain for the rest of his life. That was one hell of an alibi. And not one he'd want to question. The answers would probably make him depressed.

He withdrew a business card from the inside of his jacket pocket and handed it to Kilsgaard. "I'm sure if you ask your sister-in-law, she will reiterate the importance of getting this vigilante off the street. I don't need to deal with a body count because someone took it upon themselves to take police matters into their own hands. With this nightclub, you two have the ability to keep your ear to the ground, so to speak. If you hear of anything that can help me keep our streets safe, please, give me a call."

"Of course, Captain."

When Lucian pocketed the card, Marco stood. "Thank you for your time. I can see myself out."

Amaryllis followed him to the doorway. "Good luck, Captain. I look forward to your next visit."

The certainty in her statement sent warning bells through his head. "What makes you so certain I'll be back?"

"Do you not know The Cavern's motto? All who enter receive exactly what they need."

His shoulders relaxed. "Well, I do need to catch this criminal, so if information leads me back here, you bet I'll be back."

Her lyrical laughter made his breath catch and her palm against his cheek was soft and warm. "No, Captain. Apprehending the vigilante is what you want, not what you need. When you are ready, you'll be back. Good night."

He watched her skip to her husband's side with a serious case of the creepazoids slithering down his spine. Yep, there was definitely something strange going on with this family.

With the Kilsgaards occupied and no security guard on his ass, Marco took his sweet time making his way to the exit. Of course he believed the couple's alibi for the night of the jewelry heist. If he had a wife like Amaryllis, he'd never let her leave the bed either. But the two were holding back information. He could almost smell it on them. If he kept his eyes open, he was bound to strike gold.

Deep down in his gut, he knew that finding evidence on The Hood wasn't his only reason for poking his nose around the club. This place was a trip and he was a red-blooded man who had only had his hand for a girlfriend for far too long. If this was to be his only chance to walk around unattended, damn straight he was going to take a gander at what exactly went down in The Cavern.

Most of the doors he passed were shut, and the ones that were opened led to empty rooms, save for some kinky-looking furniture. Disappointing but not surprising. It was a week-night, after all.

A hulking shadow stomped down the hall in his direction, and Marco stepped to the side for the man to pass, only to do a double take as the figure drew closer.

Black denim jacket over a hooded sweatshirt.

The stranger was at least as tall as Lucian Kilsgaard and just as beefy with broad shoulders that appeared to span the width of the walkway. They shared similar coloring and the same square-cut features that reminded him of the comic book superheroes he read as a kid. The stern set of the man's jaw and intense focus of his gaze was a warning to all to get out of the way or become a stain on the hardwood.

Motherfucker. This had to be his guy. Adrenaline spiked in his body and made his muscles twitch to follow, but he held back, waiting several heartbeats before setting off in the same direction. The video footage of The Hood showed lightning-fast reflexes, and after Amaryllis Kilsgaard's spooky predictions, who knew what else this guy was capable of.

The Hood stepped into a vacant room and Marco held back, pressing against the wall with his cell phone out and ready to make it appear as if he were only another club-goer standing in the hall to send a text. Inch by inch he crept closer to the door until he spotted his suspect rummaging through an armoire. Strips of leather fell across his arm, swinging with his movements as he stacked brightly colored bottles in the crook of his arm. From a drawer he pulled out a long ream of condoms and held them between his teeth as he reached for more supplies.

God bless the woman he was intending to meet up with. The beast was suiting up for one intense fuck.

"Excuse me. Can I help you?"

Years of training kept him from screaming like a frightened schoolgirl. At least on the outside. Inside he jumped and shrieked like a four-year-old spotting a spider.

He turned toward the voice and felt his eyes bulge out of their sockets. "Dr. Jovanovich?"

What. The. Fuck?

The only times he crossed paths with Dr. Jasmine Jo-vanovich was in the emergency room at the city hospital when he had to interview a suspect or victim for one of his cases. Never on any of those occasions did he suspect that under-neath the blue scrubs, white coat and ponytail lurked a sex goddess.

Although her stature was on the short side, her legs looked a mile long and shimmered in the soft lighting as if burnished with some kind of sparkles. A black corset cinched in her waist, with a matching leather skirt stretching across her full hips to create the perfect hourglass shape. He had no idea her dark hair was so long as it hung loose past her shoulders and framed her pretty face. Sheer black netting hugged her breasts, highlighting the dark-pink nipples that beaded in the cool air.

Fuckin' hell. No matter how hard he tried, granted which wasn't very much, he could not take his eyes off those pretty nipples. It was as if they had tractor beams zeroed in on his retinas. He grew lightheaded as the blood from his big head raced to his little one that swelled with each passing second.

Finally, his brain couldn't take it anymore and before he realized, he muttered, "Holy shit."

The good doctor jumped at the expletive and crossed her arms over those fantastic breasts. "Captain. Wh-what are you doing here?"

"I was about to ask you the same thing. My God, woman." He scrubbed his hand over the back of his neck. He really shouldn't be staring so hard but...damn. "Making house calls?"

She shifted in her strappy high heels and shot a furtive glance around the hall. When she turned back in his direction her dark eyes blazed as she leaned forward to growl, "What are you doing here?"

Whoa, look at the little spitfire. "I'm working a case."

Oh fuck. The Hood.

He edged back to the door and peeked inside the room to find it empty.

"Damn." He slapped his palm against the wall. Now what?

The click of heels on the hardwood drew his attention back to the doc who was inching her way back down the hall.

"Wait up, Doc." Maybe all was not lost. "You haven't told me what you're doing here."

She froze. The straightness of her posture he knew was not caused by the tightness of the corset. After several heartbeats she turned his way and sighed. Her breasts shimmied oh so delicately with the movement. As if sensing his stare, she crossed her arms again. "Stop that."

"Why? You didn't wear that outfit to not be stared out. Seriously, Doc, I never realized how hot you are. I like this look." A lot.

"Look, how about we forget this little encounter occurred. Okay?"

"Hmmm." He scratched at his cheek. "I don't know. Maybe if…"

Even the flare of her nostrils was sexy. "What do you

want?" she asked through clenched teeth.

Oh, what didn't he want? Was the skin of her inner thighs as soft as it looked?

Focus, man.

Right. "A guy came down this way a few minutes ago. Huge. Black jean jacket over a hoodie. Sound familiar?"

She shrugged. "There are lots of guys around here. I can't keep track of them all."

"This one you'd remember. About the same size as Lucian Kilsgaard. Do you know who Lucian is?"

"Yes."

And... "So do you recognize whom I'm talking about?"

"Not sure."

Ooo, she was a cagey one. Unfortunately for the doc, he was not above using any means necessary to get what he wanted. With a quick flip of his wrist, he took her picture with his cellphone. The bright flash momentarily blinded them both.

"God, you're an asshole." She blinked hard but didn't move her arms.

"How's the Wi-Fi reception in here?" He held up the phone.

Her fingers curled into her biceps. "I may know who you are speaking of."

"What's his name?"

"Why do you want to know?"

"I can't tell you. Name. Or I press Send."

"Grrr." She stamped her foot and daggered him with her glare. "Bale."

"Friend of yours?"

"No. I stay out of his way and he usually stays out of mine."

His brow climbed at that. That giant obeyed this tiny woman? "Is he here a lot?"

"He comes and goes."

"Is he close with the Kilsgaards?"

"I think so."

"How?"

"I think they're all from the same town in Sweden."

Yeah, he was beginning to believe that whole Sweden story was a cover up.

"Is he a patron?" She shrugged. "Does he work here?" Another shrug. He bit back a curse and closed his eyes. "Let's stop playing twenty questions, Doc, and just tell me what you know about him."

"As I said, I don't know much. We don't converse." A sultry smile curled her lips and a teasing light flashed in her eyes. "However, I do believe his cock is ginormous, based on the wood I saw him sporting last night."

At her use of the word *cock* his own jumped and pulsed painfully behind his fly. Lordy, how he wished he could reach down and relieve the pressure. Then her words sank in. She was at the club the night before and knew the size of his dick? "Are you fucking him?"

She rolled her eyes. "No. He's hot but not submissive enough for my tastes. Look, all I know is he's close to the Kilsgaards, comes and goes as he pleases and you don't piss him off. That's all."

Not submissive enough? What the hell did that mean?

As his brain ruminated over that statement, he pulled up her photo on his phone and made a production of hitting the Delete button as he mentally kissed the image goodbye.

"Thanks for the info, Doc." He smiled. "For the record, I wouldn't have sent the photo. No one would have believed me anyway. Not that you aren't sexy," he hastily added as her eyes widened, "because you are. Holy hell are you sexy. But you don't seem to be the kinky type. You're so...efficient."

She snorted and lowered her arms. With slow, slinky steps, she walked toward him, not stopping until the hard tips of her breasts were pressed against his chest and his aching erection was cushioned in the softness of her belly.

Her eyelids lowered to half-mast and her lips pursed into a hot little pout. "If you breathe a word of this to anyone, I'll deny it until I'm blue in the face, then take my whip to your bare ass. Do you understand?"

He swallowed hard. She had to be bluffing. Wasn't she? "Sure."

"Marco." The use of his first name made his lungs catch as did the swivel of her hips against cock. "Do you understand?"

He nodded then gasped as she dug her fingertips into his side. "Yes."

"Good boy." She stepped away and walked backward, keeping their gazes locked.

She reached for the doorknob of a closed door a few feet away. For the second time that night, Marco felt as if he'd taken a baseball bat to the chest as she revealed a man kneeling in the middle of the room. He wore not a stitch of clothing, his hands resting palm up on his thighs.

"Hello, Army," the doctor greeted.

His hard cock bounced in reaction to her voice but he kept his gaze directed at the floor in front of his knees. "Good evening, Mistress."

Her smoky gaze nailed Marco as if she had reached out and grabbed him by the shaft. "Good night, Captain."

The door shut between them with a soft click.

His hands shook as he dragged them through his hair then pulled at his tight collar.

Holy fuck. She was a Dominatrix. Mousey little Dr. Jovanovich wore leather, snapped whips and tortured naked men in a sex club.

Sweat broke out across his forehead as he stared at the solid door. Curiosity possessed him, drawing him the scant feet forward until his cheek pressed against the cool wood. There was a murmur of voices, one light and seductive, the other deep and anxious. Then came the smack of a solid object hitting flesh followed by a throaty moan. Then another. And another.

Marco jumped back as if the door had burst into flames.

He wiped at his brow and raced down the hall, feeling like the biggest pervert on the planet.

A name. He now had a name. Exactly what he came for. But catching The Hood wasn't even on his radar at the moment.

Amaryllis' words from earlier spun around him in an intricate spider's web, growing thick and tight, binding him into place.

He got what he wanted, but now he had a need.

How long could he hold out until he begged to have that need satisfied?

Chapter Nine

FOR THE UMPTEENTH time that day Ari wondered what in the hell she was thinking as Bale stood behind her and brushed soft kisses down her neck. The swirl of his tongue against her pulse sent an arc of fire over her skin. At the same time she shivered at the scrape of his callus-roughened fingers parting the back of her dress.

What was she doing becoming intimate with a man who was still practically a stranger? From what she'd seen so far, Bale maybe-kinda-sort of had a job doing Lord only knew what, and he had very little to his name but for his motorcycle and a few items of clothing.

When Anthony, the scumbag, had courted her, she refused his advances for weeks, never truly believing that the smart, well-to-do, big-city lawyer was interested in the small-town girl who slung whisky and mugs of beer for a living. Little by little Anthony had made her believe she was worthy of his affections, capable of aspiring for better than her upbringing. The man had played on her weaknesses.

Maybe that had been her problem—she had trusted a man who was both a lawyer and a politician. All she had wanted was to be in a relationship with a man with a respectable job. Had that been too much to ask?

And Bale was nowhere near respectable. At least not in the traditional sense. Oh, people respected his strength and ability to kick major ass, but he wasn't the type of man you could bring home to the folks and say, "Here's my man, and he's all that and a bag of chips."

Of course, her father had disappeared before she was born and her mother's romantic history consisted of men who were either married, addicts, cheated on her or all of the above. Huh, perhaps respectability was overrated.

Still, common sense demanded she take things slow. So why was she doing a cannonball into the deep end of madness?

"You are so beautiful, Ari," Bale whispered in her ear and nipped at the lobe. "I want to spend days learning all of the ways to make you come apart in my arms."

There it was. That right there was why she was allowing him to strip her naked, inside and out.

The gentleness of his large hands as he cupped her breasts, the light in his eyes as he looked upon her as if she were a treasure he coveted for himself, yet awed that he possessed her. For the first time in her life she understood what it felt like to be cherished. To have her wants and desires attended to by someone who cared, just as she wished to do for Bale.

She smiled as she recalled the expression on his face when she opened the door earlier. In his arms he juggled a variety of sex toys and lotions, clearly eager to try them out, but at the same time his concern that he was pushing too far made him look like a little boy begging to play with his new toys. And a very naughty little boy at that.

When she had enthusiastically agreed, his delighted smile had made her heart flip and she knew then she was putty in his hands.

Like now, with his fingers massaging her breasts, making them ache for a rougher touch. She ground her backside against his denim-encased erection and lifted her arms, wrapping them up and around his neck. Her fingers grabbed the hair at the nape of his neck and tugged. She loved the way his hands trembled as he glided them over her body.

"Your hands feel so good on me. More. I want more."

The hitch in his breath as she pulled his hair and talked dirty ratcheted up her arousal until she was giddy with power. For a man who used so few words, he did enjoy hearing her constant banter.

He chuckled, his hot breath ghosting over her skin. "You shall have it."

The room spun as he turned her in his arms and cupped her backside, pulling her tight against his pelvis. His kiss was hard and hungry. Just how she liked it.

She reached under his shirt, luxuriating in the bunching of his muscles and the heat he generated. With Bale in her bed, she'd never have to worry about another cold night again.

"What wicked plans do you have for me, big man?" she asked against his lips as she raked her nails across his abdomen.

His slight frown and hard swallow instantly intrigued her.

"Tell me, Bale." She reached up and smoothed away the creases on his brow with her thumb. "The most I can do is say no."

"I—" He swallowed again. "I want to restrain you."

And... That was all? From the line of tension that straightened his shoulders she expected to hear a far more extreme request. "You want to tie me up? Okay. That's a little kinky, but not too out there. Why didn't you just ask me?"

"To give control to another requires a great deal of trust. I am not sure if I've earned yours yet," he said solemnly.

Wow. She rocked back on her heels. "Thank you for thinking of my feelings. I'm sorry to say that I'm not used to men asking me my opinion."

"Those men were beasts who did not deserve you."

The conviction in his statement made her smile and she granted him a quick kiss. "I like the idea of being at your mercy. Why don't we start small? How about you can bind my hands, but don't tie me to anything I can't run away from."

"I can do that." Anticipation darkened his eyes to a sparkly obsidian and a smile flirted on his lips.

"But I want you naked first."

The excitement dimmed. "I don't know why you insist on my nakedness."

"I suspect it's the same reason you stripped me down the moment you walked through the door. The way your body moves is highly arousing."

To prove her point, she stood on tiptoe to pull his shirt up and over his head then licked a path from his collarbone down the center of his chest to the waistband of his jeans with only slight detours to scrape her teeth across his nipples. "Admit it, you like my hands on your bare skin."

"You have to ask?" His erection eagerly sprang into her waiting hand as she released the zipper of his jeans.

With her left hand she stroked him from base to tip in a swirling motion that made his knees shake with each down-stroke while she worked to pull his pants the rest of the way off his sturdy legs.

Once he was bare to her liking, she peppered his hairy thighs with kisses and dug her fingers into the firm muscles of his backside. Mercy be, the man had a butt Michelangelo's David would envy.

Between licks along the underside of his strong cock she asked, "Do you still want to tie me up?"

His head tipped back on a groan as his fingers tunneled into her hair. With a sharp tug, she was on her feet. "Yes."

The game was on.

Perspiration dotted his forehead and slickened his bangs so they framed his eyes as they narrowed with a predatory gleam that warned her he would not stop until he conquered all he believed was his.

"Give me your hands." Hunger deepened his voice to a rumble that sent flashes of heat exploding in all her erogenous zones.

Without another word spoken between them, he used a black satin ribbon to bind her wrists together. He lifted her then set her on the middle of her bed, urging her to place her arms above her head before he stepped back and gazed at her with admiration shining brilliantly in his eyes.

He set one knee upon the bed by her side then slowly swung his other leg up and over her body, as if he were an experienced cowboy settling into the saddle for a good hard ride. The touch of his possessive gaze and the authoritative lines carved around his firmly set lips made all her senses stand at attention like fans at a rock concert climbing over each other with hands outstretched just for the chance to brush against their hero.

Holy shit. She wasn't going to survive the night.

No matter how hard she tried to hold still, her hips twitched and rolled beneath him and her torso undulated, desperate for any contact.

Bale drew a deep breath and a smugness lifted the corner of his mouth into a slanted grin. God, could he smell the cream leaking out of her pussy and soaking the sheets beneath her?

"I've barely touched you and you're ready to come."

She tried to laugh, but the sound came out more like a squeak. "I told you, you're a very sexy man."

He laid his hot hand against her sternum and she swore her heart leapt into his palm. For several long seconds he didn't move, only watched her with that intense stare as she fought the urge to scream.

Touch me, damn it!

A strangled cry broke free as tears of frustration welled in her eyes. Only then did he take pity on her and fully cupped both breasts, bending down to scrape the fine stubble of his beard over the straining tips as he laughed with evil intent.

"You suck," she gasped as she writhed.

"As you wish." He drew a hard nipple deep into his mouth.

Whoa. She hissed and arched her back for more of the delicious contact.

"Oh yes. Yes." Her whimpers turned into keening cries as he bit and kneaded her achy mounds. Around her nipple his smile widened as he watched her turn into a babbling, lusty heap.

"I love how you give your pleasure to me with such abandon." He slid his thigh between hers, prying her legs apart to make room for his torso. "Show me how wet you are."

A bitch in heat displayed more decorum than she did as she eagerly pulled her knees up and out. Did she care if she appeared as easy as a wanton slut? Hell no. Her pussy was dying of hunger and needed to be fed. Now.

Bale ran the flat of his tongue from her knee down to her open sex. Against her skin he murmured words she guessed were from his native language in that raspy voice that sent vibrations straight to her clit.

"Please, Bale. I need to be filled."

The tip of his finger teased the opening to her sheath. "No. You're not ready yet."

"Bullshit," she shouted. "Fuck me. Fuck me now. Please."

"Will this suffice?" He sank his forefinger into her pussy down to the knuckle.

Oh, that was nice. Nice, but not enough.

"More. More."

"How about this?" Two fingers plunged deep, the tips massaged the neck of her womb in little circles.

That could work. She humped against his hand, her heart ready to burst as she reached out for the orgasm dangling so close she could taste its sweetness.

Then the bastard pulled away. "Son of a bitch!"

Again with the evil laughter. She shook her head to clear the damp strands that had fallen across her face with all her thrashing and shot him a glare that should have brought him to his knees.

"I think you will enjoy this better," he said as he rolled a condom down his thick shaft.

The coiled power in his body as he moved into position sent a spike of adrenaline to her brain and her teeth chattering with the intensity. His dark gaze pinned her in place as he slowly inserted his cock into her sheath in a long, steady stroke until he could go no farther.

His eyelids fluttered and nostrils flared when she clenched her inner muscles around the invasion, pulsing and releasing as if to coax the cum from his balls.

"Thank you," he murmured, then pulled back his hips and lunged hard, driving the breath from her lungs. He snarled and hooked her legs over his arms and drove deep, again and again, in a pace that never wavered.

Tears streamed down her face as the most exquisite fire erupted within, consuming her from the inside out. The world disappeared until only Bale remained, his strength, his heat, tunneling into her soul and staking his claim. And still he never stopped, thrusting balls-deep and drawing her orgasm out until her lungs struggled for air and she wept for relief.

Sweat dripped from his brow, the sheen on his alabaster skin made him look like an otherworldly conqueror. The cock wedged in her cunt was rock hard, pulsing with the need to release his cum. He said not a word as he rolled her weak body over and positioned her on her knees. Her body was so ready, he sank every inch of his shaft with one thrust into her still-twitching core. Unintelligible words fell from her lips but the message was clear.

Take me. My body is yours. Give me your all.

The touch of his fingers rubbing against her clit ignited another blast of energy that had her bound hands clutching the bed sheets as she sent howling praises to the Lord. Consciousness faded as she struggled for air and her body continued to shake from the two orgasms. Part of her craved more of the addictive sensations while the other half was terrified she'd never survive what he planned for her next.

The sensation of cool gel oozing between the cheeks of her

ass followed by the press of Bale's finger against the tiny hole roused her attention.

She tensed at the pressure and she felt Bale freeze a moment later. Once before she had tried anal sex. It hadn't been the best of experiences, but it hadn't been the worst either.

With a glance over her shoulder she saw Bale holding himself in check. The muscles in his arms and legs twitched as if fighting against the command to hold still. His breath bellowed like that of a bull after a long hard run, his chest expanding hard with each inhale.

"Is this bad?" he gritted out, clearly at the end of his control.

"No," she whispered, unable to talk any louder. "Go. Slow."

He shuddered and resumed the gentle probing of her ass. Throughout their short history together, Bale had always treated her with the utmost care, ensuring she received everything she needed. There was no reason for her to believe that would change now. What better way to display her trust than by giving him something he clearly craved?

The generous amount of lubrication eased his way and surprisingly the penetration didn't hurt, not even when he added a second finger. Before long she was pushing back, enjoying the stretch and fullness.

"Ari," he groaned then pulled out from her altogether.

She arched in response. "Please. Ahh."

Yes. Her breath caught as he settled the head of his cock

where his fingers had been and pushed. The glide was as slow and steady as when he had taken her pussy. Against the backs of her thighs his legs trembled, his fingers dug into her flanks as he withdrew then pushed again. When his tight ball sac kissed the lips of her pussy he released a deep sigh.

"*Jesu.* You're so tight. Hot. Fuck me."

She whimpered and nodded, rocking back and forth in a silent plea for more friction.

"Ari. *Liera.*" He pressed his sweaty forehead against the middle of her equally wet back and resumed his thrusting. "Words. No words."

By the side of her head his fist was planted into the mattress. The veins and sinew in his arms bulged under the strain as he bucked and moaned her name in what sounded like a multitude of languages.

"Come again," he panted hotly against her ear.

"Don't think. I can."

"Come!" He cupped her mound and speared three fingers into her clutching channel and worked his thumb over the swollen bud of her clitoris.

Ari bit into the mattress and screamed as a tsunami-sized wave tore her asunder. Above her Bale bellowed and drove deep, pinning her to the bed as his cock flexed with his release.

Spasms continued to erupt in her pussy and ass, radiating up her spine as she sobbed. Her visions blurred in and out until it narrowed to a pinpoint of light before winking out into complete blackness.

Holy shit, she'd gone blind. Oh nope. Just crashed face-first into the pillow. She'd laugh if she had the strength, but sleep had latched on tight and was pulling her under fast.

Lord have mercy on her soul, for she wanted to do that again.

"Ari? Ari?" Bale lifted up, sensing his woman's fall into unconsciousness. "Ariel?"

Nothing. No response as he shook her shoulders and her head lolled upon her neck. His hands shook as he swept them over her body, feeling for her pulse and possible injuries. He had tried to be gentle, but once he was buried inside the velvet fist of her ass, his control had snapped. Anal intercourse was a taboo act, even on his home planet, and now he understood why after having experienced the most explosive orgasm in his life. If losing consciousness was a common occurrence, abstaining from such an act was probably best for the female's safety.

It didn't matter that Ari had been more than a willing partner. Even now as he eased from the snug grip of her ass, her channel fluttered, keeping his staff erect. Did the woman have no self-preservation?

He stumbled into the bathroom and discarded the brimming condom into the waste bin then quickly washed his hands and cock. Wetting a washcloth with hot water, he gathered another towel and dashed back to the bed to sit beside Ari's prone form.

As he sponged away the lubricant and remnants of their

orgasms from her body, his frowned deepened as the bruises on her hips and thighs darkened. His powers picked up nothing but bliss and contentment but obviously he had been too rough with his lovemaking. The fact that Ari encouraged his behavior did not make it right.

"Ari?" He untied her hands then brushed the hair away from her forehead, stroking her cheek again and again with his thumb. "Ari, please wake up. Open those pretty eyes and tell me you're all right."

Beneath his ribs his two hearts beat once, then twice before kicking up a notch as her breathing quickened and her lashes fluttered. Her gaze darted around the room before coming to rest on his face. As slow as a sunrise, a smile stretched her lips as she settled deeper into the mattress.

"That. Was. Awesome." She sighed and closed her eyes.

"Do you hurt anywhere?"

She shook her head then frowned and shifted her hips. "Not really. Just sore."

"We shall never do that again."

Her eyes snapped opened. "Why not? That was great."

"It is too dangerous."

"For who? Didn't you enjoy yourself?"

Heat blazed across his cheeks. "Ya."

"Then we will be doing that again."

"Ariel." He grunted and felt his nostrils flare. "Do not fight me on this. We will do nothing that causes you harm again."

The innocent blink and sweet smile set off his inner alarm.

"For now."

Jesu. "You've been spending too much time with Amaryllis."

She giggled and crawled with uncoordinated limbs under the bedcovers. "I should brush my teeth, but my legs don't want to work."

"That does not make me feel any better."

"That's because you have issues. I wasn't complaining." Her smile faded and he sensed her sudden insecurity as she plucked at the fabric covering her pillow. "So. Do you have to rush right off?"

Happiness infused his hearts as he read between the lines. "Are you asking me to stay?"

She shrugged. "Only if you want to."

"Silly woman. Just tell me you want me to lie beside you."

"I don't want to assume you have no other plans."

"I want—" He took a breath and voiced his secret wish. "I want you to need me."

"Oh Bale," she sighed and held out her hand. "I need you to hold me."

He almost used his powers to dive under the covers. The effervescent, bubbling sensation of her laughter felt just as good against his skin as her warm flesh did where she was pressed along his side.

"I love how warm-blooded you are." She nuzzled his chest. "You make these cold northwest nights enjoyable."

Ari made all of his nights, and days too, more enjoyable.

Just being with him, a slight weight on top of his chest, heart beating, the whoosh of her breath across his nipple. Her being there meant he was no longer alone in this new world.

Of course Amaryllis would slap him upside the head if she knew he felt that way. She found great pride in the family unit she had created and made it no secret that she considered him part of her brood.

But Ari was a treasure of his own. Her opinions were unfettered by any knowledge of the man he once was. The past, the future, nothing else existed but the peace each felt by being together in this perfect moment of the present.

How many hours could he spend memorizing the shape of her spine with his fingers or luxuriate under the light caress of her fingertips as she traced the lines and dips of his torso? Perhaps days, maybe even weeks.

"What happened here?" She skimmed the puckered line across his rib.

He closed his eyes on a sigh, enjoying the touch. "First week of training when I joined the...military. I feinted right when I should have gone left. My opponent caught me with his sword. Lesson learned."

"You still use swords in the military?"

"We were trained in all manner of weaponry."

"Hmm. See this scar here?" He opened his eyes to see her pointing at a faint tree-shaped scar on her forearm. "A shelf of liquor fell at work and glass flew everywhere. Caught a few shards in my arm. The bar patrons called me Tanqueray for a while."

"I never realized bartending was so fraught with danger. Besides that which comes from rude patrons."

"We all learn on the fly." Her cheek bunched with her smile and her fingers resumed brushing butterfly-light touches over his chest.

She cupped the cap of his shoulder, giving the firm muscle a little squeeze before trailing over the rough scar tissue of his biceps. "What happened here?"

The breath froze in his lungs and his throat closed up tight. The gnarled flesh was another example of his talent at taking something beautiful and making it ugly. Once upon a time the symbol on his arm had been one of great honor and he had been so proud when he received his mark as a royal guard.

Lucian and his family had been *Llanos* warriors for generations, dating back to the beginning of their kingdom's recorded history, while Bale's relations had always been farmers. Day laborers who earned their livelihood and muscles toiling the nearly impenetrable Skandavian soil. The monotonous cycle of planting, harvest, planting, harvest had been lost on a boy with Bale's need to push harder, go faster and be more than a farmer.

Joining the royal guard had been his ticket to adventure, to greatness. He had quickly moved up the ranks and been assigned to the king's personal retinue after three years of service. The day the crown had been added to his insignia was the day he met Natalia when his family had taken him out in celebration. She had been the quiet, calm port in the tumultuous sea of politics. The light to the darkness of his position and nature.

Then the revolution erupted and his family was destroyed. The symbol of *Llanos* had been a reminder of all he lost. Blind rage and burning guilt had barely anesthetized him to the pain of slicing the ink from his flesh in a fit of misplaced rage.

"I'm sorry if my question caused you pain." Ari's soft voice was as sharp as a fine scalpel slicing through the thick haze of his memories.

"No." He closed his arms around her when she tensed. "It wasn't your question, rather the memories that hurt. I—uh, I had a tattoo removed quite barbarically."

"I'd say. It looks like it was dug out of your skin."

She was correct.

"I didn't have access to the proper technology at the time," he lied.

"Sounds as if you were in a hurry to have it removed."

"I was."

"Hmm. Well, I see you've kept this one here. It's pretty," she murmured, while lightly stroking the starburst tattoo in the center of his chest. "What does it say?"

The innocently asked question struck him in the gut with the power of a sledgehammer. Beneath the Skandavia symbol for heaven he had imprinted Natalia's and Emmaline's names in his native language to help him keep his focus on his purpose. As much as he cared for Ari, he wasn't near ready to expose those wounds.

"It's, uh… It's the names of family I have lost. To remember them. I-I do not like talking about it," he managed to stammer.

"Oh." She dropped her hand. "Okay."

A heavy silence fell between them and the invisible band around his chest tightened and hindered his breathing. A shift had occurred in their relationship just then. He couldn't put his finger on what exactly or how, but there was a tension that vibrated between them even though they both lay quiet and still in each other's arms. It was as if Ari knew he purposely withheld information and in return locked a part of herself away from him. The closeness of only a moment before no longer existed and he wanted to weep with the loss.

"Ari," he said.

"Yes, Bale?"

He opened his mouth to reply then snapped it shut. Truth was he hadn't thought of anything else to say but her name. Meaningless conversation was not his style. Hell, he'd rather endure an uncomfortable silence than engage in inane babble. But this invisible wall that had suddenly erupted between them stole all the warmth and joy he normally felt in her presence and was a stark reminder of his solitary existence.

Ari lifted her head to look at him when he didn't answer. "Bale?"

He licked his lips and laid his palm against her cheek, his thumb smoothing out the frown line near her mouth. "Ari, I—"

He swallowed hard. "You frighten me."

Her brows shot up. "What?"

"You make me want things I—" *Don't want. Don't know how to care for. Don't deserve.* "I'm going to fuck this up."

"Fuck what up?"

"This. Whatever this magic is that's between us, I'm going to ruin it. It's what I do. And that frightens me."

"Oh, Bale." Her eyes turned liquid and the invisible wall crumbled. "Don't you think I'm a little freaked out too? Since I met you I've felt like I'm on this rocket shot into space and eventually I'll run out of fuel and crash back to Earth. It's exhilarating and terrifying at the same time."

"Exactly." Inside he laughed, for he had been in a rocket that crashed to Earth. Back then he hadn't been half as scared as he was now.

"Bale, can't we just take each day as it comes? If I start thinking too far ahead, I begin to think about supposed-tos and not about just living for the moment. Can I just enjoy being with you and leave it at that?"

"Yes," he answered slowly as his own internal conflict waged war in his hearts.

What in the seven hells was wrong with him? Here was this beautiful, sexy, adventurous woman offering him what sounded like a no-strings-attached relationship and instead of being ecstatic he wanted to howl with displeasure. Wasn't this the perfect solution? No expectations beyond the night. No chance of breaking promises that were never made. One day at a time.

However, the thought of being able to walk away with any ease burned a hole in his chest. Would Ari be able to leave him so easily if she wanted?

He had no land, no name, nothing of real value to offer her and she deserved so much more, the least of which was a man who could tell her the truth about who, and what, he was. If he had any decency, he'd end this now and allow her the chance to find a man of her own kind before their hearts became too entwined.

But he wasn't decent. Pure selfishness kept him in the bed and drew her down for a possessive kiss.

Yes, he had nothing to offer her. But pleasure.

Since words often failed him, he'd have to use his other talents to convey how much Ari meant to him. He prayed they were enough to convince her of his sincerity.

He drank in her purr of contentment as he skimmed his palms down her back and cupped the curve of her ass. Up and down, up and down he stroked her side, keeping the tempo slow when she tried to deepen the kiss. Her little growls of displeasure made him smile and more determined to love her on his terms.

"Do I need to tie your hands again?" he teased as he rolled her onto her back.

"No. I want to touch you."

"You are." He ground his cock into her belly. "And you feel so good."

She responded by scraping the edges of her teeth along his

shoulder. "I want more."

"You'll get it. When I say so."

"You suck—"

"As you wish." He took her pink nipple into his mouth, lashing the tip with his tongue. He did love to deliberately misinterpret her curses.

"Damn it, Bale." She tugged at his hair. "I want you to ravish me."

"And I want to savor you." He switched to the other breast. "You will not deter me on this, *liera*. Do not fret. I will do everything in my power to leave you satisfied."

"You always do." She sighed with contentment. "What does *liera* mean anyway?"

He froze with his mouth hovering over her skin then slowly lifted up. With a shaky hand he brushed the strands of hair off her face so he could look deep into her sparkling eyes. A lump formed in his throat but he pressed on and confessed.

"Mine."

Against his ribs he felt her heart start pounding as she melted into the mattress. "Oh."

Millimeter by millimeter he lowered his head until their mouths pressed together in the gentlest of touches. The plump pillows of her lips were satin-soft. The slight rasp of her tongue tangling with his he felt down to his bones. Ari was a sweet and rich confection more decadent than any found in the finest bakery. All her inner beauty was wrapped up in a savory package he wanted to devour whole.

When the last of her resistance dissipated and the mellow pulse of her desire engulfed him, Bale licked and nuzzled down the fine column of her neck, continuing to the swell of her breasts, teasing the undersides with his mouth. Every so often he'd look up to find Ari watching him with sex-drugged eyes and he smiled against her skin. The slow curl of her answering smile filled him with so much joy, he wanted to shout with the euphoria.

This lovely creature was truly his, and with each sigh and low moan as his hands and mouth caressed her body, he sensed her submission through his powers. Her thighs parted at the slight brush of his fingers. Wherever he laid a palm, she'd press her flesh deeper into his hold, her body flowing like warm water in his grasp.

"Bale. Please." She pulled at his shoulders and wrapped her legs around his waist. "I need you."

He knew. More than she realized.

Ari placed herself entirely into his keeping with an open heart, and the sensation empowered him at the same time it scared him to death. Not even Natalia had placed such trust in him at the level he sensed from Ari. What if he failed her? What if he couldn't be what she needed? The last woman to place such faith in him died. Dare he subject Ari to a similar fate?

"Please, Bale," Ari pleaded with a deep groan, her nails scoring lines up his back. Then she whispered in a voice so low, he barely heard, "Please love me."

Love.

Was she aware she had spoken such a powerful word? Was it possible that she had developed such strong feelings for him already? Did he even want her love?

Images of the last few years flitted through his mind. Long nights spent alone, always on the move to the next location. Days of never exchanging a single word, or a smile, or a glance with anyone. So much anger. So much sadness. Compared to the brief time he'd spent with Ari, those memories were as cold and heartwarming as a prison cell buried miles beneath the earth. Such extended isolation destroyed the soul.

A connection to another. One person, just one, who cared whether you lived or died, who thought of you, who missed you, who knew your secrets and kept them safe. One person to trust. That was what had been missing his entire life. That was what he wanted. And he wanted it with Ari. Was that type of connection called love? Hell, he hadn't a clue. He had thought he'd had love all figured out, then learned the hard way how wrong he had been.

Perhaps Ari was right. Take each day as it came. Enjoy the time they had and worry about the rest later. What was that phrase he had heard? Do not go borrowing trouble. Ari wanted him to love her? Done.

He left the bed for only as long as it took to retrieve a condom from the pocket of his jeans. As he knelt back onto the mattress, he made a great show of leisurely rolling the rubber down his hard length, reveling in the hot touch of her gaze as she watched his hand. For the first time he appreciated his inability to filter out human emotion. The bright and bold splashes coming from Ari were a drug, heightening all his senses while at the same time distorting reality until all that mattered was getting inside her heat and feeling her heartbeat.

The grip of her sheath around his cock was just as tight as ever but far more giving as he eased inside in a long, slow glide, an example of how her body already accepted his possession. They moved as one as he thrust and withdrew, her hips rising and falling in syncopation, prolonging the friction. A low flame blazed down his spine and settled in his balls as the pressure built, urging him to take her faster, harder, but he pushed the impulse aside. He had already taken her hard and rough. Now was the time for gentle, sweet. The intensity was still there. The same need to see her come undone and follow her into the mindless oblivion of release pounded in his blood as strongly as ever, but this was their time. Their time to forge that connection he desperately wanted.

He hooked her legs over his arms and pushed as deep into her core as possible. Her eyes widened and her fingers clutched his shoulders. "Oh, Bale. Ah. God. That's incredible."

The squeeze of her cunt made his eyes roll back and he fought to keep them open and focused on her flushed face. Tears of ecstasy made the light-blue flecks in her irises shimmer and the swollen pout of her lips formed a little heart as she panted and gasped beneath him. Oh, if only he could pause this perfect moment of pure sensuality in time forever.

"Ari," he groaned as her hands smoothed over the sweat-slick skin of his back and sides. The bite of her nails digging into the muscles wreaked havoc with his concentration. "Gods, woman. I'm trying to make this last."

"I don't think I'll survive." Her head thrashed against the pillow.

"Look at me, Ari." It took a few moments for her feverish gaze to meet his. "I'm right there with you. If only you knew how much of you I can feel. Right now." He punctuated his words with swivels of his hips and erupted into her depths.

"Bale." She arched her back and the black circles of her pupils dilated a split second before her pussy clamped down around his cock. Tremors rolled out from her core in long, undulating waves that lapped at his body as if she were the ocean and he stood on shore. Like a riptide she sucked him under to surf the rolling sea of their release before tossing him onto the rocks when he had nothing left to give. Through it all, their gazes remained locked, all her emotions flickering in those luminous eyes that held nothing back.

"Ah, Ariel." He pressed his forehead to hers. "Ariel."

"I know." A tear slipped down her cheek.

He rolled to his side and held her quaking body close and savored the feeling of her in his arms. Before they were ready the real world was going to barge in with guns blazing, as life was wont to do. Too few times were there these moments of perfection. Each one needed to be cherished.

Def Leppard's *Rocket* tore into the quiet with all of the subtlety of a chainsaw cutting through a textbook.

Son of a bitch.

Bale cracked open an eye and glared at the cellphone that pealed from the pocket of his jeans beside the bed.

Only four people knew his number, but only two ever called with any regularity.

"I'm sorry, Ari. I must take this call." He kissed her shoulder and reached for the offending object. "Ya."

"I apologize for disturbing you, Bale," Lucian said. "You are needed in my office. Immediately."

"For what purpose?"

"As they say around here, the shit is a hitting the fan. Come now."

The Bale he had been a year prior would have told Lucian to fuck off, followed with a right hook to the jaw, but the Bale he was now understood his former commander wouldn't have contacted him unless it was of utmost urgency.

"I'm on my way."

He quelled the urge to crush the phone and set it gently on the side table.

"Ari, I am sorry."

"I heard." She hugged him from behind. The soft cushion of her breasts against his back made him curse the intrusion all the more. "Is there something wrong? You got so tense."

"I do not know, but Lucian has called a meeting." He reached around and pinched her chin between his thumb and forefinger. "I may be gone all night."

"I understand. Really, Bale. You don't have to answer to me."

But he wanted to.

"Breakfast?" he offered. "I cannot cook, but I can bring something."

She smiled and kissed his lips. "Breakfast sounds nice."

He risked Lucian's ire by taking the time to kiss her properly goodbye then dressed quickly.

Ari followed him to the door. Wrapped in the sheet, she made it all too tempting to say, "Fuck it," and pull her back into bed.

"Be careful," she said. "With whatever it is you have to do. Stay safe."

"I will." He cupped her cheek. "You stay safe too."

"Don't worry about me. I'm going to pass out as soon as the door closes." She winked.

After another quick kiss, he was in the hall and Ari was on the other side of the closed door. Physically they were separated, yet he felt her take up residence in his hearts. For the first time in a long while he prayed to the Gods for his safe return.

✦　✦　✦

"COME IN," LUCIAN'S deep voice ordered from behind the door before Bale lifted his hand to knock.

The general stood before his desk with his arms crossed in a deceptively casual pose as he leaned against the dark wood.

Bale closed the door then stood at attention with shoulders

back and spine straight and waited. Nothing was said for several minutes as the men eyed each other—the general clearly expecting answers to unasked questions, and the solider not willing to incriminate himself.

Lucian arched a dark brow and tapped his long forefinger on the newspaper laying on the desk by his hip. "Did you read the paper today?"

"No sir."

"Here. Have a look." He stepped to the side and gestured with a grand sweep of his arm.

With one eye on Lucian, he crossed to the desk then glanced down at the paper. In bold ink the headline screamed, *The Claymore Strikes Again.* He did a double take as he saw the black-and-white photos of a hooded man gripping a large sword. Although the face was concealed, Bale knew it was him in the photo.

Even more damning, Lucian knew it as well. "What do you have to say?"

He shrugged. "The Claymore? Isn't that a long broadsword used in medieval Scotland? That's not what I use at all."

"Bale—"

"I understand," he interrupted as Lucian's face turned red and his chest rose as he gathered steam. "This is not good."

"Oh, we've only begun to breach not good." He turned the computer monitor to face them. "This man was at the club this evening asking questions about a sword-carrying vigilante."

On the screen was footage captured from the club's surveillance cameras of a dark-haired man dressed rather plainly in a blazer and jeans. By the set of his shoulders and the way his eyes constantly scanned the area, Bale could tell he had some sort of military training.

"Who is he?"

"Police Captain Marco DeWinter. He's been tasked with apprehending, well, you. He's also a former coworker of Brett's from when she was on the force. And DeWinter and his team were the men who helped retrieve Fiona when she was kidnapped by that crime lord."

"Meaning I can't hurt him."

"Meaning," Lucian frowned and shook his head, "he's met the Chameleon. Meaning, he knows there is at least one person on this planet who has extraordinary powers so it would be safe for him to assume there may be more. Meaning he now suspects that one of our family members is, or knows who, this Claymore is."

"Then I will take extra care to not be discovered."

"You still have a lot to learn about this world, Bale." Lucian sighed then sat behind his desk and furiously began to type on the keyboard. "Now that you have a moniker, you have an official fan club. Postings of your exploits are cropping up across all of the social media sites. Anyone with a camera is a potential threat to exposing your identity and broadcasting your face to the world. It's not about being careful around DeWinter or the police. You, as the Claymore, cannot be seen by anyone."

"Why not? The Chameleon is seen all over Cedar."

"Cedar is not the city, as you might have noticed. Most of the citizens there want to protect the Chameleon, while here you may be a hero one day and villain the next. And the Chameleon leaves police work to the police. At times I think you like to rub their failures in their face."

His spine straightened with indignation and he sputtered, "I take no pride when they fail, for it means someone needlessly suffered."

"Nonetheless, you have to do more than lie low." He drew in a deep breath through his nose and Bale felt as if the hammer were about to be dropped. "I'm sorry, Bale. You have to stop fighting crime."

Red filled his vision. He slapped his hands on the desk in a burst of anger that cracked the legs and shouted, "Who are you to tell me what I can and cannot do? You are not my superior."

"I am your friend," Lucian replied, barely registering the flare of anger. "I cannot let you put yourself or this family at risk."

"Then I'll leave." He shoved at the broken desk and turned on his heel.

"What about Ari?"

Lucian might as well have thrown up a brick wall directly in his path, he stopped so fast.

Ari.

If his identity as the vigilante became known, she'd discover exactly what type of man she had given her trust and love to. Learn that the darkness that lived inside him extended beyond a taste for kink.

She'll find out about the evil he had committed.

"I know you care for her, Bale. By the Gods, I can show you security footage of the club right now where practically everyone is engaged is some sort of carnal activity. When you two came together earlier this evening, you generated so much sexual energy, I was half-convinced you had bonded."

Another punch to the solar plexus. With all the secrets between them, he could never bond with Ari. He hadn't the guts to do so with Natalia, and since then he'd done so many terrible things. Even with Ari's ready acceptance of his hungers, there was no way she'd be as forgiving of the rest of his nature.

Lucian had been right. The shit was hitting the fan.

"Ariel will not be touched by my actions. This, I vow," he said without turning around.

"How do you—"

"Message received, General."

Before Lucian could say another word, Bale was out of the room and racing out the front door and down the fire stairs.

This was unfair. It was all unfair. Millions of miles and several planets away, the Gods still had the power to fuck with him. To give him a taste of paradise before wrenching it out of his desperate grasp. What more did they want from him? Hadn't he sacrificed enough? He'd lost his home, his family, his honor. Was nothing ever to be his?

He burst through a side door out onto the empty sidewalk. The clouds had opened up and released a steady drizzle that quickly soaked the shoulders of his sweatshirt. He stood with his face raised to the sky, his eyes shut tight to withhold tears of frustration. The few that escaped his tightly closed lids mingled with the chilly rain and ran down his neck to tickle his frantic pulse.

To continue seeing Ari meant to risk her finding out his secrets. To stay away would mean breaking her heart. No matter what course of action he chose, Ari was going to be hurt.

Unless he stopped being a vigilante.

If the Claymore disappeared, then there was no fear of his identity being discovered. He could still be with Ari. Crisis averted.

But what of his vow? The only thing of value he possessed was his word. Without it, he had nothing. Dare he break a promise sealed with blood?

A spiky tightness wrapped around his chest as the bitter tang of fear coated the back of his tongue. He glanced around the alley and drew in one breath, then another. Mixed in with the heart-pounding panic was the icy-cold squirming of malice slithering down his back. The sensations were sharp, fresh, definitely coming from outside and not within the building.

Without a moment's hesitation he flipped his hood over his wet head and followed the trial of emotions like a bloodhound after a fox. As he neared the source of the turmoil, he paused and crouched behind a Dumpster to better survey the scene.

A man had a woman pinned beneath him to the hood of a car. The pair created an obscene hood ornament as her stocking-clad legs flailed in the air. Her tiny clenched fists pummeled his shoulders and head as she screamed out in terror.

Adrenaline shot through Bale's veins, propelling him to move but he tempered the urge and took precious seconds to mentally feel for anyone who might also be lurking in the dark. For all he knew, this could be a setup. A sting intending to draw out the vigilante and he could be walking right into their trap.

The need to hesitate made him nauseated. A woman was in danger. A cause for immediate action. Period. As a warrior and former guard for the king, a moment's pause meant the difference between life and death.

"Enough," he grumbled, pissed over having to second-guess his actions for one moment.

He traced to the couple and grabbed the man by the back of his neck, lifting him high into the air with one hand. The man wiggled and clawed at Bale's unyielding grip as he gurgled with fear.

"Quiet! When I set you upon your feet, you will have five seconds to disappear. If I am able to see you at all, even the ends of your shoelaces, I will take you down and rip your cock off and shove it down your throat. And do not think that once you are out of my sight you are absolved of your crimes. Think about harming another human again, I will find you and carry out your punishment. Do you understand?" He punctuated his question by shaking the terrified man.

"Y-yes."

"Five. Four..." he began the countdown without setting the man down and smiled as the familiar scent of urine reached his nose. By the Gods, he did love it when they pissed their pants. Rubber soles scrapped asphalt as Bale slowly lowered his arm and the man's feet made contact with the road before he beat tracks.

As the assailant rounded the corner, Bale turned back to the girl. She had slid to the wet pavement and sat huddled in a sobbing heap. Her nylons were torn over both knees and the sleeve of her jacket was ripped at the shoulder. Since there were other holes in her clothing, he wasn't positive if they were caused by the attack or part of a fashion statement. Through the streaks of eyeliner and rouge, he recognized her as a frequent patron of the nightclub.

He kept a respectful distance and knelt on the wet pavement. "Do you require medical attention, little one?"

The cap of her short black hair sprayed water droplets in every direction as she shook her head. She began to hiccup as she struggled to control her tears.

"Are you positive? I can get help."

"I'm—I'm okay. I think. I don't know." She hiccupped. "I

just wanna be home."

"Do you have a way home?"

"Yeah." She jerked her thumb at the sedan at her back. With a shuddering breath she glanced up at him and her eyes widened. "Hey. You're that guy. The superhero."

"I'm just a fellow who was in the right place at the right time. Are you able to drive yourself, or will you require assistance?"

"I can drive. I don't live too far away." She took his offered hand and swayed on her heels. "Oh, I don't feel so good."

"Let's get you a taxi."

"No. I just want to go home." In the dark he heard her sobs begin again. "I didn't ask for this, you know. My clothes might say otherwise, but I didn't ask for this. That creep followed me. After I told him no, he followed me to my car. He kept coming at me—"

"You don't need to explain. I know none of this was your fault. There will always be assholes around who feast on preying on those they think are weaker, and I will always be there to stop them."

"Thank you. Thank you." She offered him a watery smile then dashed to the door of her car and quickly jumped inside.

He waited until she maneuvered the car safely to the corner and made a right turn without incident before he lifted his face to the rain and waited for the rush of adrenaline to abate.

Society could call him what they wanted—hero, Claymore, villain—it didn't matter. This was his destiny. The world needed his strength, his sword and his courage to step between good and evil. If his identity was discovered, so be it. The reward was far greater than the risk. Lucian, Amaryllis, all of them, would just have to understand.

And maybe one day Ari too, if she cared for him as he did for her.

He had made a vow on his wife's and daughter's lives, and he would see it through until the day he died.

Chapter Ten

"**W**HAT'S WITH THE traffic jam, ladies?" Ari scooted around the three waitresses blocking the service station and stepped behind the bar. She tried to use her boss voice, but she couldn't keep the smile out of her tone. Licking maple syrup and whipped cream off a man's abs for breakfast, and lunch, did that to a woman. "We're not that busy and there aren't any drinks in the queue."

"We, um… We had a question on the new wine list."

While the comment was directed at her, Ari noticed all three gazes were focused over her shoulder. Following the line of sight, she spotted the handsome gentleman seated at the end of the bar chatting with Ted.

He was pretty dishy, she had to admit, in a very Pierce Brosnan/James Bond-ish sort of way. Nice build, not too buff or too lean in his black-blazer-white-button-down combo. With the little bit of evening scruff on his cheeks, his style said he cared about his appearance, but not too much. He had dark hair with a touch of gray at the temples that leant him just enough credibility to be the scholarly type, but she recognized the twinkle in his eyes that indicated he could be a total badass if given a chance. Her ex had that same twinkle. A real charm-er. Dangerous.

Ari turned back to the fan club. "I can guarantee you, he's not on the wine list. So, unless you have business here, get out of my bar."

The girls gasped. "But—"

"But nothing." She smiled and shooed at them with her hands. "I get it. He's cute and not wearing a ring, but I can't have you ladies loitering in the bar. I'm sure there's sidework to go do somewhere."

"Boy, you're no fun, Ari. Just because you have a guy will-ing to bash heads for you doesn't mean we're all off the market."

Despite the protests, they marched back toward the main dining room, but took their sweet time in doing so.

Ari picked up a bar towel and wiped away the fingerprints on the taps. "Ted, go ahead and take your ten now."

"Thanks, boss." He picked up a rack of glasses. "I'll take these to the washer and pick up a fresh rack on my way back."

"Sounds good. Thanks."

With her peripheral vision she surveyed the other patrons in her area. Everyone had smiles on their faces and appeared to be having a good time, well, all but the corner table for two. Judging by their body language, she'd guess the couple was on their first date and all was not going well. The man was going to wear a landing strip through his hair if he kept running his fingers across his head.

"I tell you, the world gets stranger every day."

Ari turned her head toward Handsome and smiled. "Hard to believe, huh?" she replied while inspecting the soda gun for cleanliness. "Just when you think there can be no more surprises, wham! The powers that be will prove you wrong." She gestured to his nearly empty glass. "Can I get you another beer, sir?"

"Sir?" He laughed with an arched brow. "Sir is my father or my uppity superiors. Please, call me Marco."

"I apologize. Would you care for another beer, Marco?" she asked with a slight bow.

"No, thank you." He winked. "I need to head out soon anyway. I will take the check though."

Yep. A charmer. "Coming right up."

He gestured to the smartphone in his hand. "Have you been reading any of these stories on this crazy guy running around town like a superhero and scaring people with a sword?"

"No, I haven't, but I've heard a few customers talking about it. I knew of a group of people in St. Louis who wore costumes and walked around like they were the Justice League. The police didn't care much for their interference, but the local news stations had a great time with them." She placed the check presenter by his glass.

"I think I'd prefer costumed kids to this guy. He looks serious. I wouldn't want to mess with him." He turned the screen in her direction.

The displayed photo reminded her of something straight out of the movies. A hooded stranger with a big sword posed in a lethal-looking position, as if he were ready to behead anyone who came near.

"That's the one they're calling the Claymore?" She wrinkled her nose. "That sword looks too tiny. I'm mean it's big, but definitely not a claymore."

"I'm with you on that one, sister."

She went back to straightening napkins and restocking straws. "Is that picture even real? It looks so staged."

Marco shook his head. "It's real. I have friends on the force. They've seen this guy in person. I'm just surprised no one has recognized him. How many men do you know with this kind of build?"

"Actually, I…" She sucked in sharp breath as he flipped to another photo that appeared as if it were taken from a security camera.

There was something about the angle of his stance that brought forth the image of the first time she had laid eyes on Bale dressed all in black with a hooded sweatshirt and denim jacket as he had stared down those two hick goons. A fierce protector. Just like the man in the photo.

"Actually, I…what?" Marco's question snapped her back into reality with a jolt.

"What?" she gasped. "I—oh, um, uh…"

As she floundered to form a sentence, hysterical laughter tickled her throat.

Yeah. Right. What was she thinking? Was she seriously entertaining the notion that Bale was this mysterious crime fighter?

Her Bale. Quiet Bale. Bale without any discernible occupation who goes on mysterious missions at night and sports several scars he claimed were inflicted by a sword.

Holy crap. The room spun as she swayed.

"Are you okay?" Marco stood and reached over the bar to grasp her by the elbow.

"Uh, yeah. Yeah." She giggled and waved him away. "Sorry. I guess I've been on my feet too long today."

"You look a little pale."

"I'm fine. Really." She reached for a napkin and blotted at her sweaty forehead.

"Did I say something to upset you?"

"No. No. Not at all."

The furrow in his brow conveyed his disbelief. "For a second there I thought you were gonna say that you might have seen this guy in person."

"Me?" Her laughter sounded hoarse. "Oh, no. I, uh. I was going to say that in the restaurant business we see all types of people of all shapes and sizes. I'm certain I've seen men with similar builds before."

"I bet that a pretty girl like you has probably dated a few too."

Heat raced across her cheeks. "Ah, see, I knew you were a charmer."

He held up his hands and smiled a boyish grin. "Nope. Just calling 'em like I see 'em."

Thankfully Ted returned in a fanfare of rattling glasses, relieving her from making a bigger fool of herself. She inclined her head at their guest. "Have a good night, Marco. I hope you'll come visit us again."

He reached for his wallet. "Oh yes. I'm positive you'll see me again."

With one last nod, she focused on placing one foot in front of the other until she reached the office she shared with the dining room manager.

"Ari? What is the matter?" Amaryllis called out from her office across the hall. "You appear distressed."

"I'm fine." She drew a breath and called upon her best smile as she walked into Amaryllis' domain. She already had strangers fussing over her. She didn't need the queen of all fussers to think she was off balance too.

Amaryllis stood behind her desk with fashion magazines and fabric samples spread all about the desktop and along the floor. Miranda, her event planner, sat on the loveseat with a notepad in hand and a blue colored pencil clenched between her teeth.

For the last three days the two of them had been neck-deep in silverware and fabric samples as Amaryllis planned her latest party. The woman did love to celebrate, no matter the occasion.

"Hey," Miranda mumbled and nodded in greeting.

Ari smiled back at the woman who was dating Amaryllis' best friend. She liked Miranda, who too had been adopted into "the family" and understood how overwhelming it could be having Amaryllis as a fairy godmother. If ever Ari had a doubt that the Kilsgaards were too good to be true, Miranda was there to assure her that she hadn't fallen into a rabbit hole and landed in a world of make-believe.

"Hi. Is this all for the Imbloc celebration?" Ari plucked a scrap of white, fluffy fabric from one of the piles.

"Yes," Amaryllis replied. "What do you think of that one? Too frilly?"

"Depends. If you use little touches in just the right places, I think it will look right festive."

"See." Miranda grinned around the pencil.

"All right. Order some of the fluffy white fabric as well. Now." She crossed her arms and narrowed her gaze at Ari. "What has you so upset?"

She matched her boss' stance. "Who says I'm upset?"

"Women's intuition. What happened? And I won't let you go until you reveal all."

From the small amount of time Ari had known her, she was well aware the woman was more than capable of following through on the threat.

"Why doesn't anyone believe me when I say that I'm fine?"

Amaryllis arched a fine dark brow.

"All right." She huffed. "I've been thinking about Bale and me. There are a lot of great things going on between us and a lot of uncharted territory. I'm just feeling uncertain about the future." Which was mostly the truth.

"Bale?" Miranda spit out the pencil. "You're dating Bale? I thought you were just friends."

The alarm in her voice made Ari's scalp tingle. "We were. Are. It's blossomed into something more. Is that a problem?"

"What?" She glanced at Amaryllis, who stared back at her as if she dared her to say anything negative. "No. Not at all. That's…great. Good luck with that."

What the hell did that mean?

"Ari." Amaryllis came around the desk and took her hands. "I understand where you are coming from. Lucian and I had quite a time of it before he realized he was madly in love with me. Do you want to talk to about your concerns?"

Sure. My boyfriend may be a sword-carrying crime fighter. What do you know about that?

"Thanks for the offer, but I'm good. We're good. New. Adjusting. But good. You know how much of a sharer Bale is." She laughed.

"Oh, that man." She sighed. "He cares for you. I can tell. On the outside he looks about as involved as a brick wall. But on the inside he's seething with emotion."

"He seethes all right," Ari heard Miranda mutter under her breath.

"And soon," Amaryllis continued, "you will never have to question how he feels about you. Believe me on this."

Ari tried. She did. But what if Bale was this vigilante? What was his motive for doing something so dangerous? And what did his secret mean for them as a couple?

Or, was this entire situation caused by fear and her heart was making up an excuse to cut and run before she got hurt?

Too many questions and the only person with the answers was Bale.

A jazzy disco beat shrilled from the pink phone on the desk.

"Ooo, it's Lucian." Amaryllis pressed the Call button. "One minute, husband. I want to talk dirty to you and I'm not alone." She giggled as she skipped out into the hall.

The second she was gone Ari was in front of Miranda. "Why don't you like Bale?"

She looked up in surprise. "I never said that."

"You implied. What gives?"

Miranda set aside her notepad and stood. "Bale and I did not meet on the friendliest of terms. I agreed to give him a chance and I am still trying to do so, but that doesn't mean he doesn't scare me."

"What happened?"

She glanced toward the open door. "I don't think Amaryllis wants me to say."

"Well Amaryllis isn't in love with him." Once the words slipped out she slapped her hand over her mouth with a surprised gasp.

How was that possible? She couldn't be in love with a man she obviously didn't know.

Saints preserve us, she was. Or at least was awfully damn close.

Miranda looked just as shocked. "You're in love with him?"

"I don't know. Maybe. Probably. Fuck. Look, Miranda. I know we're strangers, but if you have anything to say about Bale, please tell me. I should know."

Miranda shot another glance at the door and stepped closer to whisper, "Bale stabbed my boyfriend."

"What?" she shouted then immediately lowered her voice so as not to alert Amaryllis. Okay. That was not what she was expecting. "Jorges? Bale stabbed Jorges? When? Why?"

"It was when Jorges and I first met, and I don't know a lot of the details. All I was told was that there was a misunderstanding and everything was worked out. The only reason I'm still freaked out about it is because Jorges is so secretive about what happened and he shares everything else with me. And you have to admit, Bale is a pretty intimidating guy. I think he knows he scares me because he's always been extra polite whenever we've crossed paths, but I've seen the scar on Jorges' side and it's not pretty."

"I can't believe Bale stabbed Jorges." She raised her hand to stop any potential objection. "I'm not saying that I don't believe you, I'm just stunned that it happened at all."

"As I said, Bale's always been a gentleman around me, but I've seen what he's capable of. Just proceed with caution."

Proceed with caution. Right. So far nothing having to do

with Bale had been about caution. For a woman who vowed to take it easy with relationships, she had blown every promise she had made to herself to smithereens.

For the rest of her shift her mind ran in circles until she was ready to collapse with exhaustion. Whom should she believe? What should she believe? Did she confront Bale about her suspicions or bury her head in the sand until catastrophe struck?

And if he was this vigilante?

Ugh, that was what made her stomach roll the most. How does one react to that type of information? Give a big thumbs-up with a "good for you" and a slap on the back, or shout "What the fuck are you thinking?" Neither option felt right.

"Thanks for the info, Miranda."

"I hope everything works out for you, Ari." Miranda patted her on the arm. "I really do."

For the rest of her shift her mind ran in circles until she was ready to collapse with exhaustion. Whom should she believe? What should she believe? Did she confront Bale about her suspicions or bury her head in the sand until catastrophe struck?

And if he was this vigilante?

Ugh, that was what made her stomach roll the most. How does one react to that type of information? Give a big thumbs-up with a "good for you" and a slap on the back, or shout "What the fuck are you thinking?" Neither option felt right.

As the clock drew closer to quitting time, Ari buried her

head further into her work. She missed Bale, but she wasn't looking forward to having to face him with all these doubts weighing on her shoulders. Maybe if she worked herself into the ground she'd pass out and wake up in Bale's arms with the entire evening being nothing but an incredibly odd dream.

So she worked and worked and worked some more until a soft knock on her office door brought her head up with a startled gasp.

Speak, or rather think, of the devil.

Bale was wearing his customary black sweatshirt and denim jacket, which immediately brought to mind images of sword-carrying tough guys. The thought did not lessen her anxiety in the slightest.

"Ari, what is wrong?" Bale crossed to her side and knelt by her chair.

Like a feral cat backed into a corner, she lashed out with bared claws. "Why is everyone asking me that today? Am I walking around with a gray cloud over my head or something? Nothing is wrong."

His eyes widened and he leaned back. "I'm sorry. I did not mean to upset you with my question."

"I'm fine, okay. Just fine."

"Ari." He pinched her chin and drew her gaze up. With his other hand he rubbed at the furrowed area between her eyes. "I am sensing that all is not well. If you do not wish to talk about whatever is bothering you, I understand. I just want you happy."

All the fight rushed out of her like water after a plug is pulled from a full swimming pool.

This man, this gentle giant who stared down at her as if she were a precious treasure was supposed to be a bad guy? The possibility was too difficult for her to believe.

"I'm sorry too." She sighed and laid her hand over his. "It's been a long day. I didn't mean to snap at you."

"You're entitled to have a bad day, *liera*. My purpose is to make your bad day go away." His soft smile, so rare, made her tear up.

"Thank you for that." She pressed a kiss to his freshly shaven cheek.

He smoothed his palm over her hair. "I've come to see if you're ready to go home. I don't want you traveling at night on your own."

"What about your bike?"

"I walked here."

"Are you planning on meeting me at work every day?" She smiled.

"Ya."

Ya. That was all. No hesitation. So Bale.

"I'm almost ready. I need to do another sweep of the bar and make sure everything is square." She shut down her computer. "Why don't you wait here?"

"I promise I will not threaten any man who looks your way, if that is your concern."

"I believe you. Almost." She dropped another kiss on his

forehead as she stood. "For my sanity, please, wait here."

"Fifteen minutes. That is all I can give you."

"Twenty, and the only reason I am willing to negotiate is because I understand you are trying."

"Agreed."

"See, look how well we worked that out." She laughed on her way out the door.

Knowing that Bale meant what he said about coming after her in exactly twenty minutes and one second, she kept her final walkthrough quick and efficient.

Sooner rather than later she was going to have to address him with her questions. How many warning signs had there been with Anthony that she refused to acknowledge and it came back to bite a huge chunk out of her ass? As much as she wished to bury her head in the comforting sand, that option was not a possibility. The uncertainty alone was already turning her into a mentally unstable fruitcake. At some point she was going to break and the damage would be irreparable.

When she returned to her office, Bale was waiting with her coat and purse at the ready. Lying in the bottom of her bag was the knife he had given her when they first met. That lethal-looking blade with the pretty stones. Was this another piece of evidence to prove her suspicions?

"Anxious much?" She swallowed down her nerves and slipped her arms into the coat sleeves. "Do you have plans for us or something?"

He trailed kisses down her neck. "Just to hold you in my

arms. The weather is turning and it's cold out there."

"Maybe you should start dressing warmer." *And thank you for providing an opening for some probing questions.* "Is that the only jacket you have?"

"Ya."

"Well…have you thought about getting a heavier coat?"

"No."

"Why not?"

He shrugged. "This one suits my purpose."

And what purpose was that? "You know, I don't think I've ever seen you in anything but a black shirt and jeans. Do you own any item of clothing in a color other than black?"

"No."

"Why not?"

"I like black."

"Oh." *Great. Okay, so just because he had a penchant for dark clothes that did not mean he was the Claymore.* "Let's go."

Bale followed her through the kitchen to the parking lot behind the restaurant. The back-of-the-house staff quieted and gave them a wide berth as they passed.

"It seems you have gotten quite the reputation around here," she said.

A soft grunt was his reply.

Outside heavy rainclouds darkened the night sky to an inky black that seemed to suck all light into its depths. Rain fell in big, fat droplets that hit the ground so hard, they popped back up to soak you again. It was a mad dash to her car to avoid becoming drenched.

"And you walked in this?" She wiped at her forehead with her coat sleeve once she settled into the driver's seat. "Bale, you really don't have to put yourself out like that."

"Seeing to your safety is not putting myself out. I do it with pleasure. If it makes you feel better, the rain wasn't that bad earlier this evening." He chuckled. "You're a Northwesterner now. You better start getting used to the rain."

She wrinkled her nose. "It does beat tornados."

"I saw one once, a tornado, several months ago when I was traveling through Nebraska. Where I am from, we have tremendous windstorms, but nothing even close to resembling that cyclone. It was a stark reminder of just how fragile humans are and their resiliency to survive."

"Well, there's not a whole lot that can withstand a good F4 or F5 tornado. Did you get caught up in it at all?"

"I rolled up behind it and was witness to the aftermath. Fortunately the injuries were minor and only a few homes sustained damage..." He trailed off and when she glanced his way, he was staring out the windshield with a faraway look in his eyes.

"Was it bad?" she whispered, unsure if her question could be heard over the sound of the wipers and rain, but she was afraid to raise her voice any louder.

He blinked and looked in her direction. "The situation could have been worse."

"You were there again, weren't you? Just now."

He nodded. "There was a child. A female with long dark hair. She was trapped inside her home on one side and her parents were trapped on the other. I could not see her, but I could hear her breathing, feel her. She didn't make a sound even though she was conscious the entire time. She just waited patiently to be rescued as I dug through the rubble. So much courage in a tiny body. She amazed me."

"She was lucky you were there to save her."

He said nothing, and as her words hung in the air, she felt the truth strike her in the heart that Bale was the Claymore. He saved that little girl, just like he saved her from those two creeps. And if the news stories were true, he saved others as well.

Again came the question of why, and what was she supposed to do with this information, not to mention the biggest question of all, was he ever going to trust her with this secret?

As she pulled into the parking garage under The Cavern, her hands shook as she turned off the ignition and climbed out of the car. A confrontation was brewing. It was inevitable. And she had no idea how to proceed.

Bale was at her side, trapping her against the door with his strong arms. "You were very quiet on the way home."

"So were you."

"I'm always quiet."

"True." She chuckled, but her smile faded quickly.

Their breathing was loud in the silent garage as they stood

looking into each other's eyes. Uncertainty flashed behind his dark irises and crinkled his brow, as if he picked up on her nervousness. He probably could for all she knew. She was never very good at hiding her emotions.

Slowly, ever so slowly, he leaned closer, as if expecting her to bolt or push him away. Both completely sound ideas. Until she heard him confirm that he was the Claymore, it was prudent to keep some sort of distance between them. But the emotion in his gaze unknotted the tie around her convictions. Whatever Bale couldn't say was in those dark eyes, and it took her breath away.

She felt like a young schoolgirl caught under the mistletoe for the first time as she waited for his kiss with her heart ready to beat out of her chest.

The first brush of his lips was butterfly soft. The second pass, a firm press that allowed her to detect the slightest hint of chocolate on his breath. Her eyes fluttered shut as she melted in his embrace, enjoying this moment of closeness before all hell broke loose. Who knew what the next five, ten, thirty minutes might bring, and it killed her to think of never experiencing his touch again if he became angry enough to leave. But there was no way she could carry on without voicing her suspicions.

Through his rain-dampened clothing she felt the flex of his pectoral muscles under her palms as he wrapped his arms around her waist. She smoothed the fabric over his shoulder then reached up to trail her fingers through his silky hair.

"Sweet Ariel," he sighed against her mouth then trailed kisses across her cheek. "Why do I sense so much turmoil within you?"

"Because I'm a complex woman." Her grip tightened on his hair, hesitant to part from him for even a second. Reluctantly she let go and took him by the hand. "Can you come up to my place for a minute?"

"A minute? I was planning on staying most of the night."

Most of the night? What else did he have planned for the evening? Walk the streets and look for criminals?

The ride up in the elevator was silent, as was the walk down the hall.

"So," she began as she led them into her apartment, making sure she kept him in her view. "I overheard some customers talking today about that superhero with the big sword."

Bale froze. It was a tiny pause so slight she would have missed it if she hadn't been focused on every aspect of his body language. Although he raised a half-interested eyebrow, she swore she felt his heart kick in his chest.

"Have you heard or read any of the stories?" she asked when he remained silent.

"I might have heard something. I don't pay much interest to local gossip."

She shrugged and went to hang up her coat in the closet, trying to play it cool. "Well, it makes a person think, you know? What's their motivation? If they wanted to stop crime, why not become a cop?"

"Those are interesting questions." He stepped closer and pulled her against his body, his head lowering for a kiss.

"Bale." She drew far enough away to look him in the eye. "What would make *you* do something like that?"

His eyes narrowed, the black slits of his irises glittered with danger. "I don't understand."

"I think you do."

"What are you saying, Ari?"

"I've seen the pictures, Bale." She drew a breath. "I know you're the Claymore."

"Pictures? What pictures?"

"The ones that are online. The ones that show a man with a sweatshirt and a jacket that looks just like yours. The ones that show a man who looks exactly the way you did the day you stopped those men from jumping me."

His fingers dug into the sides of her waist and his eyes opened wide in disbelief. "Where did you see these photos?"

"I told you, online," she stammered. For the first time she feared his size as he backed her against the wall.

"Where online? Why? What were you looking for?" The rapid-fire questions made her flinch with their intensity.

"I don't know where. There was a man at work who showed me them on his phone."

"What man?"

"A man. A customer. He asked if I had read the stories."

"Why? Why would he ask *you* this?" he shouted. "What

exactly did he say to you?"

"He—" She choked on a cough as her throat constricted. "He asked me if I'd heard the stories or if I'd seen anyone who looked like the man."

"What did you say?"

"I said I work in a bar and see all sorts of people."

"And that's all?"

"Yes. Now let me go. Please."

He gasped and let her go as if she had burst into flame and burned his hands. "I am sorry, Ariel. I didn't mean to frighten you." He scrubbed at his face. "I need you to tell me who this man was. What did he look like? Did he give his name?"

"Marco. He said his name was Marco. Oh my goodness. Is he a bad guy?" The thought never occurred to her that Bale may have a nemesis. Maybe the customer at the bar was a villain the Claymore had been hunting. "Do you have enemies?"

"Marco?" Bale turned away from her and plunged his fingers through his hair, pulling at the strands with a frustrated growl. "DeWinter. I should have known."

He prowled within the confined space of the living room as if she weren't there, wiping at his face again and emitting sounds of frustration until he bent double and stared at his boots. She held her breath and watched him with eyes so wide, she felt the orbs begin to dry out, but no way was she going to blink and miss his next move. What was going to happen now that he knew she was aware of his secret?

Just when she thought her heart was going to burst with anticipation, Bale began to laugh, a deep self-deprecating chuckle that was in no way jovial. He shook his head and straightened with a weary sigh.

"The arrogance of man will always be his downfall," he said then speared her with a hard look. "And here I foolishly believed I could tell you on my own terms."

At least he wasn't going to insult her by saying she was crazy and deny everything. "I just want to understand why, Bale. Why with the hood and freaky-long sword and the nickname?"

"I never intended for *this*." He circled his arms around in a great arc. "For you, the media, that stupid nickname. None of it."

The thought chilled her to the bone, but she had to ask. "Are we through? Now that I know your secret, are we done?"

"You don't know," he whispered, closing his eyes and shaking his head. With a clenched fist, he tapped at his sternum, right over the starburst-shaped tattoo. "You don't know it all. You don't know anything. You don't know about them. Here. Natalia and Emmaline. My wife and child."

Wife. Wife? "Oh my God. You're married?" she shrieked.

She knew it! She knew everything between them was too good to be true. How could this be happening again? Had she offended God somehow and was doomed to always fall for married men? And a child too? How many lives was she destined to ruin?

Now she was the one pacing the room with her arms wrapped around her middle and plaintive groans spewing from her mouth.

"Ari."

"Oh God, I'm cursed. I have to be. Why? Why me?"

"Ari."

"How could you?" she shouted. "How could you do that to your family?"

"Ari, it's not—"

"Don't touch me." She jumped away from his outstretched hand, but he was faster and caught her around the arms.

"They're dead, Ari. They are dead."

As his words finally registered her brain stopped with all the subtlety of a car smashing into a brick wall at seventy miles an hour.

"Oh, Bale." Heat ignited across her face. "I am so sorry. I-I didn't know."

"I know." Right before her eyes, the Bale she knew aged. Across his forehead and around his mouth, lines of remembered grief carved into his skin. "I know."

Fuck. Fuck. Fuck. This entire day was just one fucking fubar mess. And it seemed as if every time she breathed, she just kept making things worse. She clenched her hands at her sides and pinched her lips together. Maybe if she pretended she were a statue, she could avoid making a bigger ass out of herself.

"Ah, Ari. I promised myself I wouldn't make the same mistakes with you as I did with Natalia, yet it seems as if I cannot break the pattern. Please, sit down." He guided her to the nearest barstool. Once she was perched on the edge, he backed away and ran his hands through his hair.

As much as she wanted to ask him a million questions, she held her tongue. This was Bale's story, and she had a feeling very few heard the tale, if any.

As was his fashion, his mouth opened and closed several times before he spoke. "I was already in the guard when I met Natalia. Her father owned a farm that was in the same colony as my family. We met when I had returned home to share the news of my assignment. As the youngest daughter, her options for marriage were limited, all her father wanted for her was security and felt I would be a good match. Natalia was delicate and sweet. Everything that I am not, and when our Emmaline came along, she was just like her mother, so fragile."

The language he used confused and ensnarled Ari at the same time. The way he spoke, it sounded as if he came from the medieval period and not this century. No matter the words, it was obvious by his solemn tone that even though his marriage was arranged, he cared for his wife.

"They were my light, so bright, so pure." His stare turned hard. "You have seen my darkness. Know my hungers. Seen my temper. I couldn't show that around them, share that side of myself with my wife. I—I did not trust her enough to share all of me. I loved her, but was too afraid of what would happen if she knew the real me. So, I sent her and Em to live with my family, visiting when I could, but keeping them as far away from my darkness as possible. And then the revolution began."

Revolution? In Sweden? Weren't they like the happiest people on Earth? "I don't understand."

"Our king had lost favor with the people. First it was rioting, then it became all-out battles to dethrone him. As a member of his guard, I was often dispatched to squelch the opposition."

Now she was definitely confused. "Wait, wait, you lost me. How could all of that happen in Sweden and no one over here heard of this? How could that not make the news?"

"This wasn't in Sweden. It was in Skandavia."

With the way he said that with his head down, as if braced for a blow, scared her to ask, "And where is that?"

He sighed. "It is the largest of Saturn's moons."

"Saturn?"

He nodded.

Did she hear him correctly? "As in the planet?"

He nodded again.

She sucked in one breath, then another. The words stuck in her throat until she forced them out. "Are you telling me that you're an alien from outer space?"

"Ya."

"Okay. I'm not sure if I'm more upset about the fact that you were married and never told me, or that you're claiming to be an alien."

Whoosh. Faster than she could blink, Bale raced around

the room in a streak of movement. When he came to a stop, he lifted the couch up over his head without a breath of sound or the slightest grimace before gently setting it back down.

"Those are some of my powers," he mumbled.

Breathe, Ari. Breathe.

There had been a few times in her life when she had been struck dumb. This was a thousand times worse than all of them put together. It was as if her body were in a coma, yet her brain was wide awake and her eyes open so she could see and hear everything going on around her, yet she couldn't move.

"I'll, um, get to how I came to Earth in a moment," he said.

Sure. Fine. Take your time. She might have said it out loud, but she was certain all she managed were a few unintelligible squeaks and a faint nod.

"The revolutionaries did everything they could to gain the backing of the people, resorting to force if necessary. My retinue received word that several colonies were to be targeted in a massive siege by the opposition, including the castle and my home colony. I wanted to protect my family and go with the unit that had been dispatched. The soldiers were new, young, and the people of my colony were simple farmers. They knew nothing of war and fighting. But as part of the king's retinue, my commander forbade me to go. In my gut, I knew all was not well, so I disobeyed the general and left."

As his eyes watered, her stomach turned.

"It was too late." The catch in his voice broke her heart. "The soldiers that had been sent were all dead in the town square. Every farmhouse was burned to the ground. My father and mother, slaughtered. I found Natalia in the field, her body curled around the babe's."

"Stop. Bale, stop." She leapt from her seat and laid her hands on his cheeks. In his eyes she saw he was trapped in the past. Seeing his family where they had died all over again. "I don't need to know the details. I'm sorry. I'm so sorry. I can't imagine anything so horrible."

"That is why I fight, Ari. To protect those who cannot defend themselves. People like Natalia and my Em. I was too late for them, but I can save someone else. Someone like you."

"Wow. Just. Wow. Then how did you get to Earth?" She choked on the word. His story was too much to process.

He grasped her hands, holding them tight in his. "When my family died, I went to a dark place. A place so dark, you lose your soul. Anger, devastation, nothing comes close to describe how I felt. I wanted to die, but I wanted everyone who I felt had a hand in my family's deaths to suffer first. Every revolutionary who had remained, I killed. Every soldier who had been there, I tracked and eliminated. No man was left standing but one, my former commander who held me back."

"Your commander." Chills shot down her spine and she tried to pull away, but his grip kept her at his side. "Oh my God. Lucian?"

"Yes."

"You wanted to kill Lucian?" It was all too much. This was a man she thought he considered friend, practically family, and he had wanted him dead?

"I was beyond devastated and willing to do anything to obtain my goal. When I heard there was a contract out on Lucian's life, I took it."

"You took money to kill? Like a hit man?"

"That's what I was. That's how I earned enough money to survive and have my revenge. I was an assassin."

The ease with which he said the word, the utmost certainty in his statement stole the last of her sanity.

"You killed people for money?" she asked, yet the words sounded muddled in her head.

He nodded.

"You killed people for money."

"Ya."

"You have killed people. Dead. Like dead-dead. For money," she repeated slowly, enunciating each syllable.

His Adam's apple bobbed as he swallowed and the little emotion that had shown on his face completely disappeared as he said clear enough for her to have no doubt, "Yes."

Okay, so her boyfriend was not only a vigilante but also an alien with superpowers, oh and *killed people for money*.

Fuck the straw that broke the camel's back, this was a frickin' bulldozer dropped on a tiny glass figurine. She was done.

Bile rose in her throat and she swayed on her feet as the room closed in around her. "I'm gonna be sick," she mumbled.

Red and black swirled in her vision. Somehow she managed to stumble toward the bathroom, ricocheting off the doorjamb into the wall. The doorknob nailed her in the side as she fell to the floor.

He killed for money.

The contents of her stomach ran up and down her esophagus as the words barreled like a runaway freight train in her mind.

He killed for money.

To fall for an adulterer was one thing, but a murderer? A hired gun? What was wrong with her! What kind of person falls in love with someone who has no regard for human life? Human. Ha! Maybe that was the key. He was a fucking alien from fucking outer space!

Her throat was raw, her abdomen on fire and her head fit to explode as she struggled for air and collapsed against the cool plastic toilet seat.

"Ariel?" Bale rested his hand on the middle of her back.

A murderer's hand.

"Don't touch me. Don't touch me," she repeated in a shriek and batted his hand away.

How could she ever have thought his hands were gentle? Hands that had brought her to a pleasure so high, she never wanted him to let go. Blood stained those hands and now they stained her conscience.

He came at her again. "Ari—"

"Don't fucking touch me!" Her shoe flew off as she kicked in the direction of his shape. Next was the wastebasket, an easy-to-reach projectile, then the toilet brush. Whatever she could lay her hands on she threw at him as she screamed for him to leave until she tasted blood and her vocal cords gave out.

Even after the front door closed and she was left alone, great gasping sobs ripped from her throat. The reaction was irrational, insane, completely over the top. Any moment the men in white coats were going to burst in and lock her away and she'd completely understand why, but no matter how hard she tried to gain some semblance of control, her brain refused to process the command, too fried to comprehend the slightest bit of information. Well, all except for one fact.

He killed for money.

Ever so slowly, her vision returned and the outline of the ceiling fan came into focus. At her feet the bathroom door stood open, revealing an empty living room where Bale had stood and shattered her world. She worked her foot around until her toes touched the door and she pushed, shutting her inside the darkness.

That was two doors between her and Bale's ugliness. How many more would it take before she could find the strength to lift her head? To move? To breathe?

To live?

Chapter Eleven

BALE LAY IN the hallway outside Ari's apartment and dropped the barrier on his emotions to be doused in all her pain. Tears streamed down his face and his throat ached in sympathy as Ari wailed inside. Her howls were much the same as his had been when he had found the bodies of his family. His vocal cords had healed, but his voice had never been the same again, just as he had never been the same.

Just as Ari would never be the same. The world she knew no longer existed, and he was the destroyer. Another death that rested squarely in his hands. While he never struck her physically, she now carried the scar of her injury for all to hear every time she spoke.

Of course he knew Ari's reaction to his truth was not going to go well, but the absolute devastation that tore her asunder flayed him to the bone. But it wasn't her anger at him that stabbed him in the heart but the hatred she harbored against herself.

He could hear her thoughts now. How could she have let a monster touch her, love her? She must be broken or twisted in order to have felt affection for such evil.

He wanted to scream at her, shake her until she realized that nothing was wrong with her, that she was perfect. That her love for him was magic.

And now it was gone.

Even if he had wanted to keep the truth from her, deep down he knew he was on borrowed time. Sooner or later he'd have to come clean and face the repercussions of his actions, both on Skandavia and Earth. Prolonging the ruse was only going to make the moment more difficult, impossible as it was to imagine. As it was, he felt as if he were stripped of his flesh and dipped in acid.

"Bale." The soft sweep of a hand against his cheek brought his eyes open.

Amaryllis knelt by his side and Lucian stood behind her. Both had the same expressions of worry and devastation carved upon their faces.

"What happened?" Lucian asked. His gaze went to the door as Ari's cries came to an abrupt end.

"She knows." He shook his head and curled into a ball. "Everything."

"Everything?"

"All of it. The fucking Claymore. Skandavia. Natalia and Emmaline. The killing. All of it," he gritted out.

"*Jesu*. No wonder the poor girl sounds gutted."

"Lucian," Amaryllis gasped.

"It's the truth."

"Doesn't matter. Bale." Her hand moved to stroke his hair.

"Do not fret. All will be well."

He grunted and shook his head harder. "She hates me. But she hates herself more."

"That's not true. She loves you. That is why she's in so much pain. In time, she will remember why she loves you and will forgive you."

"No. No. Can't you feel her? She's shattered."

"And she will heal." She pulled his hair when he tried to argue. "The girl has been dealt quite a shock. Have faith, my friend."

Faith? The only faith he had was that Ari would hate him forever. What person in their right mind would ever love…him?

"Do not give in to self-pity, Balellanos. I can feel you slipping away. I will not allow you to lay about on the floor and believe the worst. Lucian, take him to our home. I'll stay with Ari." She cupped his face between her hands. Her eyes burned bright with determination until they glowed with silver light. "I am not saying it will be easy or quick, but Ari will see the truth of your heart. And hers."

She had seen the truth and it broke her.

But he bit his tongue. It was useless to argue with Amaryllis. If tenaciousness had royalty, she'd be the undisputed empress of all. Any attempt to convince her otherwise was just wasted effort.

He waved away Lucian's outstretched hand and slowly climbed to a stand. Using the wall as a crutch, he shuffled toward the waiting elevator with Lucian trailing behind as a parent would do with a toddler just learning to walk. As the doors slid shut, he saw Amaryllis slip into the apartment.

"You do know that Amaryllis will not leave Ari's side. No matter how much Ari may protest."

"Ya." That was what he was counting on, otherwise he wouldn't have dared leave Ari vulnerable in her condition.

"Will you fight for her, Bale?"

He turned a confused eye toward his general. "Ari? There is nothing left to fight for."

"Then you never appreciated what you had and don't deserve her."

His hand clenched into a fist, ready to strike the bastard in the face. If this was his way of trying to make him feel better, his delivery was shit.

"Look, Bale, no one hates you more than you, and until you stop with the self-flagellation, you will never be able to accept that another can find you worth loving." He snorted. "Loving. I should say worth giving a shit about. Prove to Ari that you are not the monster you painted yourself to be. Prove you are worth her love. I speak from experience. The sooner you forgive yourself, the sooner she will forgive you."

It wasn't that simple. The blood on his hands would never wash away.

"Hey." Lucian laid a hand on his shoulder. "Remember when Amaryllis whipped us? She said that we were blessed with the gift of today and the promise of tomorrow. Be thankful for that, Bale. Make tomorrow better than today. You are a *Llanos* warrior. Handpicked by me, and when I was in command, the *Llanos* never gave up."

Lucian's reasoning was too simple. While the *Llanos* may have not always won, it wasn't for lack of trying. But how did one begin to remove the taint of such sins? To pay for the crimes committed on another planet?

"Believe, Bale. Believe in Ari."

"I broke her."

"And you can put her back together, just as she has done with you. She is a strong woman. Have faith."

Faith. To Bale faith was as elusive as striking the last paper match while standing in the deepest, wettest cave and expecting it to last long enough to guide your way to the light. Faith was for those who had nothing.

Just like you.

He sighed. Yes, he did have nothing. Well, nothing but love for a woman who probably rued the day she ever met him. Perhaps he and Ari were through, but the least he could do was prove that she wasn't the broken one, that her love for him made him want to be a better man. The question now was how?

The idea stuck so fast, he jerked with the impact as the elevator doors slid open on a hush, revealing the front door of Lucian's apartment. With a jaw clenched in determination, he pushed the button for the ground floor.

"Keep in contact," Lucian said with a smile. "I'll update

you if there is any change with Ari."

He nodded. "Thank you. Brother."

Lucian slapped him on the back and wished him luck as he ran out into the night. Transportation was not important, for he knew exactly where to go and once he arrived, he wasn't going to be leaving anytime soon.

Two miles away he reached his destination and sprinted up the concrete steps, striding through the door with a decisive swagger. The few people occupying the lobby backed away with wide eyes and open mouths, allowing him unfettered passage to the front counter.

"Can I help you?" the woman asked through the safety glass with a tilt of her head. He noticed one of her hands remained under the countertop, her finger probably resting on the button of an alarm.

"Tell Captain Marco DeWinter he has a visitor."

"Is he expecting you?"

His lips twitched. "Oh, he's expecting me all right."

WHEN IT CAME to holding perfectly still, Bale was a master. It was his ability to wait and watch without making the slightest flicker of movement that made him so good at his previous occupation. But sitting on the worn-out loveseat in what appeared to be a waiting room of the city's police department was driving him to insanity. His skin itched as sweat trickled down his hairline and his hearts raced. He flicked so many glances at the closed door, the muscles of his eyes were starting to tire and his jaw ached from clenching his teeth to keep from fidgeting.

Something was amiss. When he had announced his arrival at the police station, he anticipated a dozen, if not two, armed officers to instantly surround him with weapons aimed at his head. To be politely escorted to a waiting area and offered a cup of coffee had not been a possibility. The reaction was strange, and strange was bad. Strange meant endless possibilities and endless was dangerous.

The click of the doorknob turning made his spine straighten. Captain DeWinter entered the room, looking cool and unruffled. Well, at least his demeanor appeared unruffled. His blazer and shirt were creased as if he'd been sleeping in his clothes, but nothing of what he was feeling showed on his face. Even his emotional signature was steady, revealing more curiosity than triumph at closing a case.

DeWinter pushed the door shut and turned the lock before taking a seat in the chair directly facing him. "What are you doing here?"

Odd question. Odd was bad too.

"I am the Claymore you have been searching for and I am turning myself in."

"I can see that, Bale… Do you have a last name?"

"My name is Bale."

"Fine, Bale no last name. Why are you turning yourself in?"

"I must pay for crimes I have committed."

"Why?"

He bit back a surprised gasp as his head jerked. "What do you mean, why?"

"I mean why? You've been running around town, looking more than content about doing your own thing. Why turn yourself in now?"

"What does it matter?" Who was the insane one now? The man was being given a gift and he questioned it?

"I'm curious."

Then he could damn well stay curious.

With that, the stare down began. Two foes locked in a silent battle for domination of the situation.

DeWinter was good, he'd give him that. A slow blink now and again, but otherwise the man didn't flinch as their gazes locked as if they were engaged in an arm-wrestling match with both sides pressing flesh to flesh with all they had and neither giving an inch. However, the captain never spent two years zipping through the galaxy enclosed in a capsule meant for a man half his size. He didn't stand a chance of winning this battle.

At the eight-minute mark DeWinter broke his stare with a smile. "Gonna make me guess, huh? Hmm… I think… I think I got to your girlfriend. Ari, right? She's cute. Smart too. She might not have known about your alter ego, but when I showed her your photo, I noticed she pieced it together right away. So she confronted you, threatened to leave if you don't put an end to it, and now you're here trying to make her happy. You must care for her very much."

The captain's observations hit him like poisoned-tipped arrows. The guessing game was a waste of time. He had come to accept his punishment, not sit and discuss his motivations.

He rose to a stand and held out his hands. "I am here to pay for my crimes."

"Sit down, no name." DeWinter waved his hand and settled back in his seat. "Look, believe it or not, I don't give a shit as to whether you're captured or not. So you've stopped a few crimes here and there and have crippled some dumbasses who probably deserved it. I don't care about them. You'll get, what, a year, for obstruction of justice? Community service if you have no priors? A slap on the wrist for reckless endangerment? Big deal. The only reason the city's after you is because you're making the suits at the top look bad."

"What about you? You've been tasked to capture me. Don't you want to succeed?"

"I did catch you." He laughed. "That's why you're here. I just didn't get the chance to arrest you and make the information public."

"Arrest me now."

DeWinter shook his head. "You're not who I want."

The sudden shift in his tone and emotions from curious to deadly serious made Bale's entire being go quiet as he waited for the captain to continue.

"I was pulled off a case to hunt you down. A case I'd been

working on for three years." He tilted his head. "Does the name Smithwick ring a bell? If you're as close to the Kilsgaards as I think you are, it should."

He gave a slow nod. Just what was the captain after?

"Tell me what you know."

"He's a crime boss. Drugs, human trafficking. Very elusive."

"And…"

"And what?"

"The Kilsgaard connection…" he led.

"He had Fiona Kilsgaard kidnapped last year."

"Correct." DeWinter leaned forward and rested his elbows on his knees. "When I helped your friend the Chameleon with her release, that was the closest we came to nailing Smithwick. You call him elusive. I say he's slippier than a greased pig at the county fair. I have this hunch that even after I close the case on you, I won't be back on the Smithwick case. Right now my commander is burying it deep in the cold case files, never to be seen again."

"Why?"

"Time, money, manpower, ability to make the charges stick, he's on the take. Perhaps all of the above. They're going to let that man walk and be content with putting out the little fires caused by the sparks of Smithwick's operation instead of snuffing out the source."

"And what does this have to do with me?"

"I've seen video of you in action. You move like the Chameleon. I can't touch Smithwick, but you can. You can track him down and finish him once and for all."

His stomach soured as his nostrils flared. "What exactly are you asking me to do, Captain?"

"I want him gone. However you make that happen, is up to you."

"Whatever you may think of me, I do not kill for sport," he spat.

"I hope you don't kill, period, otherwise we will have issues. I just want Smithwick somewhere he can't do any more business."

He released a slow breath and with it some of his anger. He should be used to people thinking the worst of him by now. "This case has become personal to you."

DeWinter raised a surprised brow. "What makes you say that?"

"A soldier follows orders. Only when it becomes personal, strikes a nerve, does he disagree and fight. Smithwick has become personal. Why is that? I do not sense it is about your pride at not being able to close this case."

The captain shifted in his seat. "He's a bad man and needs to be taken off the street."

"I am not a child, Captain. You are asking me to commit a crime. Why?"

He sighed and seemed to deflate in his seat like a party balloon. The touch of gray in his hair seemed more pronounced as did the lines around his mouth as he said, "Because I'm tired. I'm tired of adding another name of a girl who has disappeared during a night out with her friends to the long list of missing persons. I'm tired of having to tell another family member, like my sister, that their boyfriend, husband, son, brother, died of an overdose from drugs they bought from one of Smithwick's dealers. I'm tired of scraping another would-be thug off the street because they thought they could run with the big man and failed. I am tired."

"You get rid of Smithwick and another will take his place. Men like him are like a hydra. Cut off one head and out sprout three more."

"But *this* one will be gone."

Bale shook his head. "I cannot do what you ask. My actions have hurt Ari enough. I am to pay for my crimes, not commit new ones."

"That's noble. Misguided, but noble. Look, without your confession, the DA has no solid evidence to prosecute you with. If I were to have arrested you and you fought the charges, the only things they'd have is a video feed without a clear shot of your face and eye witness accounts, which are spotty at best. The case against you is weak. As I said, you'll get a slap on the wrist, maybe a spanking. If you really want to atone for your sins, you'll help me put an end to Smithwick."

Damn it. Bale clenched his jaw against a scream. Why was it that whenever he begged for punishment, his wish was never granted, yet when he wanted nothing but peace, his world tumbled down in fire and brimstone?

If the captain was to be believed, the sacrifice of his free-dom would be minimal at best. And unfortunately for him, there was nothing in DeWinter's demeanor that suggested he wasn't telling anything but the truth. To prove his contrition to Ari, his gesture needed to be grand. He needed epic.

He needed to not break the law again.

"I cannot, Captain." He placed his hand on his chest and pressed against the ache. "I cannot hurt Ari."

A flare of frustration whipped from DeWinter like a hot lash. "Think of the girls you will be saving. The girls you have saved. Women like Ari. Bale, why be the Claymore in the first place? Why have you been doing what you have?"

"To protect those who cannot protect themselves." The response was so ingrained in his psyche, it came readily to his lips.

"And that's what I'm asking you to do now." He rose and straightened his blazer. "I'll give you some time to think it over. Help me nail Smithwick, then the Claymore can disap-pear forever. If I don't hear from you by five tomorrow night, I'll be right over at The Cavern and will arrest you on sight."

And with that, he left Bale alone to wallow in his self-pity. This feeling of impotency made his blood boil over like an acidic reaction, propelling him from the room as if shot from a cannon. He burst out of the closest exit onto the street and ran. And ran. And ran. Screaming like a siren as his rage consumed him to the point of violence. Only his unspoken vow to Ari to do no harm kept him from tearing the nearest building down with his bare hands.

How was he going to prove to Ari he could be a better man and pay for his mistakes if no one allowed him to? The only person who had ever come close to delivering the punishment he deserved had been Amaryllis—

Amaryllis.

He pulled up short as the tiniest flicker of hope sparked in the darkness of his hearts.

Yes, his princess always knew what a person needed. She helped him see the truth when he had come to take her life and punished him accordingly. The tools still existed to help him again. Fortunately, he knew who had access to those tools.

From his jacket pocket he withdrew his phone and found the number for his potential savior. As the line rang, he held his breath. Thank the Gods, there was a quick answer.

"Bale?"

"Jorges, I need your assistance. I need you to meet me at The Cavern. Bring the chain."

"The chain?"

"*The* chain."

There was a long pause with only Jorges' gentle breathing disrupting the silence. His worry and curiosity reached across the distance as he asked in a hushed voice, "Who's it for?"

"Me."

"What's going on, Bale?"

"I will explain later."

"Explain now."

He grunted with frustration. "Ari knows everything. She's broken. I need to pay for my crimes and the police will not cooperate. I know you have the chain and I know Amaryllis and Lucian will disagree with my wishes if they know what I have planned. Please, help me, Jorges. You're the only one who can."

He sighed loudly. "Okay. We're just finishing up with dinner. I can be there in half an hour."

Relief made his knees buckle. "Thank you. Meet me in the locker."

"Damn, you are fighting some demons. See you there."

He tapped the end of the phone against his forehead and released a long breath. There was every possibility Jorges could expose his plan to the princess, but he prayed the man understood his desperation and allowed him the opportunity to make things right in his own way.

The skies split open and rain pelted the earth in a furious waterfall. The deluge was either a sign that his soul would be cleansed or an omen of ill yet to come. With his luck, both were possibilities.

When Jorges met him twenty-seven minutes later in the basement far beneath the nightclub, the tension in his muscles began to abate. Finally, salvation was within his grasp.

"Thank you, Jorges," he said with a firm handshake.

He nodded. "I can't pretend to know what you're thinking, but I know you'd rather cut off your nuts than ask for help, so I figured this must be serious."

"You would be correct."

Jorges unlocked the door and pushed it open. "After you."

The locker was the affectionate term for the storage unit in the basement of the nightclub. Cold, damp and with a single light bulb for illumination, it was the room where spare furniture and decorations from events past lived until called upon for service again. Since Jorges rarely reused his ideas, very few people came down this hall, which made this the perfect location for Bale's purpose.

Jorges set down a leather bag and withdrew several yards of thick chain. "How do you want to do this?"

Bale surveyed the room, up, down and all around until he spotted a line of straight-back chairs hanging from a hook screwed into the ceiling. "That might do."

With Jorges' help he moved the chairs. Once the task was finished Bale nodded at the hook. "Hang on and see if it will hold your body weight. If I try at full strength, I'll rip it out of the ceiling."

Jorges leapt into the air for the hook. He hung on for fifteen seconds before dropping back to the ground. "Felt good. Not even a squeak."

"Good. Let's do this." He stripped off his shirt while Jorges climbed onto a chair to secure the center of the chain to the hook.

"Arms up or down?"

"Up. I'm not doing this for comfort."

Bale lifted his arms and Jorges wound the chain around

each wrist then pulled until his torso stretched out long before continuing to spiral the ends of the chain around each arm. While Jorges finished wrapping his legs, Bale felt the molybdenite leech the strength from his muscles. The last time he had been bound in such a manner, he had been unconscious and missed out on the rolling nausea and dizziness that came with losing his powers. It was terrifying being parted with his ability to defend himself, but the terror was nothing compared to the pain Ari felt when faced with who he was. If it made the situation any better, he'd suffer the loss a million times over.

"Is this what you wanted?" Jorges asked as he stepped back.

"Ya."

"How long do you want me to wait before I tell Lucian and Amaryllis?"

The question almost made him smile. At least Jorges was granting him this small boon. "A year?"

"No."

"A month."

"We both know that's not going to happen. I guess it will be up to me to decide when you've had enough time to settle in before calling Mom and Dad. The anticipation will be part of your self-inflicted punishment."

"Thank you, Jorges," he slurred as the effects of the chain seeped into his bones. Fire bloomed in his shoulders as his body weight pulled on the chains.

"Keep that in mind when Amaryllis lays into you. Good

luck, Bale."

His eyelids grew heavy and his vision blurred as Jorges' footsteps faded into the darkness. The descending silence went beyond the absence of sound. Without his powers he no longer was able to sense emotions. For the second time in his life he wasn't bombarded by the constant noise of living. No buzz, no hum. Absolute nothingness. Numb, as if dead.

After all he had done, death would be a reward he didn't deserve.

✦　✦　✦

THE SOUND OF a whistling tea kettle roused Ari from her nightmares. Bale had stood in her living room and calmly declared himself a murderer. The image had been the most horrible thing she ever witnessed.

Wait. Tea kettle? Was Bale still in the apartment with her?

She sat up with a gasp and frowned when she realized she was laid out on the couch. In the kitchen Amaryllis hummed while she poured boiling water into two mugs.

"I was wondering how long you'd be asleep," she said by way of greeting.

Ari rubbed her cheek as if she could still fill the chilly bathroom tile against her skin. "I'm so confused. Why are you here? How did I get on the couch?"

"I carried you. And do you seriously have to ask as to why I am here?"

"You carried me? But how…" The words died as Amaryllis

came into the living room with a knowing smile on her lips, as if it were no great effort to have carried a grown woman across the room. "You're like Bale, aren't you?"

"Meaning am I from another planet and have special powers? Then yes."

Well fuck. She sank into the cushions. "Is it true? Is what he said true?"

"Well, I don't know exactly what he told you, but judging by the sobbing heap I saw in the hallway, I would say yes to that too."

"Who was sobbing?" she asked and watched as Amaryllis set one of the mugs on the coffee table.

"Bale. He was devastated by your reaction."

"He's killed people, Amaryllis. For money. How was I supposed to react?"

"Just as you have. I was not belittling you for your feelings, Ari. Believe me. Here, take this. It will help steady your nerves and sooth your throat." The scent of orange and cinnamon tickled her nose as Amaryllis offered her a steaming mug.

"I don't think I should," she croaked and stuck her shaking hands under her butt. "I'll spill and burn myself."

"Give me your hand." She pulled at her wrist and guided her fingers around the warm mug and held them with her own. "Wrap them around the ceramic. Let the warmth seep into your hands and travel up your arms to your heart. Breathe and know that all will be well."

In the swirling depths of Amaryllis' all seeing-eyes, Ari

desperately wanted to believe her, but the notion was impossible. "How can you say that? What does that even mean? I can't unlearn what I've learned." Distress made her voice squeak. "I am in love with a murderer. How sick does that make me? I'm like those women who form fan clubs about mass murderers and marry them in prison."

"Don't be so melodramatic. You are perfectly normal. You fell in love with Bale as the man he is today, not the man from the past. And the man you fear was only who he was for a brief moment in time and not who he truly is."

"You're speaking in riddles to try to confuse me and make this whole mess seem not that important."

"No, I'm only trying to give you perspective. How would you like it if I called you an adulterer because of your affair with that married politician and treated you with disdain?"

She flinched as if slapped. "That's not fair. I didn't know he was married, and I ended the relationship the second I found out."

"But you were still involved with a married man and caused anguish to his family. Ari, you cannot choose to live in shades of gray when it suits your purposes. Now, Bale told you his story. Let me tell you mine. Settle in, *lebshone*." She sat beside her on the couch and covered both of their laps with a fleece blanket. "When a kingdom is at war it affects everyone, no matter their station, and there is no escape from its reach. Bale is a warrior. Born to fight and protect and he is very good at it. That is why he was selected to serve on my father's guard."

"Your father? Wait, the king?" Holy crap. "That means you're—"

"Was." Her smile was bittersweet. "Was, darling. My father was a king who came from a long, long, long line of kings. He was a good king but also a very arrogant one. He was naïve about the lives of his people. My mother did all she could to connect him with those they ruled, but she was female. What do females know of politics and leadership? As I said, arrogant. The people revolted, but those who led the revolution where no better than my father and his lords. Lives were destroyed. Families torn apart, like Bale's and mine. For my protection I was sent to Earth. My exile was a blessing and a curse. I knew I would never see my friends or family again but here I have so many more freedoms than I did back on Skandavia. Earth is my home and I love it here."

Ari held her breath as Amaryllis' eyes filled with tears before she looked down at her lap. Her pink-tipped nails plucked at the fluffy fabric.

"My mother was killed while trying to make peace with the revolutionaries. Lucian's brother was the head of her guard and was punished for his failure. He was offered banishment or death. He chose banishment. Lucian stood by his brother's side, and they were sent here." A small grin broke free. "He wanted to keep an eye on me. But that's another story. Without Lucian, my father's crown fell and he was executed. To ensure that no member of the royal family existed to retake the throne, the new regime hired an assassin to come to Earth and kill me."

"Bale. Bale was sent to kill you?"

"And Lucian and his brother."

"That's insane." She jumped off the couch, so stunned she barely registered the hot tea as it sloshed over her hands. "And you still speak to him? Invite him into your home?"

"Ari. Sit down. This is my story." She reached out and grabbed a fistful of skirt, tugging her back onto her seat. "I haven't reached my point yet."

"This better be the holy grail of all morals."

"You'll see." She laughed. "Yes, Bale was sent to kill me. But he wasn't acting on greed for money or the thrill of the hunt. He was angry. He was wounded. And he was severely misguided. Did Bale explain our powers?"

"No. Not really."

"The strength and speed we inherited when we arrived on this planet. On Skandavia the only power we have is empathy. There are many instances where verbal or visual communication is limited, so our species have developed the ability to read each other's emotions. That power is magnified a thousand-fold when a couple chooses to bond and meshes their emotions together. The bond is so strong, it lasts vast distances, even time." She smoothed down a lock of her sable hair and smiled. "I used to have silver hair, but then I bonded with Lucian and inherited his hair color, and his green eyes turned lavender. All bonded mates share coloring to reflect their connection."

"Wait a minute. So all of this time you've been able to know what I'm feeling?" The horrible realization stabbed her through the ribs. "Bale has known what I've been feeling?"

"Yes. That is why your grief affected him so greatly. As a human, you have no filter on your emotions, and Bale has a difficult time handling such purity. Even from my apartment I was able to sense your pain like I was trapped in an avalanche of rocks underwater. For Bale, you absolutely leveled him, but that's not my point. You see, Bale never bonded with his wife and that was why he was so angry at the world. Once bonded, your entire being is opened to the other. There is no hiding, no secrets, and Bale didn't trust his wife with truth of the darkness that lives inside a *Llanos* warrior. There's a hardness, an infinity for violence and an intense sex drive, which you've experienced, and he felt she was too delicate to understand who he was. When she was killed, he felt as if he failed her as a protector and a husband and the guilt drove him mad."

"That doesn't excuse him from trying to kill you."

"No, it doesn't. But I forgave him. Once I was able to make him realize that killing was not the way to honor his family, that is when he turned into the vigilante. To protect those who could not protect themselves. But he fights with that guilt every day. Believe me when I say no one hates Bale more than himself."

"But I don't hate—" She sucked in the words before they spilled into the air where they could never be taken back.

She did hate Bale. Didn't she? By all rights, she should despise him because... He made bad choices in the past and had the audacity to try to make up for it? God, that made her sound so shallow. But she was supposed to hate him, right?

She dropped her face into her hand and groaned. "I don't know what to think anymore."

"Let me add one more thought to consider."

"Must you?"

"Yes." She patted her on the knee. "War makes monsters out of even the best of men. Whether they are a villain or hero depends on which side they are fighting on. A soldier in combat is instructed to kill the enemy. What if that enemy is just a man, much like the soldier, who was forced to fight by his government or watch his family be killed? He may not believe what he is fighting for, but he has no choice so he takes up arms. Aren't these soldiers paid to defend and protect? Aren't they paid to kill? It is all about prospective, Ari. Not everyone is one hundred percent guilty nor one hundred percent innocent. There is no black and white but an infinite number of shades of gray."

Ari sighed and rested her head against the back of the sofa. "This sucks. I don't want to be an adult anymore. Even the crappiness of my childhood was easier to traverse than this mess."

"But not nearly as much fun." The chirp of Amaryllis' cellphone interrupted her laughter. She frowned at the display before she answered. "Hello, Jorges."

The way Amaryllis stilled and her gaze shot in her direction made Ari hold her breath and the hairs on her arms stand on end. Whatever Jorges was saying had to be about Bale.

"We're on our way. Thank you, my friend." Amaryllis ended the call and closed her eyes. She let out a slow breath as she shook her head. "Oh, Bale. The man is fortunate I love him so. Come along, Ari. We are needed."

Chapter Twelve

A MARYLLIS ALLOWED HER just enough time to change out of her work clothes into a more comfortable skirt and ballet flats before pushing her out the door and toward the elevator.

"Explain now." Ari stood before the closed elevator doors with arms crossed in defiance. She refused to enter a situation without any hint of preparedness.

"We'll talk while we walk."

"Where are we going?"

"There's a storage unit down on the lowest level. That's were Bale and Jorges are." The doors opened and they stepped inside. "I told you, no one is harder on Bale than Bale. From what Jorges has discerned, Bale wanted to prove to you he can atone for his crimes and tried to turn himself in to the police. Apparently that plan didn't turn out well and they declined to arrest him."

"Seriously? If he confessed, why not?"

"We'll have to get that story from Bale. With the attempt to prove himself to you foiled, he contacted Jorges to bring him the chain."

Chills ran down her neck as images of gladiators swinging lengths of chain at each other in dark, humid rooms with blood and sweat flying everywhere flashed through her mind. "What does *that* mean?"

The elevator doors opened, revealing a hallway with concrete floors and walls that looked as welcoming as a prison cell. The dampness and creepy shadows did not help her nerves.

"By accident Lucian and his brother discovered a mineral here on Earth that steals our powers."

"You mean like Superman and kryptonite?"

"Similar, yes. There was a man who discovered a way to harness the strength of this mineral on its own and fashioned several products, including a chain we used to restrain Bale when he was bent on his revenge. Afterward we gave the chain to Jorges for safekeeping since none of us from Skandavia are able to handle it."

"So Bale asked Jorges for this chain to what, steal his powers?"

"My guess is that's part of the reason. Believe it or not, Bale is an honorable man. He wanted to be punished for his failure to protect his family. I gave that to him. If he is seeking punishment for the crimes he has committed afterward, this may be his way to obtain it."

They rounded a corner and saw Jorges standing in front of a closed door. He crossed to meet them and placed a hand on each of their shoulders, bringing them into a huddle.

"How is he, Jorges?" Amaryllis asked in a hushed tone.

"Quiet and determined, which is not unusual for Bale, but something about the way he's acting makes me want to hug the guy. I take it you two had a fight?" he asked Ari.

"Kind of. Sort of." She let out a huff. "I found out…things. Scary things."

"Ah." He nodded. "I understand. I'm afraid of what's going to happen if Miranda ever finds out about all of this Saturn business."

"You've never told her?" How could he have kept such a secret so quiet? Especially since she worked so closely with Amaryllis.

"It's not my secret to tell."

"Tell her, Jorges."

The both looked to Amaryllis in surprise. His eyebrows rose to his hairline. "What?"

"Tell her." She laid her hand on his cheek. "She's family and has earned the right to know the truth."

"Okay. But if she takes it poorly, I'm not going the Bale route."

"Were you ever an assassin?" Ari asked.

"No."

"Then she won't take it as poorly as me."

"Good point. So I can leave our boy in your hands?"

"Definitely." Amaryllis kissed his cheek. "Thank you."

"Anytime." He squeezed Ari's shoulder. "Good luck."

As Jorges walked away, Ari turned to face the closed door to the storage room and felt her heart climb into her throat.

"What now?"

Amaryllis settled her hands on her hips and cocked her head. "Well, the last time I used a whip to help him break through his guilt."

"You whipped him!" Would the mental shocks never end?

"Do not fret. I didn't beat him. I didn't even break the skin. I told you, he wanted punishment for his failure, and the pain helped him to break away from his perceptions and see the truth. It appears he may need that lesson again."

"So you're going to go in there and whip him?"

"No. You are."

"Are you insane?" she hissed. "I'm not whipping anyone."

"Ari." Amaryllis grabbed her around the biceps and gave her a shake. "Bale needs you just as much as you need him. I know you've received a lot of extraordinary information in a very short time, but I know you are strong enough to handle this. You don't have to whip him, but you do have to go in and see to his needs. Only you will be able to provide that for him. I have faith in you."

There was no controlling the tremble in her voice. "I have no idea how to handle a restrained alien with masochistic yearnings."

Amaryllis smiled. "Maybe. Maybe not. But you know how to handle Bale. You can do this. Now go."

Ari stumbled as Amaryllis gave her a friendly shove. The solid steel door grew larger and larger with each timid step. What was waiting for her on the other side? The possibilities made her shudder as adrenaline raced through her system. The fight-or-flight instinct was most certainly kicking in. Too bad she couldn't decide which path to choose.

"Ari. If I had asked you to tell me how you felt about Bale before tonight, what would you have said?"

She glanced over her should and saw in Amaryllis' smile that she already knew the answer. "I love him."

"Why?"

"Because." She swallowed as the undeniable truth burned her throat. "Because he fights for those who cannot fight for themselves. And because he has done nothing but try to give me everything I wanted."

"I believe you." Amaryllis nodded with encouragement. "He's worth the second chance."

Ari sucked in the positive reinforcement. Damn it. Amaryllis was right. No matter how much Ari wished it to be otherwise, her feelings for Bale weren't going to shut off and disappear as if they had never existed. At some point she was going to have to confront her feelings for the big man. Now was just as good a time as any, however this rip-the-bandage-off method was destined to be painful.

The handle was a block of ice against her palm as she opened the door and crept inside. Boxes and stacks of chairs created an eerie maze of shadows in the dimly lit room. From the corner she heard the soft rattle of chain-on-chain and she inched her way in that direction.

Around a stack of short cocktail tables, she stopped suddenly as she caught sight of Bale.

In the chilly room his face and torso glistened with sweat and his head lolled to the side to rest against his arms that were stretched to the sky. A thick chain wound around his wrists and snaked down each arm, crossing over his chest before continuing down each leg. His skin had lost its golden glow and his lips appeared pale and parched.

Bale wasn't just weak, he appeared as if he were dying and her heart lurched. He asked for this? He wanted to suffer? What was he thinking?

Fear for his health propelled her into the small pool of light. "Bale, what are you doing?"

He started and cracked opened his eyes. "Ari? What are you doing here?"

"I asked you first." She gestured at the chain then around the room. "What is this? Why did you ask to be hurt this way?"

He shook his head and sighed. The movement rattled the chains and the sound set her teeth on edge. "I sullied you with my darkness. I broke you and that is unforgiveable."

"You didn't break me. Shocked the hell out of me, yes, but I'm not broken."

"Aren't you?" he spat, although he appeared more angry at himself than at her. "You got sick. Your voice is damaged. I did that to you."

"You didn't—" Tears choked her as she processed the implication of his words.

Was she broken? Forever changed, absolutely, but was she broken? And what did broken mean? Obviously she was able to function, but was she now damaged, like he claimed? Would she no longer be able to face the world? No longer be able to exist as a loving, compassionate, trusting person again?

God, the thought was depressing. And weak. He made her sound weak and frail and that just pissed her off.

She was Ari Rayner. Each time life knocked her on her ass, she got up, dusted herself off and got back to living. Her mother with her revolving door of husbands and Anthony's betrayal hadn't kept her down, and by God she wasn't going to allow Bale and all of his whatever-you-call-it prevent her from getting up every morning and having a happy and productive life.

"I am injured. But make no mistake, I am not broken. Now explain to me what all of this," she waved her hands around, "is about."

"The man you spoke to at the bar." He shuddered and swayed on his feet. "He is a police officer and was tasked with capturing the vigilante. I went to him and turned myself in."

"Why would you do that?" If what Amaryllis said was true, his work as the Claymore was his sole reason for living.

"I wanted to prove to you that I am willing to pay for my crimes."

"So you were willing to give up your work? Just like that?" She snapped her fingers.

"For you. Yes."

"What about your wife?" she whispered.

The air stilled and she saw every muscle in Bale's chest and arms tense as his eyes widened. The chains rattled as he began to shake and his mouth moved as if trying to speak, yet he didn't say a word.

"What about your wife, Bale?" She stepped closer. "All night long I've been hearing about the vow you made to honor her. How all of the bad you've done has been in her and your daughter's name. And you're telling me that you were willing to give up that vow? For me?"

The harsh in-and-out of his breathing brought her to tears, but she refused to break her gaze. Damn the man. The words were there, swimming in his dark eyes and hovering behind the tremble of his lips, all he had to do was say them.

"Tell me, Bale."

"I—Ari." He closed his eyes and hung his head.

"Damn it, Bale. Tell me," she shouted and closed the distance between them and cupped his face. Her fingers curled with her frustration, but she restrained the urge to claw at his cheeks. If there was any hope for them, he had to talk to her. This was too important to guess at his reasons. "Why would you break your vow?"

And still he remained silent.

Frustration bubbled over into anger as he continued to shake. "Are you fucking kidding me? Just tell me. Or are you too much of a pussy?" She pushed against his chest and as the chains swung him back in her direction she slapped at him again as her anger erupted. His relieved sigh drove her into a blinding rage.

"Is that it? Amaryllis said she had to whip you into a confession. Is that what I have to do? Beat you senseless?" She slapped at his right arm, then his left, over and over until her palms stung. "You sick fuck."

The dam broke inside her and a great sob burst forth followed by another then another as she fell to her knees.

What was she doing? What had she become? Giving in to the violence wasn't going to solve anything. Couldn't he see she was willing to hear him out? If he cared about her one bit, he'd try to help her understand his thoughts, his motivations. He would confirm that her love was not one-sided and that all this shit she was going through was not in vain. She needed to be secure in the knowledge that if she forgave him of his past, it wouldn't come back and bite her in the ass later. The future was never for certain, but he had to give her something to go on. Where was her hope?

"Ari, love, please don't cry." Bale's plea brought her head up. "I love you. I'm sorry. I love you and you don't deserve this. I'm not worth your tears."

At his profession her hands flew up to press against the ache in her chest.

He loved her. Did he really? The Bale she thought she knew would not have said those words unless he meant them. So why wouldn't he answer her questions?

For her, love meant pushing aside all rational thought for

the slightest chance of happily ever after. Love meant walking through fire for another. Love meant entering a dark room not knowing what lay in wait to confront a man you want to give everything to with the knowledge that blood stained his hands. Love meant risk and here she was stripped bare, trying to understand him, and he couldn't even muster the courage to answer her with the truth. He was the fighter, yet he wouldn't fight for her. Wasn't she worth the effort?

"You're right." She stood and swiped at her cheek with her sleeve. "I don't deserve to be used as an excuse for you to be a fucking martyr. Obviously this has nothing to do with me."

"No. Wait. Don't go," he cried as she turned. "This has everything to do with you. Ari...I don't have the right words to say. I can't phrase it perfectly."

"Any words are better than none. They don't have to be perfect. They only have to come from the heart."

"My heart." He chuckled without mirth. "In my case that is two hearts, and I mean that literally and figuratively."

Silence descended while she waited for him to continue. And waited and waited as the chains creaked and her teeth chattered. With a last sigh, any hope she had that he would finally open up died. He was never going to change.

As her foot shifted to leave he pinned her with a hard stare that froze her in place. His eyes glittered with his tears as he croaked, "I love you, Ariel. And I love my wife. Reconciling those two thoughts has not been easy for me. You two are so different. She was delicate and calm. You are strong, a fighter, a force of nature that frightens me at times with your intensity. But you are both kind, compassionate, and unfortunate enough to have me fall in love with you. There is nothing I wouldn't do for you. Absolutely nothing."

Like kill. Neither of them said it out loud, but the implication hung there as heavy as a lead balloon.

But he was talking. Thank God, he was finally talking.

She crossed her arms, fighting the chills that rattled her bones. "So you feel guilty for loving me? Like you're being unfaithful?"

"Yes," he sighed as if relieved that she understood. "She's dead. I know that. I know she is never coming back. And you make me want to live. You make me want to be a better man. Natalia did too, but I was too afraid to be that man. She deserved better than me. You deserve better than me."

In her heart the walls shifted and all the love she felt for him poured out. Here was a man trying to make right and going about it all the wrong way. God, men could be such idiots.

"What kind of man do you think I deserve, Bale?"

Surprise flashed across his face, but his voice was sure as he answered, "A good man. A man who doesn't need to fight unless it is to protect you. Who loves you with his entire being. Who will do everything he can to see to your happiness. You deserve a man who is loyal and will never give you cause to cry. Who will tell you every day with his actions and words that you are the most precious treasure in existence."

Tears welled as he proved her right. He knew exactly the right words to say. "Before this evening, those are the words I would have used to describe you."

"But I am not that man."

"Yes, you are. And then some."

He shook his head. "I am evil."

"You're not evil. Yes, you've done bad things, but I don't believe you are evil." And that was the truth. An infinite amount of shades of gray, Amaryllis had said, and she was right. Bale had done wrong, but in his heart he wasn't evil. "Did you take any pleasure while you were killing?"

"Only when I terminated the men who killed my family," he said without glee but with definite satisfaction.

"Okay. I can understand that." She didn't want to ask her next question, but she needed to know. "When was the last time you killed anyone?"

"A year ago."

She sucked in a sharp breath but pressed on, despite the urge to run away. She had to learn the entire truth of who he was. "Was that here on Earth?"

The muscles in his jaw tightened as he nodded.

"What happened?"

He swallowed hard then licked his lips. "I have the power to read another's emotions."

"I know. Amaryllis told me."

"I have a feeling Amaryllis told you a lot of things."

"She did, but continue."

The corner of his mouth kicked up for a nanosecond. "When I arrived on Earth, I had difficulty filtering out the purity of human emotions. I still do. But back then the on-slaught was overwhelming. I crossed paths with a street gang that had beat up a man who they felt betrayed them and were going to attack his sister. I stepped in to defend her. But I was already running on a high of anger and frustration and could not contain my rage. I maimed and killed several of the gang members."

"Were they all bad guys?"

"Does it matter? Ari, I shouldn't have killed anyone."

"I know. I just—" She laughed. "I can't believe we're hav-ing this conversation. I guess I would feel a little bit better if I knew they were all bad guys. Like they deserved it, somehow."

"If they did, I shouldn't have been the one to carry out the execution. Ari, I love you, but you need more than I can provide. You were right to push me away. You should leave."

"I should leave." She drew in a breath. "But I don't want to."

In two steps she was before him and wrapped her arms around his waist. Against her cheek his skin was cool, not nearly as warm as normal and she hugged him tighter.

Bale lowered his head to nuzzle her as if he were a giant cat. "Ariel. This is no place for you."

"Or you." She fingered the thick link of chain. "What are you doing here? I thought you turned yourself in."

"I did. The captain didn't want me as a criminal. He wanted the Claymore's help to capture a bigger threat. I told him I would not commit any more crimes. He gave me the night to reconsider his offer."

"Why the chain? Are you in pain?"

"No pain. Weak. A little nauseated and uncomfortable. But at least I am locked away where I can't hurt anyone. Especially you."

"So this is your grand plan? Stay chained up in here for, what, forever?"

"As long as it takes to pay for my crimes."

"And who determines that?"

"You."

She stepped back and laid her hand on his cheek. "And if I think you've suffered enough?"

"Eternity would not be long enough."

Of course he'd think that way. And here she thought she was the one who leaned toward the dramatics. As she stroked her thumb over his skin, she noticed the way he swayed into her touch. Despite all his talk and insistence on remaining sequestered, he still craved contact. Until Bale believed he had completed his penance, they were at an impasse. Talk wasn't going to convince him and she sure as hell wasn't going to whip him. For one, she didn't have a whip handy, and two, those things were dangerous. She was just as likely to injure herself as well as Bale.

Out of the corner of her eye she spotted several dowels of various sizes leaning against the wall and her heart kicked up a gear. According to Amaryllis, pain had been the catalyst that broke through his guilt the last time he fell into the pit of self-pity. Who was to say it wouldn't work again? But did she have it in her? Could she give him what he needed?

She licked her lips and tucked her hair behind her ears. "Just so we're clear, you insist on remaining here, tied up, as a punishment for contributing to my freak out?"

"Ya."

"And even though the duration of this punishment is up to me, you don't think you've served enough time?"

"Ya."

"Okay." She rubbed her hands together and walked over to where the dowels rested behind him. The one she chose was two inches in diameter and about three feet in length. The stick was light and when she swung an experimental arc, a soft whoosh followed in its wake.

Wow. Oh Lord. She released a long breath and looked at Bale. The broad expanse of his back flexed as he shifted his weight. As quiet as ever, he didn't ask what she was doing, but his head was cocked as if to listen for her movements to give her away.

She stepped up behind him and reached around his waist for the buckle of his belt.

He jumped. "What are you doing?"

"You want to be punished?" She pulled his jeans and boxer-briefs down to his knees. "That's what I'm doing. Spread your feet apart."

"Ari." He turned his head left and right to try to catch a glimpse of her.

"No Ari. Now spread 'em." She popped him on the butt with her open palm. "You're at my mercy now."

With a sideways glance, he shifted his feet. Before he settled into place she struck the first tap to his firm backside.

It wasn't a hard blow, but a light, testing smack that didn't even leave a mark. She swung again and this time his flesh rippled and a pink welt blossomed. On the third strike Bale moaned and leaned into the hit.

Whoa. She blew a strand of hair out of her eyes and wiped her damp palm against her skirt. Okay. Testing done. Now was the time to get serious.

With each hit he let out a short groan as the muscles of his ass flexed and clenched and a soft blush spread beneath the scattered blows.

The balance between pain for punishment and pain as cruelty was a thin edge she never before traversed and she approached with extreme caution. This wasn't about hurting Bale, but to give him a release from the emotions he didn't know how to process.

Every few seconds she looked to him for any signs that she had crossed the invisible line. His eyes were closed and his head hung low. A slight grimace twisted his lips with each strike, but other than that, the only sign of his discomfort was the sweat that slickened his skin and his reddening butt cheeks.

Bale was a warrior and was trained to withstand the harshest of environments, plus she knew that if she asked him about his welfare, he'd refuse to answer and ask for more. But his cock couldn't lie and right then it was saying a lot about his state of mind.

As she continued to rain blows, his hips jerked and his erection bobbed in the air. Swollen and red, the tip grew wetter by the second and his balls drew up tight. Above their heads his hands clutched at the chain and his entire body tensed and she recognized the clenching of his jaw as a sign of his impending orgasm.

She dropped the dowel then ran her fingernails down his back and over his hot ass. He hissed and bucked, her name falling like a plea from his lips, but either in prayer or a curse, she couldn't tell.

"Can you take more?" She stood on her toes to whisper in his ear. In her flats, she was barely able to peek over his shoulder. "Or have you had enough?"

"Whatever you desire," he panted.

"I desire more."

Actually she desired a lot more. Between her thighs she was slick and her core pulsed with hunger. But this was not about sex and her needs had to wait.

She reached around and grabbed his cock at the base. Twisting her wrist, she rubbed up and down the hard shaft, stopping just short of stroking the wet crown.

Bale began to moan. "Please stop."

"You don't like this?"

"I love it," he gasped. "But I don't deserve this pleasure."

"What about this?" She stuck two fingers into her mouth then pushed against the tight opening of his anus. Slowly she worked the tips up into his body until they were buried to the knuckles.

In her hand his cock twitched and a spurt of pre-cum shot from the tip. The fingers buried in his ass scissored and searched for that magic spot that would make him beg for more. She didn't know if his species had a prostate gland, but she was gonna do all she could to find out.

When his cock bucked again, she squeezed the base of his shaft and stilled her probing fingers. He shuddered in her arms and his knees buckled. She slid her hand down to massage his balls as he caught his breath. He sucked in a long draw of air between his teeth and she began again, jacking him off with one hand while fucking him with the other.

Against the backdrop of his animalistic growls, the chain squeaked and rattled in rhythm with their movements. His cock kicked and she froze and tugged his testicles, which made him howl with frustration.

Twice more she worked him to the edge of release then pulled away at the last moment. Pressed against his sweaty back, her shirt adhered to her chest like plastic wrap and her hair clung to her neck in ropy strands. Her arm slipped over his side and her lungs burned as she rode the wave with him. Only his bound hands kept them on their feet as she clung to his slippery body. She closed her eyes and absorbed the sound of his cries, the up-and-down motion of his billowing chest, and the play of muscles of his back.

The scent of man and sex filled her nostrils and made her weep with the need to take him down from his restraints and quench both of the fires turning them into ash, but this wasn't about her. The touching, the stroking, all this was about showing Bale she cared enough about him to give him what he needed. She cared enough to break him down to his base self, to unravel the layers of self-recrimination to expose the man who craved touch. Her touch. Her love.

Bale's trembles turned into a full-on spasm and his head tipped back with a roar. This time she didn't stop his orgasm. She sank her teeth into his back and milked his cock. It took all her strength to hang on as he jerked in her arms. In her hand his cock spurted over and over and she used the wetness to ease him off his high as she gentled her strokes until his erection softened and his cries ceased.

Her hands shook as she unwound the chain from his legs. When she reached to release his arms, she lost her balance and fell against his back.

"Sorry," she mumbled, still struggling to catch her own breath.

She wasn't tall enough to free him from the rest of the chain, but she hoped it was enough for him to regain his strength. As she stepped around to face him, she wiped at her face with the hem of her shirt. Bale looked completely undone.

His face was pale but for the red flush across his cheeks and his swollen lips from where he had bitten them to hold back his cries. The muscles of his chest, arms and legs twitched independently of each other as if attached to electrodes. But his eyes, oh. His eyes burned bright with myriad emotions. Disbelief, love and most of all hope.

The sparkle dimmed as she spoke, "Never again, Bale. I love you. I love the man you are and the man you want to be, but I can't do this again. Bondage, a little spanking while playing together, fine. But this is too much. I don't have it in me to hurt you in such a way whenever you can't communicate. I'm not a Domme. I'm just Ari, who loves you and wants to work our differences out. If you can love me as I am, come find me."

Without a backward glance, she left him hanging on his hook and let the door close behind her with a soft click.

Chapter Thirteen

A RI STEPPED OUT of the shower and stood on the bath mat for several long minutes with her eyes closed and her hands down by her sides. All her focus was on drawing in one slow breath, then another, allowing the coconut-scented steam to fill up her lungs.

The sound of her beating heart filled her ears, reminding her that all of life started with the basics. Blood moving through the veins. Touch. The tickle of each drop of water as gravity pulled the molecules down her body. Starting at her toes, she wiggled each digit, digging them into the cotton shag, then flexed each muscle in her legs from the calves to her thighs. All the way up her body she worked tendon and tissue, stretching, twisting, bending her limbs.

Wasn't one supposed to be thankful for the little things in life? Here she stood, able to function and move with ease. She had a roof over her head and a job to pay the bills and keep food on the table. Those were the important things, right? Everything else was fluff. Inconsequential bullshit that meant nothing and stayed behind once you died.

Bale. The Claymore. The entire assassin-from-outer-space

situation were complications, not insurmountable obstacles that prevented her from living a fulfilling life. She alone was in control of her destiny and future happiness.

Just as Bale was in control of his.

Yes, everyone needed to let off some steam, but the extent to which he wallowed in his guilt was not healthy. At some point he was really going to break and she had no idea how to sweep up the remains of an explosion destined to hit epic on the Richter scale.

An itch began in the middle of her right palm and radiated out through her fingers. She pressed her thumb into the center and turned her hand to the front and back, searching for any visible sign of her altercation with Bale. The power she had wielded with the dowel had been frightening and empowering. To have that much control over another's well-being was a heady sensation and had the ability to blaze out of control in a nanosecond. Bondage, a little rough sex, she was ready and willing, but the night had turned into something deeper, darker, much more dangerous for the uneducated. And she had the feeling she had gotten lucky earlier and all had turned out as she planned. If she and Bale were to continue as a pair, instinct was not going to be enough to keep either of them from getting hurt.

If Bale and she were to continue...

Big if. No, she hadn't gotten over his past history, but she loved him. She ached for him. She was willing to take a chance. Focus on the now, just as she did her breathing. Could Bale?

The last of the big droplets of water settled into a fine mist and the cool air sent bumps across her skin. She tugged a towel around her shoulders like a blanket. Her limbs were active, but carried all the strength of pudding. There were what, fifteen, twenty steps to the bed. Lord help her make it to the soft mattress.

The bedside lamp glowed bright and cheery in the corner. Normally that would be a welcome sight, but wrong since she hadn't bothered to turn it on when she had stalked straight to the bathroom when she'd returned.

"Ariel."

Bale stood in the bedroom doorway. His hair was damp as if he had just showered as well. A black shirt stretched across his chest and the soft-looking exercise pants made a smile tickle her lips. Wow. He actually owned a pair of pants that were not jeans.

Deep lines bracketed his mouth and his dark brows were lowered with uncertainty. One bare foot was pointed toward the exit as if he expected to be kicked out at a moment's notice. He was beautiful and tragic, and if she had the strength, she'd weep for all that had happened to him. As it was, all she managed was to shake like a naked poplar tree that had all its leaves blown away by a storm.

"I understand now, Ari." He sighed and crossed to her side to scoop her up in his arms. "I need to hold you. May I?"

Exhaustion and her own need to be held made her compliant. The fact that his body was toasty warm and eased her chills was an added bonus she was too greedy to deny.

Neither made a sound as he tucked her beneath the sheets and molded her to his side. While he stroked one hand along her spine, the fingers of his free hand traced a delicate line from her brow to her chin. With one of his broad hands he could completely cover her face or crush her bones with one blow, yet his touch was so gentle, so tender and reverent her heart ached all the more.

In his eyes she saw his fear that she would still reject him, his regret at not being able to voice what was in his heart, his love, his apology.

"Ariel," he whispered, his voice breaking as moisture made the black of his eyes glitter.

She whimpered and tears she didn't believe she had left trickled down her cheeks. Funny. Here she thought she needed a litany of words but in actuality, she just needed one. In that one word she heard his love. Heard the emotions he didn't know how to verbally express unless he was beaten into submission. Just the sound of her name coming from his lips told her all he felt in his heart.

"You undo me, *liera*." He gathered her close and dropped light kisses to her trembling lips. "I swear I will do all that I can to never give you cause to cry anything but happy tears."

"I am happy."

"I know otherwise."

Shit. That was right. He could read her emotions. However, reading and understanding were two different things. "I'm overwhelmed and exhausted. Confused and pretty much out of my mind right now."

"And yet you still claim to love me," he said with disbelief.

"Yeah, I do. Crazy as that seems." She scraped her fingernails over the stubble on his cheeks. "Do you—Do you think you'll be able to love me? Even though I'm not your wife?"

"Ah, Ariel." He touched his forehead to hers. "I love you for your differences as much as your similarities."

"But her death drove you to madness. You killed for her."

"I will kill for you too."

"Bale—"

"Ari, I love you so much that at times I-I—" He choked and his lips curled over his teeth. "You are mine to love. Mine to protect. No matter the cost. My thirst for revenge is no more, but make no mistake. I will protect you to the death, whether it be mine or whoever threatens you. This I vow."

The fierce intensity of his promise brought forth more tears. "God, what is wrong with me that I can't stop crying? I need to be more like you. Strong like a rock."

"No." His brow furrowed as his nostrils flared and the muscles in his jaw tightened. With an open palm he tapped at the center of his chest. "Inside," he rasped and swallowed hard, slapping his chest again. "Inside."

The rawness in his voice broke through the last of her reserves and she melted in his arms, wrapping her limbs around them as they both shook with emotion.

Bale was the man for her. This broken warrior who loved

so deep, he allowed it to consume him. This man who spoke very little, but lived by each word. There was no doubt he would fight against any demons out to harm them, just as she would battle the demons of his past and keep him in the light. Together, they were unstoppable. As long as they trusted in each other.

"Bale, promise me." She rubbed her cheek against his chest. "You'll let me know how you feel. You don't have to say anything, just let me know, somehow, that you're okay. We're okay. I don't want to be going along, thinking everything is fine and dandy then come home to find you hanging from the ceiling in chains. Please."

"Done." He kissed the top of her head.

"If only I had your power to sense emotions. It must be nice to have that knowledge about someone."

In her arms Bale tensed. His hand paused mid-sweep down her back and she swore she heard his heart skip a beat.

She froze along with him. Obviously she had said something that struck a nerve but damn if she knew what it was. After all they had been through that night, and all the things he'd confessed to, what had she said to make him tense up as if she had asked him to shed his skin?

"No." He hugged her tight as she tried to move away. When he tipped her chin up, she saw that pinched expression on his face again. "Do not pull away. You know, for a human, you are quite adapt at picking up on my emotions, but I understand what you are saying," he drew in a breath, "and there is a way."

She didn't move, didn't dare blink as her throat tightened. Surely he wasn't going to suggest the merge or mind-meld or whatever it was Amaryllis called it?

"We could bond."

Shit. That was the word. "Are you serious?" she screeched.

Did she want to be with him? Yes. Did she want to be confident of his feelings for her? Of course. But to go from dating to bonded mates was a huge leap. "Why would you even suggest that?"

He jerked back in surprise. "Do you know what it means to bond?"

"Yes. Well, a little. Amaryllis filled me in. You join our emotions together. Forever. In an unbreakable bond."

"That is correct."

"It is a bond so strong it can transcend death."

"Ya."

"Ya," she repeated with a hysterical chuckle. "Are you saying you want to bond with me?"

"Ya."

"I don't understand. Why? Why me? Why me and not," she laid her hand over the tattoo on his chest, "and not her."

Bale sighed and lifted her hand to place a kiss on the knuckles. "I didn't trust Natalia with what I carried in my soul. I never gave her the opportunity and that is a decision I will always regret. I know what it feels like to lose everything. I don't want to lose you, Ari. You have seen my darkness and you're still here. Touching me. Loving me. I may be stupid, but I'm not a fool. I learn from my mistakes. You are what I need, and more importantly, I want to be what you need."

When he gazed upon her and stroked the curve of her cheek as if she were the most precious object in existence, it wasn't difficult to fall even more in love with him. Her brain cautioned her to step back and consider the matter for, like, years, while her heart pounded with the urgency to say yes and claim him for all time.

"You and me?" she asked, still in disbelief as to what he was proposing.

Bale nodded.

"Forever and ever?"

"If you wish."

She held her breath, as did Bale. As her heart thumped he didn't make a sound or do anything to sway her decision. Their future together was entirely in her hands.

Stars floated in her vision as she released a breath. "I wish."

Bale blinked once, then twice and shook his head to try to stop the ringing in his ears. Did Ari agree to be his bonded mate? Of course that was what he wanted, but was his dream really coming true?

"You wish?"

The loveliness of her smile blinded him in the shadowed bedroom. "I wish. I choose you, Bale. I choose us."

Euphoria rippled up his chest and he felt the muscles of his face stretch into the biggest smile he'd bet money he'd ever produced. "You are certain?"

She laughed "I'm certain. Can't you tell?"

"Ya." Bubbles wrapped around his body and kissed his skin. "But I want to hear it from your lips."

Those wonderfully full lips curled into a grin before she lifted up to kiss him. "I want to be bonded to you."

Tears stung his eyes as he laughed with unadulterated joy and held her close to his hearts, thanking the Gods for granting him a second chance. Hell, more like the seventh or eighth, if he were to be honest.

Ari had been the last person he had expected to walk into that storage room earlier that evening. Of course he figured she'd hear about his self-imposed punishment from Amaryllis, but never did he dream she would confront him so soon.

Gods, she had been magnificent, staring down a killer with nary a flinch. So strong, so powerful in her convictions even though he felt her terror at facing the unknown crawl beneath his skin. Yet she had stayed with him, argued with him and loved him with an intensity that cut him off at the knees. She had displayed more bravery than most of the revolutionaries he had fought. She was his match. Instead of his darkness overpowering her light, her brilliance banished the shadows. Until his dying day he would put his all into being worthy of her trust.

"Come here, *liera*." He drew her to the edge of the bed and knelt on the floor between her knees. The quest to worthiness began with asking her properly. Taking her hands, he placed them on his chest over each heart. "Ariel Rayner, will you do me the honor of speaking the Sacred Vows and becoming my bonded mate?"

A warm, velvet clasp of love wrapped around him and stole into his soul as she smiled down on him with love shining in her sapphire eyes. "Yes, Bale…Llanos? That is your name, right?"

He laughed and dropped a kiss into each of her palms before sealing his lips over hers, drinking in her love and giving his in return. Ari sank into his embrace, but her hands were strong as she guided him to lie on top of her and wrapped her legs around his waist. With a frustrated growl, he pulled away and whipped his shirt over his head. The barrier of his clothes between their skin was too much to bear for a second longer.

"What's your rush?" She giggled as he tore at his pants.

"We don't have much time before I am taken away. I want to spend every possible second in your arms."

"Wait. What?" She sat up. "Taken away?"

"Do you not remember?"

"Obviously not."

"Captain DeWinter expects my answer at five p.m. tonight otherwise he will seek me out at The Cavern. Either I help him capture a criminal, or he will arrest me for the crimes I've committed as the Claymore."

"Oh, right," she groaned and pulled at the ends of her hair. "I know this is a stupid question but… Do you want to run? I know." She held up her hands when he raised a surprised brow. "Stupid. But I thought I'd ask. What are your options, really?"

"At this point I have only one. I turn myself in. I will no longer break the law or interfere with its process. The risk to you and the others is too great." He sat on the bed beside her. "At least when I am gone, we'll have our bond to keep us together. I find great comfort in that."

She hugged him around the waist and kissed his chest. "How long do you think you'll be gone for? Seriously, what can they charge you with?"

"I do not know. DeWinter claimed my punishment would be minimal, but even an hour away from you is too long. Whatever the courts see fit to give me, I will abide by."

"And I'll stand by you."

"Thank you, Ari." He rolled her onto her back then trailed kisses down her neck and sternum. "No more talk about the Claymore or jail. Now is for you and me."

She drove her fingers into his hair. "So, how does one bond? Is it like a wedding or a spell or something?"

"I will speak the Sacred Vows while we engage in the most intense sexual experience we've ever had," he explained between nipping kisses to the underside of her beast.

She arched into his touch. "More intense than we've been having?"

He let his smile be his answer.

"Oh shit. I may not survive." She shivered, but the wicked gleam in her eye let him know she eagerly anticipated what was to come.

He buried his nose into the cushion of her cleavage and drew in the enticing scent of coconut and hibiscus soap and Ari's own unique fragrance. For the rest of his life, the smell would always remind him of home and her loving embrace.

With his hands, he worshipped her. With his lips, he left praises of gratefulness to be granted the opportunity to love her. Her soft sighs and stilted groans caressed him as surely as her hands on his back as she raked her nails across his flesh. She had such sensitive nipples and they puckered so prettily when he took them between his teeth.

The baser, male part of him wanted to plunder her quivering body, claim what was his now before she regained her senses and realized he wasn't good enough, but the lover in him wanted to steep in the slow boil of her desire. Stoke the flame within her until her world consisted of nothing but him and the pleasure he provided.

"Lie back, love," he said as he settled between her thighs. "I'll take care of everything."

The slick petals of her sex easily parted beneath his thumbs, revealing the ripe, pink berry of her clitoris to his hungry gaze. His mouth watered as he lowered his head and touched the tip of his tongue to the swollen bud. Alternating between licks and nibbles, he worked his bride into a frenzy, reveling in the sheen of perspiration that made her skin glow like alabaster and the mewling cries that rolled down his back in a liquid satin wave. He pressed two fingers into her sheath and the tight tunnel rippled in welcome, bathing his hand in her sweet cream.

Ari stretched her arms over her head, abandoning her body to his will and he took her offering with great delight.

How magnificent was the female body? How soft and pliant she became under his lips and hands. He explored the satin lining of her sheath, memorizing the different textures. Right before her cervix he felt the tiny impression of rings against his fingertips and he rubbed the area in small strokes. Ari gasped with a jerk of her hips. He did it again, then again, and smiled as she melted into the mattress. Her fingers dug into his hair, holding him in place as she writhed against his face.

"Don't stop. Please, Lord, don't stop," she panted with her eyes squenched tightly shit. "If you stop, I swear to God I will kill you."

"We can't have that." He chuckled and went back to worrying her clit and stroking her walls.

An electric current ran from her body to his mouth and down his torso to wrap around his balls and squeeze in a deliciously painful grip. Against his stomach his cock leaked, ready to spill onto the sheets with the slightest brush, but he diligently ignored the incessant throbbing and concentrated on Ari and the power that radiated from her core.

She stared blankly up at the ceiling, moaning broken words and grunts that grew louder as the pressure grew within them both. His eyes crossed as she pulled his hair, but the pain was worth the overwhelming tide of her impending orgasm as it sucked them into the vortex. So close. She was so. Damn. Close.

Then she hit the wall. With a guttural cry her thighs tightened around his head. Sweet water flooded his mouth and her belly rippled with spasms he felt in his gut. The wave rolled on and on and his balls churned, desperate to come. At this rate he wasn't going to last long enough to thrust inside her, let alone bind them as one.

He rose to his feet, hooking her knees over his arms and gripped her by the hips. Lining his dripping cock up to her sheath, he lunged and pulled her onto his shaft.

"Ah, Gods," he gritted from between clenched teeth.

Without the barrier of latex between them, her pussy was scorching hot against his dick. And wet, by the Gods, he had never felt anything as sublime as her drenched cunt sucking away all his rational thoughts. Whatever deity had conjured the Sacred Vows was either a supreme prankster or a fucking genius. A man would have to be incredibly motivated to bond with his mate in order to remember the vows and not spill his seed at the first touch. As it was, he could barely remember to breathe, let alone all the parts of a ritual he had only heard spoken of and never seen in practice.

Focus, Bale. Focus.

Ari's bouncing breasts drew his gaze. Oh, how he did love the way the soft mounds shook with his every thrust. Ah. Breasts. Right. He reached up and cupped a palm full of flesh. Although she lacked the second heart his race carried, her solitary organ beat hard enough to feel the vibration against his hands.

"Ari, love. Look at me," he grated.

Her head lolled against the mattress and she struggled to lift her eyelids. He twisted his hips, sending his cock deep into her core. The action made her eyes widen in surprise as she screamed his name.

"Ariel." He wet his lips and searched his brain for the words to bind them together for eternity. "Ariel, *en la nire de demos, Y tesktsen a mi band brigde.*"

At his words, Ari gasped and reached out, scoring his forearms with her nails as she struggled to hang on. "Bale. God. What's happening?"

He groaned and fought to ignore the pressure in his balls. "Ariel, I claim you as my bonded mate. In my hands I hold your life and your love. Two precious gifts I ask you to entrust in my care. Ah, fuck."

Sweat dripped into his eyes and his lungs burned as her pussy milked his cock. "Fuck, Ari, stop coming around my dick."

"Don't stop. God, don't stop." She writhed in his grasp, completely oblivious to his plight. "I feel you. Bale, I feel you."

Damn it. He wasn't going to make it. "In return." Fuck. "I promise. To be all things. You need."

Sparkly white lights appeared in his vision as he felt her heart beat right out of her chest and into his palm. Her cries became his cries. His fire, hers. With each plunge of his cock, he felt the answering thrust spear up into his belly. The ripple of her sheath against his length drew the first spurts of cum he felt splashing the mouth of her womb.

One more sentence. *Jesu*, just one more sentence.

"Say you accept me. Say you accept my gift. Bond as one for eternity."

"Bale," she screamed. "Bale!"

"Say it! Do you accept me?"

"Yes. God, yes. Bale."

White lightning tore him in two as his cock erupted over and over again. From the center of his soul he felt the cleansing burn of their union scour the darkness of his past and radiate out to encompass their shuddering forms. The bite of her nails into his back and her teeth into his chest where she sobbed against him was a welcome pain, for the all-consuming depth of her love for him eased the ache.

She was inside him now. A living, breathing entity, hovering at the edge of his consciousness, forever in his care. Just as he lived inside Ari and experienced the wonder and awe at their joining with shared intensity.

All his warrior finesse was shot to hell and he collapsed on top of Ari in a graceless heap, pressing their pelvises together to burrow as deep inside her as possible. With their union he experienced the crush of his body as the weight stole her breath.

"Sorry," he mumbled and slid to the side.

"That's nifk," she slurred and weakly patted his chest while her legs remained locked around his waist in an alligator death-roll hug. "We died. Didn't we?"

His throat burned when he chuckled. "Ya."

"Knew it."

Even with exhaustion tugging at his consciousness, he sensed Ari's thirst and discomfort. The need to tend to his bonded mate swept him away from the abyss of sleep and was the only thing that blasted him from the bed.

"Where do you think you're going?" She clutched him tighter.

"You have needs."

"Yeah. I need you to hold me."

He dropped a kiss onto her forehead. "Water. I'm getting us water."

"Oh, all right." She buried her face against the mattress. "Hurry," came the muffled order.

"Of course. Whoa." His knees buckled as he attempted to stand and he fell back onto the bed. "Let's try this again."

"That was awesome." Ari laughed with her face still buried in the bedding.

"Do not laugh too hard. I'd hate to accidently spill a full glass of cold water on you."

"You would too. I can feel your certainty. That's so weird. How I can feel you inside me? All around me, actually."

Weird? No. Miracle? Yes.

He used his super speed to make it a quick trip to the sink and back and handed Ari the glass of water. "Here you go."

"Thanks." She reached out blindly and struggled to sit up enough to take a healthy swallow of cool liquid. She glanced up in his direction with a smile then promptly spewed the water all over like a geyser. "Holy shit," she gasped.

He froze in stunned silence for several seconds with water dripping off the end of his nose before reaching for the sheet to use as a towel as Ari climbed to her knees in horror.

"I am so sorry, Bale." Her sorrow was overcome with laughter as she tried to help him dry off. "I, uh—" Her sentence broke off into another fit of laughter that she attempted to stop with her hands clapped over her mouth. Over her fingers her dark eyes danced with merriment.

Dark eyes? Wait a minute. He looked again. Sure enough, gone were the dazzling sapphire gems of her irises and instead the color was a deep brown, almost black. Like his.

Like his.

Which meant…

He jumped to his feet and raced to the dresser, skidding to a stop in front of the mirror.

"*Jesu*," he exclaimed and tugged at the burnished red lock of his bangs then swiped a hand over the red hair covering his chest and eyed the trail all the way down to his cock before muttering, "The carpet matches the drapes."

"Come on." Ari scrambled off the bed, wiping the tears of laughter from her eyes. "It's not that bad." She caught her first glimpse of her new eye color and her brows shot up as she leaned closer to the mirror. "Wow. Okay, this will definitely take some getting used to."

The man who looked back at him from the mirror was completely unrecognizable. Gone was the permanent frown and the visible strain on his face and instead was a man who had been granted the gifts of love and hope. A new look for a new beginning. A happy beginning.

"Having second thoughts?" Ari asked at his side.

"You know I'm not. Quite the opposite in fact."

He drew her into his arms and clasped her to his chest. In the mirror, their reflection displayed the perfection of their mating, with his red hair blending seamlessly with her fiery strands as he rested his cheek against her head. A peace unlike any he'd ever known stole over him as his bond with Ari created a buffer against the volatile emotions of the human race. Her emotional strength stole inside him, lifting him into the heavens where contentment was within his grasp.

Never again did he have to second-guess his place in Ari's heart for her love surrounded him in its warmth, ebbing and flowing with his love for her in a symbiotic wave so inter-meshed there was no line of demarcation. They were truly joined in the most intimate of ways. Even if they were to become separated, they'd never be alone in the world. The connection was pure magic and he was damn lucky to be blessed with such a miracle.

But perhaps his fortune was too grand. What did he do to be granted such a gift when there were others far more deserv-ing than he?

"Bale, you've grown so sad." Ari lifted her head and frowned. "Why are you crying?"

"I do not cry."

"Sweetie." She wiped her thumb against his cheek and showed him the wet skin.

He glanced in the mirror and was stunned to see tears streaming from his eyes.

"You were thinking of her, weren't you? Natalia."

"I robbed her." He sucked in a stuttered breath. "I was a selfish bastard and robbed her of her happiness."

"You were young and insecure and did the best with the knowledge you had. You didn't know what was going to happen."

"I should have known. I should have been stronger."

She laid her hands on either side of his face. "Bale. Through all my short years of living, the biggest lesson I've learned is that hindsight is a malicious bitch. Should've, would've, could'ves will put you in the grave, and I've had my fair share of them to know. I've heard you say over and over again how you weren't strong enough. Well you know what? She wasn't strong enough either. If she wanted more of you, she should have demanded more, and you can bet your sweet ass that I'm going to demand everything from you."

He pressed his palm against the ache below his throat and shook his head. "It's not fair to you. This guilt won't leave me be." He dropped onto the bed and dug his fingers into his hair. "My bonding day should be the happiest day of my life and

I'm allowing my guilt to ruin it. We're bonded, but I'm still fucked in the head."

Ari sat beside him. "Did you honestly think that becoming bonded would erase a lifetime of neuroses?"

He nodded.

"Has bonding been known to do that?"

He began to nod again then paused. "Actually, I do not know."

"Oh my God," she sighed and wrapped her arms around his shoulders. "Emotional damage is permanent. I don't care if you are from another planet. Once you've been dented, you are never the same, no matter how you much work goes into the repair."

Her optimism drew a smile, a weak smile, but still a smile. He pulled her across his lap and kissed her lips. "You are a treasure, Ariel."

"I know. And I love you. Even though you're fucked in the head, I still love you. I made a promise to stand by you, Bale. And I will. Never doubt that."

"Never. You are the best part of me."

She wiggled her backside against his cock and grinned. "Not exactly. But I don't mind being second best."

"Woman, you've drained me dry once. You cannot be ready to do it again."

"Yes, I can." She straddled his lap, grinding her slick sex along his rapidly hardening length and touched the center of his chest. "I want to be as close to you physically as we are here. Our forever starts now, and I don't want to waste a second of it."

As refreshing as a summer rain, her love washed away the dust of his guilt. "If you wish."

"I wish," she whispered then claimed his mouth in a slow, deep, toe-curling kiss.

As he flipped her onto her back, he caught sight of the clock sitting on the night stand. Twelve hours, thirty-six minutes until DeWinter came for his answer. Twelve hours, thirty-six minutes he had control over how he spent. His mate was right. Forever started now.

He lowered his head and pressed kisses to the faint finger-shaped bruises around her breast left by his claiming. He would have felt bad about that too except he sensed her pride at bearing his possession, just as he bore the scratch of her nails on his arms. Before his time was up, he wanted to be adorned with more of her markings. When he walked into that jail, he would wear her marks like badges of honor. If his luck held out, he'd be back in her arms before they healed.

Luck. The Gods were probably tired of bestowing favors upon him. But he did have hope and Ari's love. That was enough.

It had to be.

Chapter Fourteen

BALE SAT ON the couch and watched Ari whirl around the kitchen. The yellow-and-orange floral print of her skirt created a kaleidoscope as she twirled from cabinet to cabinet, arranging trays of snacks. He didn't need to be nervous about the upcoming meeting with DeWinter for she was anxious enough for both of them. Try as he might to project a calm front, she wasn't having any of it.

She lifted a silver bag and a red box up into the air. "Do you think he'll like some tea? Or does he prefer coffee?"

"I don't know."

"But what do you think?"

"I haven't a clue. In our brief meetings we've never discussed his preference of beverages."

She tossed the bag of coffee at his head, which he caught without a flinch. "Don't be an ass. I'm hoping that if we are nice to him, he'll be nice in return and not take you to jail. Help a girl out."

Her logic made him smile. "He's a very driven man. I don't think the best coffee in the world will sway him."

"Well I have to try something." She adjusted a plate of

cookies to catch the light to her liking. "I'll make both. And have the whisky ready. Maybe he likes a little Irish in his coffee. Oh, hey. Can you bring me back that bag?"

He tossed the bag from hand to hand as he sauntered to her side. "You are cute when you worry."

"And I'm annoyed when you're calm on the outside and boiling on the inside." She stood on tiptoe to kiss his chin. "I can feel you, remember."

"That is why I am striving for indifference. We both cannot be on edge. It does neither of us any good." He pulled her arms to encircle his neck and drew her in for a hug. "If these are to be my last moments of freedom, I'd rather spend them kissing you than having you run around making food for my soon-to-be jailer."

She sighed and ran her fingers through his hair, scraping her nails in light strokes against his scalp. "This sucks. I understand why you're doing this, but I don't want you to go away."

"I'll be with you. Always. Just because you won't be able to see me, does not mean I won't be here. Feeling you. Experiencing your day with you."

"I'll do my best to not have any fun," she teased but her smile wavered.

"I appreciate the sentiment, but please have fun. Live, Ari. Make us a home for me to come back to."

A tear slipped down her cheek. "Fuck, Bale. I love it when you say cheesy things like that."

She jumped and wrapped her legs around his waist and met his mouth in a desperate kiss. His fingers dug into her flanks as he set her on the counter and held her still to grind his growing erection against the soft pad of her belly while she drank from his mouth as if she were dying of thirst.

Their last few couplings had been colored with the same sense of urgency, manifesting in clawing, reaching hands and deep, biting kisses. More than one bite mark marred his neck and chest, and if he timed it right, he might score one more.

The carefully arranged tray of vegetables was about to be sent to the floor with a sweep of his arm when a sharp rap on the door stopped him mid-swing.

"Break it up, you two and get dressed. You've been at it all day," Amaryllis shouted from the other side.

"*Jesu*," he groaned and struggled to catch his breath.

"How does she know what we've been doing?"

"She's Skandavian. She and Lucian can sense us."

"Oh my God!" She slapped at his arm. "Why didn't you remind me? I would have made an effort to control my reactions."

"Precisely why I didn't." He winked and crossed to open the front door, revealing a beaming Lucian and Amaryllis. "Should I be put out that you are interrupting us or thankful that you granted us this much alone time?"

"Yes," Amaryllis answered before throwing her arms around his neck. The bottle of champagne in her hands *thunked* him in the back of the head. "I knew it. I knew you two were a match. Congratulations."

"Thank you, your highness."

"And Ari." Amaryllis swept across the room to engulf Ari in a big hug. "Welcome to the family. My word, *lebshone*, your joining was powerful. Lucian and I haven't fucked like that since our own bonding. He came so hard I would be shocked if he didn't impregnate me."

Ari's jaw dropped. "Wow. TMI, Amaryllis. T. M. I."

"Oh please. If we are to reside under the same roof, you'll have to get used to sensing what is going on behind closed doors. We know everything."

"Fantastic."

"Bale." Lucian gestured at his head with a grin tugging at his lips. "I like your new look. It's different."

"Good different?"

"Yes, good different." He held out his hand. "Congratulations."

After Bale clasped his forearm they bowed toward each other in a *Llanos* warrior's greeting. Before he could let go, Lucian dragged him into an embrace and landed three solid slaps to his back.

"Well deserved, my brother." His eyes shimmered as he drew away. "Well deserved."

The lump in Bale's throat prevented him from answering, not that he had the right words to say if he wanted to. He nodded his acceptance and tapped the center of his chest. Lucian's watery smile told him the message was received as intended.

"When is Captain DeWinter due to arrive?" Amaryllis asked.

He raised a surprised brow then chuckled to himself. Of course the Kilsgaards knew everything that went on within their domain. "Any moment. Jax is to escort him here when he arrives."

"Then we arrived in the nick of time." She flounced to an armchair and settled herself on the seat as if it were a throne.

"Your highness, with all due respect, my appointment with DeWinter has nothing to do with you."

"Nonsense. Balellanos, you are family. If there is any threat to our family, we will face it together. Always. Do not make me have Ari take the strap to you again to remind you."

"Princess—"

"Bale." Lucian placed a hand on his shoulder. "We are not here to interfere but to lend our support. Both to you and Ari. Amaryllis will keep quiet. I promise." He said the last to his wife with a silent warning in his smile.

"I will do my best," she said without an ounce of conviction.

"May the Gods take me," Bale muttered and wiped his hand down his face.

He glanced over at Ari and the breath whooshed from his lungs, and suddenly he was thankful for the others' presence for that meant Ari would not be on her own when DeWinter arrested him. His woman was brave, but even the strongest of souls benefited from the love of a friend.

With only a glance, Ari raced to his side and hugged him around the waist. For several long seconds he basked in her warmth and the scent of her skin. When the heavy knock pounded on the door, the entire room tensed.

He smoothed his hand down Ari's back and crushed the silky strands of her hair in his palm one last time. "I'll answer that."

Captain DeWinter stood at the entry, looking more rested then the last time they had met. His cheeks were freshly shaven and his black slacks bore a crisp pleat down the legs. Anticipation had replaced the exhaustion from the night before and the man looked ready to move mountains. The determination in his firmly set jaw was a good indication that the captain was going to press the Smithwick issue and not allow him to surrender.

"Captain," Bale greeted.

DeWinter began to nod in response then his gaze flew to Bale's hair. Deep lines carved his brow and his mouth opened and shut without sound until he shook his head and muttered what Bale thought sounded like, "Damn Swedes."

"Please, enter." Bale stood to the side and swept his arm over the threshold.

"Thanks." DeWinter entered the apartment and drew up short when he saw the contingent stationed in the living room. He tossed Bale a surprised look over his shoulder. "Did I need to bring backup?"

"My family feels as if they have a vested interest in our upcoming discussion. And I agree. Mostly."

"I see." DeWinter smirked and greeted Lucian and Amaryllis before addressing Ari. "Ms. Rayner. Nice to see you again."

Ari crossed her arms over her chest and sent him a scowl fierce enough to gut a man.

"I see the sentiment is one-sided. Understandably." He turned back to Bale. "So. Is the Claymore going to help clean up the city, or do I take you in?"

Bale held out his hands. The soft intake of Ari's breath almost made him pull back and agree to anything to remain with her, but he stayed the course. "I will not commit any more crimes."

DeWinter bit back a snarl. "You can do more good on the street than behind bars."

"I made a promise to my mate. I will not break my vow."

"And while you're tied up in bureaucratic bullshit, what happens to your girl? What about all the girls Smithwick hurts?"

"Unfortunate casualties in a war I didn't start and I alone cannot end. I'm sorry, Captain, but it will have to be up to the police to finish their job."

"Well isn't that great that you've gained some moral ground now of all times. Fuck," he spat then ran his hand through his hair, his arms shaking with restrained anger. He reached behind his back and withdrew a set of handcuffs from his pocket. "I've told you the case has been tabled. The police won't put an end to this asshole. The city needs help."

Over the captain's shoulder, Bale met Ari's unwavering gaze. The silent message was clear. Whatever he decided, she would support him one hundred percent. DeWinter's passion was admirable, inspiring even, but Bale knew the more he put himself in harm's way, the more he endangered Ari. Fiona Kilsgaard was the perfect cautionary tale as to what happened when caught in Smithwick's crosshairs.

"Captain," Lucian interrupted. "I'd wish to propose a trade."

"A trade?" Bale and DeWinter asked at the same time.

"The Claymore for the Chameleon."

"I'm sorry. What?" DeWinter shook his head as if to clear his mind while Bale stared at his general as if he'd gone daft. What was Lucian plotting?

"The Claymore wants to make a fresh start and you want to capture a criminal. The Chameleon owes you a favor for the assistance you provided last year. Allow me to contact the Chameleon. I am certain he will agree to serve in Bale's place in return for giving him the opportunity to have a new beginning."

Bale shook his head while the general spoke. "No. I cannot ask...the Chameleon to take my place. This situation is of my own making."

Lucian smiled. "Bale, the Chameleon owes you a boon as well, remember?"

After Fiona had been rescued from Smithwick's lair, news of her relationship with Dhavin, acting as the Chameleon, had spread across their small town like a plague. To keep her safe the masked hero ended their affair in a very public demonstration witnessed by many of Cedar's citizens, including all of the Kilsgaard clan. But Bale posing as the superhero in order to fake break up with a girl in no way equaled the danger Dhavin or Lucian faced going after Smithwick. They had mates as well depending on them. It wasn't fair to ask them to take the risk.

"Lucian. No."

The general waved his protest away. "Do not fret. There will be some stipulations on his assistance."

"Really?" DeWinter propped his hands on his hips. "And you know what those will be already?"

Lucian matched his stance. "Yes, because he is an honorable man. As am I, and I hope as are you. The Chameleon's role will lie solely in surveillance. He will pinpoint the location of Smithwick's whereabouts and create a list of associates if possible, but he will not confront Smithwick or any of his men directly. That is police business and will stay that way. If Bale decides the Claymore can participate without breaking his vow, then I am certain his assistance will be appreciated."

"Wow." DeWinter issued a dry chuckle that grew as he pulled at his hair. "Wow. Sounds as if I should be taking orders from you too."

"The general has had much experience issuing orders," Amaryllis chimed in, slipping her arm around her husband's waist.

Lucian patted her hand with a proud smile. "This is your operation, Captain. The Chameleon will only act as an informant. The decision to proceed is entirely upon you."

DeWinter looked to each person in the room, settling last on Bale. "My beef with you has never been personal. I only want to get this scum off the street, not make your life miserable. I will gladly take the Chameleon's assistance. And yours."

"What about the Claymore? You can't go after Smithwick until you've captured him."

"If I provide proof that the Claymore has disappeared, or perhaps is spotted in another state, I can request to close the case and be assigned a new one. Do you think that's possible?"

"Perhaps. I have an idea. Wait here one minute."

Bale raced to his apartment. The layout was exactly the same as Ari's unit, and that was where the similarities ended. For a year he hadn't done more than update the contents of the refrigerator. The décor had remained the same generic furnishings that existed before he had moved in. Not like Ari who had added her own touches with fluffy throw pillows in bright colors, scented candles and knickknacks that graced every available surface. As he entered the cold, impersonal unit, he knew it was going to be for the last time. Ari was home now, and wherever she laid her head, so did he.

In mere seconds his essentials were packed in a bag and he was back with his family in less time than it took to exhale.

"Why did I know that when you said one minute, you

meant that literally?" DeWinter remarked.

He dropped his bag near the front door and strode toward the captain with his sword and jacket in hand. "Will these suffice as enough evidence of the Claymore's disappearance?"

Amaryllis gasped out loud while Lucian's silent surprise crackled down his spine. A warrior was never without his weapon, and for many long years all that Bale was had been defined by the actions of his sword. Even Ari, who held no knowledge of the *Llanos* ways understood the significance of the gesture and rushed to his side.

"Bale?" she asked. "What are you doing?"

"This sword belonged to an angry and confused man. I am not that man anymore. I am entrusting this sword in your keeping, Captain."

DeWinter grasped the hilt and faltered with its full weight when it Bale relinquished it, nearly dropping the heavy weapon. "Whoa. It's a lot bigger than it looks in pictures. Thank you, Bale. I'll keep it safe."

"Do we have an accord then?"

"Accord?" DeWinter scoffed. "You guys and your fancy talk. Yeah. We have a deal."

The pact was settled with a handshake then DeWinter was overtaken by two bubbly women who peppered his cheeks with kisses while avoiding the sharp edge of the blade.

"Lucian, pop the champagne," Amaryllis ordered. "Captain, you must join us for a toast. There is much to celebrate."

"Ah, no thanks. I have the disappearance of a vigilante to

plan." He gestured to Bale and Ari. "You all enjoy your hair-ritual-whatever-the-hell-you've-got-going-on…stuff. When can I expect to hear from the Chameleon?" he asked Lucian.

"I'll contact him right away. You should be notified within the hour."

"Uh-huh. Right. Thank you for your assistance. I'll just leave you now and try to get to my car without anyone noticing that I'm carrying a gigantic sword." DeWinter covered the weapon with his jacket then gave him a tight salute before exiting the apartment.

"Is it over?" Ari asked. "Really? That was it? You don't have to go to jail?"

Bale drew her close. "Are you disappointed?"

"No, just afraid to believe that the threat is over." She buried her nose against his chest and held him tight.

"Me too," he admitted. He met his commander's gaze. "Thank you, Lucian. I am forever in your service."

"I have plans for you, do not doubt that." He smiled. "However, the only thanks I need is for you to live a happy life, Balellanos."

"I will." His shoulders relaxed and he released an easy sigh. "Starting now. If you don't mind, please take your wife and return home."

Lucian laughed. "Absolutely. Come, Amaryllis."

"What?" she screeched. "I was just pouring the champagne."

"Do not fret, your highness," Bale said. "It will not go to

waste."

"But Ari and I have so much to talk about. We need to plan a party in their honor and figure out new living quarters. They should have a bigger home. Lucian! Put me down. I haven't even heard how he asked her about bonding. Lucian."

The princess pounded on her husband's back as he carried her over his shoulder. With a jaunty wave he left them in silence as Amaryllis' protests echoed down the hall.

"Is that going to be us in a few years?" Ari asked.

"That's going to be us now." He dipped low and flipped her onto his shoulders.

"Bale!" Her fingers dug into his backside. "Is this really necessary?"

"No." He picked up the open bottle of champagne on his way to the bedroom.

As an afterthought he made a quick detour to the bathroom and ripped down the shower curtain liner.

"Why did you do that?"

"I plan to use your body as a vessel. We might make a mess."

"Might?"

He set her on her feet and dove in for a breath-stealing kiss. When his lungs screamed for air, he raised his head with a smile. "We will definitely make a mess."

"Well hell, why don't we just bypass the bed altogether and lay everything out on the floor?"

"I like the way you think."

Together they laid out the curtain and a few sacrificial pillows on the carpet. Bale pulled Ari down to lie on top of him, drinking from her lips as he slid the zipper of her dress down her back. One hand rested on the warm skin of her spine while the other he used to cradle the back of her head. The urgent desire to join their bodies together cooled as he took the time to savor the weight of her body on his, the silkiness of her hair between his fingers and the steady sound of her heart beating as he nuzzled her neck.

They were free to be as one now. Truly free.

Euphoria raced through him as Ari gasped, "Bale. Can't. Breathe."

"Sorry." He loosened his hold. "I'm just so…I…"

His eyes watered, blurring Ari's beautiful face as she lifted up to look upon him with adoration. "I know, Bale. I know."

As lovely and intelligent as she was, she was wrong. Ari would never fully understand—not even with their bond—the depth of his love, gratitude and happiness.

He placed his hands on either side of her face. It took several attempts for him to manage to squeeze past his constricted throat the simplest of statements but nonetheless true and one he would never hesitate to speak for the rest of his life.

"I love you."

Epilogue

"AGAIN, MRS. DUBOIS." Bale adjusted his grip on the padded nightstick and nodded at the woman staring timidly up at him from the other side of the blue exercise mat. "This time with passion."

Mrs. Dubois worried her lower lip and pulled at the hem of her t-shirt. "I'm trying."

"No, you are afraid, and therefore do not follow through with your actions. What are you afraid of?"

"I don't want to hurt you."

At five foot two, the plump fifty-year-old didn't appear capable of harming a piece of paper. Two months prior her bridge club had joined his self-defense class after one of their own was mugged while doing their holiday shopping. With her genteel Southern upbringing and doting husband, she had been fortunate enough to never have to fight for her life, which also made it difficult to inspire the warrior spirit within her.

He thumped on his chest. "I am here for you to hurt. For you to grow strong. An attacker lives to hurt you. Your fear and pain is a drug they feed on. The only thing standing between you and death is your will to live. Will you fight, Mrs.

Dubois? Or will you let a stranger steal you away from your family?"

"I-I—" she sputtered. Her eyes widened with terror as he stalked closer.

"I am your attacker. Fight or die. What shall it be?" He grabbed on to her arm in a tight hold, but was careful not to snap the delicate bones. "Give me what I want or I will hurt you with this weapon."

"No!" she screamed and stomped on his foot while twisting in his direction. Her knee connected to the inside of his thigh with enough force to make him lose his grip.

She stumbled back and looked up at him with bright eyes and a pink flush across her cheeks as her breath whooshed in and out.

He nodded. "Better. Not good, but better."

"Thank you, Mr. Bale," she said in a breathy voice.

"Go to the bag for ten minutes. I want you to treat it like the scum that it is."

"Yes sir." She trotted off, slapping high-fives with her friends as she passed.

He bent down to straighten the mat at his feet. "Who else wants a go?"

"I do."

Ari stood across from him with her feet apart and knees bent, ready for action. She held out her hands and waved her fingers in a "come and get me" motion as she waggled her brows.

As always, his world stopped when he gazed upon his wife. The rest of the room faded away until there was only Ari and the love in her smile. The sun in his universe.

He blinked hard to focus his vision and looked around the room. "Where are the children?"

"On the gymnastics equipment with Roxanne." She nodded to the corner of the room.

Roxanne, their family friend, spotted five-year-old Lucas as he swung back and forth on the uneven bars while his younger sister marched on top of the toddler-sized balance beam. Gleaming red curls spilled from her ponytail and bobbed about her tiny shoulders as she leapt with a grace far beyond her three years of age.

Lucas laughed and his eardrum-piercing squeal bounced off the walls of the community center's gym, hitting a crescendo each time Roxanne pushed him higher. The sound was perfection to his father's ears, but little Rosaline glared daggers at her brother before pulling her shirt over her head.

When Bale had first offered the self-defense classes, the women Captain DeWinter referred to him had often come from situations where they had already experienced a violent attack. His size and intensity had frightened many of them from returning to his classes, but Ari, who had been six months pregnant at the time, had convinced them to try again, and soon became a fixture in all of his beginner's classes. Once his students witnessed the tenderness and love he felt for his growing family, he ceased to be so scary and now they treated him as a loveable giant, except when he came at them with a club. They knew it was time to get serious when the stick came out.

"Hey. Come on, big man," Ari taunted. "Are you afraid to come at me?"

He twirled the club in his hand and shot his wife a wink. "Never. Tackling you is one of my favorite pastimes."

"Ha ha. I'm serious. I've learned some new moves. Come at me. If you dare."

"Ooo," the students cooed and gathered around the edge of the mat to watch the interaction.

A smile flirted with his lips as he gave Ari his fiercest stare, then with a battle cry that had made many a man wet his pants, he ran at her full-bore with club raised in the air.

She lowered her stance and as his arm swung down she blocked the blow with her forearm and followed it up with an upper-cut to the gut. Using her momentum, she dug her shoulder into his stomach and knocked him onto his back where she finished by punching him directly in his cup-covered groin. The plastic diminished the blow, but it still caused him to suck in a harsh breath while his eyes watered.

All the ladies gasped, and from the corner of his blurred vision he saw Lucas cup his own groin in sympathy.

Ari jumped up with a triumphant crow and dusted off her hands. "A fine warrior once told me to know exactly where to strike your enemy and to not hesitate. Whatd'ya think?"

"I think he did not mean for his wife to use that tactic upon him," he wheezed. "Who taught you that?"

"Amaryllis."

"I should have known." He staggered to his feet and pulled her in for a hug. Over the top of her head he addressed his students. "Ladies, let this be a lesson. A larger opponent is not unbeatable. And if my own wife will gleefully strike me in the balls, you should not be afraid to use your full force on me. I am here to teach, and you are here to learn."

Ari sputtered with laughter against his chest. "Admit it. You're proud of me. Just a little. I can sense it."

"I am very proud of you, but you do know that I expect you to pay appropriate homage to my manhood and apologize profusely in a manner of my choosing." He lowered his head and covered her smile with a kiss that quickly blossomed into an all-out blaze that pained him to stop, however one second longer and the cup was going to fail in hiding his erection.

"I will do all you ask and more. After the family dinner."

Jesu. He closed his eyes on a groan. The monthly family dinner. As much as he loved his extended family, when his woman was in his arms, his only desire was to spirit her away and make love all night long until the children demanded breakfast at dawn. Not even Fiona's chocolate-mousse cake made up for missing a few hours of Ari's kisses.

Huh. Now that was an idea. Chocolate mousse cake and sex with Ari. Would anyone notice if he squirreled a few slices away to take home?

"How I wish I knew what you're thinking." Ari ran her

tongue up the side of his neck.

"I'll surprise you later tonight."

"Not even a hint?"

His cheeks bunched with his Cheshire grin. "We're going to need a new shower curtain."

Ari's laughter burst across his skin as Mrs. Jenkins waved her hand at her face like a fan. "I don't know if it's all of this exercise or watching you two together that makes my blood hot, but when I get home from class Mr. Jenkins is always a very happy man."

Heat singed his cheeks and he knew his face grew as red as his hair. Whenever he was around Ari, he often forgot to see if there was an audience before indulging in a public display of affection. "All right, ladies. That's class for this evening. I will see you next week."

"Daddy. Daddy." Rosaline ran up to him and lifted her arms as she jumped. As always, he caught her mid-leap. "You okay? Mommy got you good."

"She sure did. When you're older, she'll teach you that move. I can see it coming in handy in your future."

"Cool. Wha-wha." She sliced through the air with her pudgy hands with ninja precision then giggled when he kissed her cheek.

Together he and Ari worked with the synchronicity that came with years of practice as they bundled up the children in winter coats and mittens and collected teddy bears, sippy cups and the stray Cheerio in preparation for transport. With all the enthusiasm of a dozen small boys, Lucas scurried around the couple, jumping on every piece of equipment to the door and chattering nonstop.

"Dad. I need my sword. Not the plastic one either but the wood one." He swirled an imaginary blade over his head.

"Why?"

"Uncle Dhavin said he'd teach me how to fight like a warrior."

"That pansy-ass? I'm a much better swordsman than he."

"Bale, language," Ari hissed. "I swear, I'm going to have to kick your ass to remind you not to swear in front of the children."

"Yes, darling." He bit his lip to hold in his chuckle then sucked in a breath as a jolt of distress struck him in the chest.

Ari's eyes widened, signaling she felt it too. "What was that?"

"Keep the children inside." He drew the hood of his sweatshirt over his head and strode toward the door.

"Bale."

"I'm only investigating. Keep your phone at the ready." He burst out onto the sidewalk and squinted up at the rapidly darkening sky and the fine mist of rain that hovered in the air as finely as cobwebs.

His feet beat tracks to the parking garage and the source of the emotion. It had been over six years since he last donned the mantle of the Claymore, yet he still reached toward his hip for the sword he no longer carried. He glanced down at his empty hand in confusion for half a second, then continued on. The lack of weapon was not going to stop him from lending his assistance.

Twin shots of adrenaline raised the hair on his arms as he ran up the stairs to the second level and came to a halt at the landing.

"Mrs. Dubois?" he asked in disbelief.

A man lay sprawled facedown upon the concrete while Mrs. Dubois kneeled on his back and tightened a plastic zip-tie around his wrists.

"Mr. Bale!" She leapt to her feet and ran to throw her arms around his neck. "I did it. I did it, Mr. Bale. Just like you said. He jumped out of the shadows and tried to push me into the car and I snapped. I screamed then kneed him in the balls and flipped him to the ground. Oh, I can't believe I did it."

While Mrs. Dubois clucked like a hen, the stranger lifted his head in confusion and met Bale's gaze. Bale bared his teeth with a silent growl and feinted with his head. The man's jaw dropped then he lay back on the ground.

"Are you injured, Mrs. Dubois?"

"No. No. I'm just—I'm just a little shaken and wow. Wow. I can't believe I did it."

"Bale?" Ari's voice preceded the sound of her footsteps up the stairs. "Is everyone all right?"

"Ari? What are you doing here? Where are the children?"

"They're with Mrs. Jenkins." She appeared on the landing. Her red hair was a splash of light in the dark. "I figured you had everything under control. I called 9-1-1 on my way here. They're on their way."

"Ari, oh Ari, I did it. Just like Mr. Bale taught me. See, and I even used the zip-ties he told us to carry in our purse. You know, at first I thought that was a crazy idea, but look. Look. Oh my. Thank you. Thank you so much." She hugged him again.

Ari smiled at him and her pride blossomed with a bonfire glow to warm his heart. When the police arrived a few minutes later, they stood to the side in silent support while Mrs. Dubois gave her statement.

"Look at that," Ari spoke from the corner of her mouth while they watched on. "Who needs the Claymore when the city has you teaching everyone how to be their own hero?"

"It was up to Mrs. Dubois to apply the knowledge."

"And it was you who gave her that knowledge. Your family would be proud of you. Especially her," she whispered.

Natalia might have been the motivation but Ari was the compass, showing him the way to keep his vow while maintaining his soul. She was the true hero.

He slipped his arm around her waist. "Thank you, Ari. For believing in me."

"You've made it easy." She stood on her toes to kiss his cheek. "I've just been privileged to watch you grow."

"You are wrong. I am the privileged one to be on this great journey with you, *liera*."

"I do love when you say cheesy things like that."

"I'm going to say a lot more later tonight." He gestured toward the police officers. "It looks as if they're almost finished. Let's collect our children and go home. I need my family close to me."

"I'm ready when you are."

"Officer?" he asked. "Are we free to go now?"

"Sure. Thank you for your statement."

"My pleasure."

"Hey." The officer stopped them as he turned. "Did anyone ever tell you that you kind of look like that Claymore guy who ran around here a while ago?"

He raised his brow. "No."

"Huh." He shrugged when Bale left his response at that. "Well you do. At least, you look like the pictures I've seen." He turned to his partner. "I wonder whatever happened to that guy."

Ari smiled slyly up at him while they walked toward the community center. "I've wondered that too."

"I know what happened." He squeezed her side. "He went home."

About Anna Alexander

Anna Alexander is the award winning author of the Heroes of Saturn and the Sprawling A Ranch series. With Hugh Jackman's abs and Christopher Reeve's blue eyes as inspiration, she loves spinning tales of superheroes finding love. Anna also loves to give back and has served on the board for the Greater Seattle Romance Writers of America as chapter president and on the committee for the Emerald City Writers Conference.

Sign up to receive news about Anna's latest releases at http://eepurl.com/Q0tsz

Website

annaalexander.net

Facebook

facebook.com/pages/Anna-Alexander/282170065189471

Twitter

twitter.com/AnnaWriter

Newsletter

http://eepurl.com/Q0tsz